Also by Cassandra Page

The Lucid Dreaming duology
Lucid Dreaming
False Awakening

The Isla's Inheritance trilogy
Isla's Inheritance
Isla's Oath
Melpomene's Daughter

CASSANDRA PAGE

www.cassandrapage.com

First published in Australia 2017 by
Cassandra Page

The right of Cassandra Page to be identified as the author of this work has
been asserted by her under the *Copyright Amendment (Moral Rights) Act 2000*.

Cassandra Page
www.cassandrapage.com

Cataloguing-in-Publication data available from
the National Library of Australia www.nla.gov.au

ISBN: 978-0-9944459-9-5

Set in Bookman Old Style 10pt

Formatting and cover design by KILA Designs
www.kiladesigns.com.au
Cover image: ©Shutterstock.com

To Craig, Ali and Karen. You know what you did.

How would, I say, mine eyes be blessed made
By looking on thee in the living day,
When in dead night thy fair imperfect shade
Through heavy sleep on sightless eyes doth stay?
All days are nights to see till I see thee,
And nights bright days when dreams do show thee me.

– Sonnet 43, William Shakespeare

Chapter One

An unfamiliar sound jolted me from sleep, pulling me from a dream about green cranes and ventriloquist puppets. My eyes flew open, searching the unfamiliar room as I lay still, trying to calm my speeding pulse. My ears strained, but the rest of the house was silent. Gradually, each of the shadows turned into something I recognised: my washing basket, a chest of drawers, a stack of unopened boxes.

No figure leaned over me. No hands clutched at my throat.

Beside me, his breath in the deep and even cadence of sleep, lay Brad. A sliver of moonlight that had eased through a crack in the curtains highlighted the gentle contours of his face. His hair was a scruffy, uneven pile on top of his head and one hand curved beneath his cheek—one of the same strong hands that had caused me such dread months before.

I smiled, the confused terror fading as I regarded him,

glad he'd agreed to stay over. His lips formed a pout he'd never wear during the day. I wished I had a camera—my old phone didn't have one.

I'd just about decided the sound that woke me had been my imagination when I heard it again. But, awake, I was able to identify it: the snick of a Stanley knife, followed by the long tearing sound of a blade slicing through packing tape.

I rolled over, ignoring muscles that screamed a protest, and stared blankly at my bedside table. No clock radio stared back; it was still in a box. Fumbling, I found my phone and pressed a button to activate the screen and check the time.

Just after four in the morning. Dammit.

Moving slowly so as not to wake Brad, I slid out from between the sheets and eased the wardrobe open, finding my dressing gown. My bunny slippers were in the tumble of shoes I'd emptied there the day before. I poked my toes into them and, hugging myself to stay warm in the chilly night air, walked up the hall to the kitchen.

The overhead light was on, filling the space with a warm yellow glow that made the benchtops seem greener, the pale tiles on the wall shinier. In the corner, Jen's and my old fridge hummed, content in its new home. And in the middle of the space, moving like a melancholy ballerina, was my mother.

She stood amidst torn scraps of newspaper, a box on the bench before her. As I watched, she pulled a newspaper-wrapped bundle from the box and set it on the bench, stripping the paper from a mismatched crockery set with graceful efficiency.

"Couldn't sleep?" I asked, moving fully into the room.

FALSE Awakening

The rest of the boxes we'd left in the corner before bed had been emptied.

She looked up at me, a small smile tightening the lines around her tired eyes. "A few hours. Then I woke and that was the end of it. I thought I'd finish the kitchen. Any news?"

I shook my head, and her fine-boned shoulders drooped. Feeling guilty, I took a plate from her and swiped at it with a tea towel before placing it in the cupboard. I shouldn't feel bad. The lack of an update from the world of the Oneiroi, or dream spirits, wasn't something I could control. But Ollie, my Oneiroi father and a former fugitive, was gone, probably to be tossed into an Oneiroi prison. Mum's dreams were empty in a way they hadn't been for two decades.

Mum had been cured of her hypersomnia by Dad's departure, and her sleep had mostly returned to normal. Her doctor had proclaimed her cured without looking too hard at the reasons why; her nursing home probably hadn't wanted to admit that one of their staff may have been drugging her. And, since Mum no longer needed the around-the-clock care the home had provided, she'd discharged herself. When she'd invited me and my best friend, Jen, to move into the house she'd bought with her trust fund payout, I hadn't known what to say. I'd never lived with my mother, wasn't sure I knew how to … but she was lonely. We'd find a way.

When the last of the crockery had been dusted off and put away, I helped Mum collect the scraps of paper. We tucked them into the top of an overstuffed box by the door and washed our hands, all in silence. "Did you want me to help you sleep?" I asked her finally, pressing the back of my hand to my mouth as though to prevent a yawn escaping.

Her hazel eyes narrowed. "If I say no, will you stay up with me?"

"Yes."

"And if I tell you not to, will you listen to your mother?"

"No."

She sighed. "Then yes. You can help me get back to sleep."

I smiled and followed her up to the master bedroom. She'd suggested I take the biggest room, but I'd refused. It was her house, bought and paid for; she should have the ensuite. Besides, Jen and I were used to sharing a bathroom.

Once my mother was tucked back under her blanket, I leaned over and kissed her forehead. "Goodnight, Mum."

"Goodnight, Melaina." She blinked eyes gone misty with tears. "My darling girl."

I breathed gently on her face and watched her slip back into slumber.

She had always looked younger when she was sleeping, and it was still true now: the tension drained from her shoulders, the curve of her neck. There were differences, though. Before my father had been arrested by my childhood friend and dragged away, she'd always seemed happiest when she was asleep. Not anymore.

Grimacing, I turned the lamp off and crept from the room.

Despite my faked yawn, I didn't think I'd be able to sleep again. My heart was too heavy. The sun wouldn't rise for more than an hour, and the air outside was frigid—it was only the first month of spring, and I wouldn't

be surprised if there was a touch of frost on the grass come dawn. It had been a hard winter, and the season seemed reluctant to loosen its grip just yet.

Instead, I made a coffee and drank it in the lounge room as I unpacked and arranged our DVDs and books on the meagre shelves. Jen and I had owned enough furnishings for our tiny two-bedroom flat; they didn't come close to filling the space in this roomy, if somewhat tired, three-bedroom house. And Mum didn't own anything beyond clothes and toiletries. The dining room was empty except for a teetering and uneven pile of flattened moving boxes.

I shucked the dressing gown and took advantage of the empty space to do some stretches, trying to loosen muscles knotted from all the lifting and carrying I'd done the day before. Then I ran through a yoga workout to try and lift my spirits and stretch out the last of the kinks.

Brad found me just as I was easing my way out of a reclining spinal twist onto my back. He eyed me, an appreciative curve to his lips, and I grinned back before flattening my shoulders against the carpet and lengthening my spine. I was conscious of the image I must present: thin cotton pyjama pants and comfortable T-shirt, unbrushed black hair with a shock of blue in the fringe, painted toenails pointing out towards each bare wall.

Still, Brad didn't seem to mind. When I stood, he slid his arms around my waist and kissed me, slow and deep. His lips were soft, his faint stubble a rasping counterpoint. Heat flared in my belly and, for a moment, I considered dragging him back to my bed so we could try out the new bedroom. But the sound of movement down the other end of the house made me sigh. It was probably Jen, not my mother—but my bedroom shared a wall with Mum's. How long would my spell of sleep last, anyway? Mum was a lucid dreamer, like me; I couldn't assume she would stay under for as long as someone with no awareness of their dreams would.

I hadn't thought through all the implications of moving in with her, I realised with a sinking feeling. Resting my forehead against Brad's chest, I grimaced into his shirt.

"Want to come back to my place later?" he asked, his voice smoky as he ran his hand up and down the curve of my ribs through the fabric of my shirt.

"I really do," I said. "But I should stay here and help get things squared away. Jen has an exam tomorrow. She needs to study."

"Your mother could get everything sorted. She doesn't have to work..." There was a question in his voice, and I shrugged, muscles relaxing as his hand found a persistent knot in my shoulder and massaged it.

"I know. Once we're settled, I'm going to see if I can help her find a job somewhere. I feel bad, ditching her, but..." I looked up at him "...I suppose I could spare an hour. We could do a round trip." I gestured to the boxes.

"Okay," he said with a grin. Then he licked his lips, tipping his head to the side. "You've had a coffee already?"

I nodded. "It's just instant. Want me to make you one?"

He wrinkled his nose and then nodded. "Now you have the bench space, I might buy you an espresso machine."

"You can't," I said. "You've done so much for us—for me—already. Hiring the truck, helping us move..."

"That *is* true." A twinkle in his eye, Brad tapped a long finger against his chin. "But this wouldn't be for you. This is enlightened self-interest."

FALSE *Awakening*

I collected my empty coffee mug from the lounge and walked back to the kitchen, putting the jug on to boil. As it hissed to life, I bent to fetch a mug from the cupboard underneath, plonking it on the bench beside mine. Brad grimaced.

"What is it?" I asked.

He nodded at the second mug. "You have mugs from Wattle Tree Park?"

"One. The staff gave it to Mum as a parting gift when she left. Why?"

His gaze slid away to look out the window. "No reason."

Like hell. I crossed to his side and touched his chin, that strong jaw I loved, turning his head to face mine. "What's the matter?"

"Belinda is dragging me out there to visit my grandad later this afternoon," he said. "I hate that place. I hate it twice as much now I know he's got a … a thing inside him. Belinda always holds his hand, even though I've warned her about the breeder blight, and I'm terrified she's going to catch a blight from him. It gives me the heebie jeebies."

Guilt and anxiety tightened my gut. I didn't think it was that easy to pick up a blight infestation from a person infected with a breeder blight, but I didn't know for sure. Blights had to be the most common dream-world predators for a reason. "If she starts having nightmares, even the tiniest ones…"

"I'll tell you. At least she's careful to wash her hands properly after we visit. I just…" He looked away again, and I let my hand fall to my side.

"If there was anything I could do about the breeder on my own, I would. But Leander said we'd need a dozen

Oneiroi to deal with it." I turned to the fridge, shuddering as I remembered touching Brad's grandfather's dream. The breeder blight had nearly swallowed me whole. "I believe him."

"And there's been no sign of Leander?"

Not since the last time you asked. "I haven't seen hide nor hair of him since the day he arrested my father. And I have no idea how to get in touch with him. Mum's been asking too." I bit my lip as I poured the steaming water. Leander was my only Oneiroi contact, and he was as flighty as, well, a moth. "I'm sorry."

"Hey." Brad's warm hand squeezed my shoulder. "I'm not blaming you. I was just asking. I'm sure he'll show up soon. In the meantime, I'll let the nursing home staff think I've developed a handwashing obsession. They already reckon I'm a little bit nuts."

"You aren't?" I asked, raising my eyebrows at him.

With a wicked glint in his eye, he picked up the tea towel I'd used to wash off the plates and twisted it between his hands, turning it into a crude whip. I danced away, laughing.

Chapter Two

The little girl sat in her grandmother's oversized armchair, her black-shoed feet dangling from the end of the couch cushion. She wore a knee-length school uniform and plain grey tights that looked comfortably warm. I wished I'd worn tights underneath my jeans; clearly Mrs Blackwood didn't believe in running her heater once winter had finished. Goosebumps prickled along the outside of my arms.

"I like your hair." The girl regarded me with wide eyes. Her own hair was the colour of a polished copper coin; her curls clung to the couch upholstery.

"I like yours too."

The girl returned my smile, although hers didn't reach her eyes. "Gramma, when I'm older can I have blue in my hair?"

"We'll see, my sweet," Mrs Blackwood said with remarkable calm, setting a tray bearing a floral tea set on the coffee table. "How do you have your tea, Miss Armstrong?"

"Please, call me Melaina. And just a splash of milk, thank you."

Mrs Blackwood poured three cups: mine, plus two that were milkier and sweet. She handed one of these to the little girl, who blew on it, regarding me solemnly.

"Thank you for coming." Mrs Blackwood eased herself back into her chair, at the other end of the three-seater couch I perched on. She was dressed neatly, in blue slacks and a collared shirt. "My friend Mim spoke most highly of you. Said you did wonders in curing her nephew's nightmares."

I nodded, inhaling the tea. The aroma of bergamot and lavender filled my sinuses as I remembered the trouble I'd unleashed by helping Larry three months earlier. He'd been possessed by a blight. The creature itself had been easy to deal with, but in doing so I'd attracted all sorts of unpleasant attention.

Remembering the creature, I studied the little girl. She was pale, but it was hard to tell whether it was as a result of winter pallor and her fair skin, or due to lack of sleep. The dark smudges under each eye were likely to be sleep-related, though.

Dragging my thoughts back to the conversation, I turned to her grandmother. "How do you know Mim? Is it through Wattle Tree Park?"

Mrs Blackwood frowned. "The nursing home?"

"Yes. She volunteers there. With her dog. A poodle-y looking thing?"

"Oh. No, we both volunteer at a charity shop in Woden."

Maybe Felice wasn't blight-infested after all. "Have you been sleepwalking?" I asked the little girl.

Felice tipped her head to the side. "How would I know?

Wouldn't I be asleep when it happened?"

"Usually you'd wake up somewhere different. Other than your bed."

"Oh. Then no. I don't think so?" She glanced at her grandmother, who shook her head and smiled reassuringly. "No," the little girl said again, more firmly.

"Can you tell me about your nightmares?" Felice bit her lip and didn't answer. I pressed a little harder. "Are they always the same?"

"It's alright." Mrs Blackwood reached over to take the still-full cup from her granddaughter's trembling hand. "Melaina's here to help."

"Okay." Felice's voice was so soft I could hardly hear her. "They're mostly the same. The scariest ones are."

"What can you tell me about the scariest ones?"

"I dream about Mum and Dad. About the night they—" her voice dropped to a whisper "—went away."

I glanced at Mrs Blackwood, whose lips had compressed into a thin line. "Felice's parents died in a car accident last year. A drunk driver on the Princes Highway."

I swallowed hard, trying to dislodge the sudden lump in my throat. It didn't work. "And Felice...?"

"Was in the car. Yes."

"I..." For a moment, I was at a loss for what to say. The memory of my uncle's funeral—of my cousins' grief at losing their father—flashed before my eyes. I shook myself, looking between the girl and her grandmother. "I'm sorry for your loss." The rote words felt awkward and inadequate.

The older woman nodded, her gaze flicking to my own before returning to her granddaughter's face.

I also turned back to the girl. Felice avoided my gaze,

picking at a loose thread in the hem of her skirt, twisting it around her finger until the fingertip turned red. She seemed even smaller in the armchair than she had before, lost amidst the abstract patterns. I squared my shoulders and forced myself to focus. Mrs Blackwood wasn't paying me to pity her granddaughter.

Felice had plenty of reasons to be having nightmares, all on her own, and she wasn't sleepwalking. She probably didn't have a blight infestation, then—they tended to gradually assert control over their host.

But I wouldn't know for sure until I walked in the girl's dreams.

I glanced at Mrs Blackwood. She held her tea cup in one hand, but her posture was stiff, protective. Small chance I'd be able to get her to leave the room for long enough for me to use my Oneiroi magic to put her granddaughter to sleep. On the other hand, she'd come to me. She knew my reputation ... didn't she? "What are the other nightmares about, Felice?"

"There are lots. Sometimes I'm lost at the mall and can't find anyone. Sometimes I'm being chased by a bad dog. Sometimes the kids at school tease me because I don't have a mummy and daddy anymore."

That nettled me. "I hope they don't really do that."

"Sometimes they do..."

"When I was your age, kids teased me about that too," I told her in a gentle voice.

She looked up at me. "Don't you have parents either?"

"Felice," Mrs Blackwood said, gentle admonishment in her tone, but I waved her off.

"I don't have a daddy." I'd met him once. It didn't count. "My mother is alive, but when I was a girl she was very

sick, so I didn't live with her." They also said she was crazy, locked up in a mental institution … but that was more than Felice needed to hear. "It's hard when people pick on you, especially when it's for something that's not your fault."

A shadow crossed her face and was gone. "Yes," she mumbled.

I sipped my tea and set it back on the tray, before sliding out of my seat to kneel before Felice's chair. "I'm going to hold your hands. Is that alright?"

She nodded mutely, and I untwisted the thread from her finger and took her hands in my own. They were so small it was as if I held a baby animal in the palm of each hand: fragile and likely to bolt. She was the youngest customer I'd ever had. "Do you know what I do in my dreams when something bad happens?" I asked. She shook her head, and I smiled, leaning over her. "I fly away."

"I can't fly." A frown marred Felice's smooth brow.

"I can't either, in real life. But I can in my dreams. Want me to teach you?"

She nodded, and I leaned over her. "Okay, sweetheart, close your eyes and take a deep breath." Felice did so, and I pursed my lips and breathed a thin stream of air over her face. Slowly, her head lolled to the side, coming to rest against one of the chair's fat, padded arms.

I sat back on my heels. Mrs Blackwood's eyes opened wide when she saw her granddaughter was asleep. "That was fast. What did you do?"

"I need her to be dreaming. Then I can go into her dreams myself, see what is going on."

"But how? Was it hypnosis?"

"Something like that." I returned to my seat. The older woman narrowed her eyes, and I sighed. "Put simply, Mrs Blackwood, I'm a psychic. But not a very good one. This is my one and only trick. I can't read thoughts or see the future or anything cool like that."

"Mim never said..." She hesitated.

"That I was a crackpot?" I smiled grimly when Mrs Blackwood's cheeks reddened. "I've never talked to Mim, but I'd wager she believes in this sort of stuff. Am I right?" Mrs Blackwood nodded, one corner of her mouth pulling tight. "So she wouldn't think of me that way," I said. "Still, you're not the first sceptical client I've had, and I'll tell you the same thing I tell all my customers. If I can't help Felice, it won't cost you anything."

"That isn't my concern." Her tone carried a mild reproof. "I'm worried about Felice. She's been through so much."

I felt a pang of guilt at that. "Of course you are. But I haven't given her anything chemical, if that's what you're worried about. If you shook her arm right now, she'd wake up—although I'd be grateful if you'd wait ten minutes. I was wondering, though, is she seeing anyone for the trauma from the accident? I can help with the nightmares themselves, but I'm not a psychologist."

"Yes, she has been seeing someone," Mrs Blackwood said. If she was surprised I was recommending traditional medicine instead of meditation and chakras, she didn't let it show.

"Good. Now, what I'm going to do is touch Felice's dream." Mrs Blackwood opened her mouth, and I made an appeasing gesture. "This is where the 'psychic' thing takes effect, I'm afraid. It will look like I've fallen asleep too, but if you shake my arm, I will be harder to wake

than Felice would be. If for some reason you need to wake me up, your best bet is to wake Felice. That'll bring us both around."

"Why ... that is, what would be a reason to wake you?"

"If there's a fire," I said with a smile that I hoped was reassuring. "I'm not anticipating any issues on my end."

"Oh." She hesitated and then nodded. "Very well. It's worth a try. Just ... be gentle with her."

"I will," I promised, settling back into the chair and closing my eyes.

I stepped into Felice's dream.

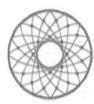

I was standing on a school oval. Long, dry blades of grass scratched my calves, and poked through the holes in my sandals to stab at the sensitive arches of my feet.

Sandals? What?

Grinning, I saw I was wearing a school uniform: sandals, a blue tartan skirt and a pale blue polo shirt. Brad would no doubt approve. At least they'd been scaled to fit ... but I spent a thread of energy to change the shoes to a replica of my usual black leather boots with their purple laces. My butt-kicking boots, as Jen called them.

Now that the grass was no longer irritating me, I looked around for Felice, not really expecting to find her. I didn't often meet dreamers during my therapy sessions; usually, when I put someone under and stepped into their subconscious mind, they weren't there yet—it took them time to start dreaming, to enter REM sleep. But the girl was at the oval's far side, trudging along a footpath, dressed in the same school uniform as me. Her hair was curlier than it had been in the real world, a coppery gold cloud of frizz around her head. A heavy backpack made her look like a turtle trying to carry its house on its back.

Somewhere, a dog barked, a staccato burst of sound. She stiffened, looking around. Her panic was clear not just in the lines of her body but in the dream all around me. The sun grew wan, like it had passed behind a cloud, and the shadows under the trees darkened until they were almost impenetrable. The grass beneath my feet transformed, growing unkempt and full of weeds: sticky, clinging grass seeds, and brown patches of oversized, sun-dried bindi prickles that wouldn't just scratch but would tear the skin of the unwary like a rasp. Glad for my boots, I strode across the oval towards the girl.

The dog's bark grew louder, each inhaled breath a snarl. Felice ran.

Looking around, I didn't see a dog, but in dreams things didn't need to obey the laws of physics. The animal could literally appear out of nowhere. Speaking of which … I willed myself to the girl's side and caught her hand. "Felice!"

She regarded me with wide, panicked eyes. "Let me go. It's coming!"

"I'm here to help." I narrowed my own eyes, and the sound of the dog cut off, mid-bark, like someone had paused a recording. She stared around, her hair flying about her face. "It's okay," I said, keeping my voice calm, like I was trying to sooth a skittish animal. "The dog is gone."

The colour returned to her cheeks and to the dream world around me. The shadows grew less threatening, the weeds smaller and more manageable. "Do … do I

know you?"

"We've met. My name is Melaina."

"I like your hair."

"I know." I smiled. Her confusion, the memory's imperfect ability to cross between the dreaming and waking mind, wasn't unusual.

"Are you an angel?" She peered around me.

That was unusual. "No, sweetheart."

"But ... oh. I thought you had wings. Where did they go?" She frowned at me and I realised my mouth was hanging open. "What's the matter?"

I stretched, trying to look casual, and ran one hand along my other shoulder and as far down my back as I could reach. It was smooth, and I felt a twinge of disappointment. Most Oneiroi, including my father, had moth wings sprouting from their shoulders, and a second pair they called hindwings emerging from the bottom of their shoulder blades—or where the shoulder blades would be on a human. The wings were so long that they would brush the ground as they walked if the Oneiroi didn't keep them lifted.

I'd never had wings, although when I used my powers in a dream, sometimes a ghostly reflection of them flared at my back, casting a shadow I could see before me. They never lasted long. Still, that was probably what Felice had seen.

I recalled my offer to the little girl. "I don't have wings, but I can fly. Do you want to know how?"

"Yes, please." Felice dropped her backpack onto the ground with a thud and tipped her heart-shaped face up to me expectantly.

"All you have to do is imagine you're lighter than air,

like Superman," I said. "Can I have your hand?"

She slipped it into mine and I closed my eyes briefly, reaching deep into her subconscious mind. *You can fly in your dreams,* I told it. *You just have to will it.*

"Supergirl," Felice corrected.

I opened my eyes. The girl had her free hand on her hip and was giving me a disapproving look. "Sorry, what? Oh, yes. Supergirl." Normally, changing someone's dreamscape used my own energy, but I'd learned through experimentation with Brad that, if I was physically touching the dreamer in their dream, changing the dream didn't cost me anything. It meant we could both be superheroes.

"So I go like this?" She punched towards the sky with her fist and gave a little jump. The scrape of her sandals on pavement was followed by a squeal as she bobbed two feet into the air, tethered by my arm like a balloon on a string.

"Exactly like that." I grinned, hopping into the air myself. I felt as light as a feather, as a joyful thought. Felice took my other hand and together we rose above the trees, the roofs of the houses, until the oval was a patch of green, the school roof a bright terracotta like something out of a storybook.

Awake, I was sure I'd feel dizzy, looking down from such a great height with no obvious means of support. But, in the dream, I was in control. My elation was enough to send us flying into the fluffy, cartoonish clouds above our heads.

Felice's face was level with my own, so I saw the shift from nerves to giddy delight as she took it in ... and then to alarm as the sky grew dark and a new sound emerged.

The hiss of tyres on pavement. The steady thrum of a car engine. "Felice?" Her hands tore from mine. The world went black around us, and I struggled against a restraint that slithered over my shoulder and across my chest, pinning me down. *"Felice?"*

Blinking rapidly, I managed to clear my vision. I was strapped in the back seat of a car, a too-tight seatbelt pressing into my shoulder hard enough to bruise. *What the...?* I glanced down and realised I was sitting in a booster seat. That was why the seatbelt was too tight. Grumbling, I loosened it ... then looked to my left. Felice was sitting in an identical seat on the other side of the car, white-faced and trembling. Judging by the slanting light, it was either just past dawn or just on twilight; the sun was behind us, glinting like fire off the rear-vision mirror and bathing the back seat in a warm golden hue.

"It's okay, Mummy," Felice whispered. "I'm not thirsty."

"Hang on, sweetheart," the woman in the front of the car said, a faint thread of exasperation weaving through her voice. "I'll just..." She leant forward, and there was the sound of a rustling plastic bag. "Where is that bottle?"

"I'm not thirsty," Felice said again, louder this time. Her hands were twisted in the flat strap of the seatbelt, and tears streamed down her face.

"She's getting it, Felice. Hold on," a man in the front seat said. He had Felice's coppery hair. I caught a glimpse of a goatee as he glanced over at Felice's mother. "Did it fall down the side of the—"

"Daddy!" Felice's scream pierced the air just before tyres squealed, right in front of our car. Another vehicle.

Oh god. "STOP!" I flung out my hand, energy spilling from me as I froze both cars—as if they were a DVD and

I controlled the remote. Fatigue rolled over me in a wave. Leaning to the side, I examined the car in front of ours. It was so close I couldn't see its tyres. The driver was a shadow, malevolent and strange, with eyes glowing as red as taillights.

Of course he was a shadow. Felice hadn't seen him. She'd only seen her mother trying to find her a drink; her father, distracted.

Beside me, Felice burst into tears, her sobs tearing from her throat.

I reached across to her, my hand trembling with fatigue. "Felice. It's okay. It's just—" I stopped. I'd been going to say it was just a dream, but it wasn't. This was a memory. Sure, it was distorted a little, but it was real all the same. "Sweetheart, give me your hand."

She looked up at me, pale face blotchy with grief. "Supergirl?" she hiccoughed.

It took two tries before I could reply to her. My throat ached with shared grief. The poor, sweet child. "Yes."

"Can we fly away from here?"

"In a minute." I wiggled my fingers, and she reached out, again slipping her hand into mine.

I closed my eyes and moulded the dream to my will.

"Oh, bunny," the woman said, her voice warm and soft. The scent of vanilla threaded through the cabin: whether it was perfume or body wash, I didn't know. The memory had come straight from Felice's subconscious "What happened isn't your fault."

"Mummy?" Felice's voice was tiny.

"It was the other driver." Her father had a pleasant voice, sad as it was. "He did something stupid, and was on our side of the road. See?"

FALSE *Awakening*

I opened my eyes in time to see the man gesture towards the windshield. He and his wife were moving normally, but the car outside was still frozen, inches away from disaster.

"But if I—"

"Even if I'd seen him swerve, there is nothing I could've done. It happened too fast," he said. I wasn't sure whether that was true, but it was what Felice needed to hear. "You did nothing wrong. You were just thirsty. You didn't make it happen."

"I …" Felice pulled her fingers from mine and slipped out of her seatbelt to reach for her parents. They each took one of her hands as she clambered forward. Her mother kissed her fingertips, one by one. "I miss you both."

"And we miss you," Felice's father said. "More than anything."

"Gramma said the man who crashed into us might go to jail," Felice told them, a hint of fire in her voice.

"That's good, bunny," Felice's mother said. "But even if he doesn't, he will regret what happened for the rest of his life. I'm sure of that."

"We love you, Felice." Her father took her in a crushing embrace. Tears prickled my eyes as I watched the ephemera—the fragments of dream that looked, sounded and smelled like Felice's parents—smother her with kisses and murmured words of adoration and forgiveness.

Finally, when fatigue tugged at me and I knew I couldn't hold the dream together for much longer, I reached out and brushed my fingertips against the dreaming girl's shoulder. "Come on, bunny," I said. "It's time to wake up."

Chapter Three

I leaned my head against the bus window. The engine's vibration, felt through the glass, made my teeth rattle. I wedged the caramel lolly between my teeth so I didn't swallow it too soon and choke. The sugar always helped restore my energy after a session in someone's dreams, so I kept a little packet of lollies in my bag for situations such as these.

By the time we reached the bus interchange in Civic, I was feeling a little better—less like a wrung-out rag, at least, although nerves made me fidgety. I stomped down the stairs and, after checking the bus timetables, made my way to another arrival bay to wait for Mum.

I'd called her as I was waiting for the bus following the appointment with the Blackwoods. She'd surprised me by offering to meet me in town for dinner and, delighted at this sign of her reengaging with the world, I'd agreed before thinking it through. Her first week outside the home and she wanted to catch a bus? At peak hour? On her

own? I should have said no, pled a prior engagement.

"Boyfriend, love?" a man with a shock of silver hair and a three-day growth asked me, his pale eyes alight with amusement. The interchange was crowded with public servants waiting to head home for the day; he stood out in his paint-stained jeans and flannelette shirt.

"What?" I stared at him, unblinking, and his smile wilted a little.

"You waiting for your boyfriend? You look worried. That's the third time you've checked your phone. Doll like you, I'm sure he won't stand you up."

Bristling at his tone, I opened my mouth to snap something at him, and then closed it without speaking as I realised how I must look: nibbling my lip, shifting from foot to foot, face tight with lingering grief at Felice's awful memory.

I was saved from having to answer by the arrival of the bus, which groaned and sighed its way into the bay. Conscious of the man's twinkly-eyed stare, I tried not to look too anxious as I scanned the passengers through the windows as they moved to disembark. I spotted Mum's long, black hair immediately. When she clattered down the stairs, I hugged her enthusiastically; her brows rose with surprise.

"Anyone would think you hadn't seen me just this morning." Smiling, she swatted me with a rolled up piece of paper: the bus timetable, a distinctive green stripe down one side. "You shouldn't worry so much."

"When was the last time you caught a bus?" I looped my arm through hers and gave the silver-haired man a pointed look. He shrugged a shoulder, looking the pair of us up and down. *Ew.*

"Before you were born," Mum admitted, her cheeks flushed and her eyes bright with delight. "They have heating now!"

I laughed, steering her away from the interchange and the guy checking her out. "Some of them do." Relief coursed through me, leaving me giddy. Despite my apprehension, I wanted her to acclimatise to life on the outside. It had just been so long.

"Anyway, I haven't been living in a total bubble," she continued as we wandered towards City Walk. "We *did* have TV, you know."

I snorted, and then tried to hide it behind my hand, pretending to scratch my cheek. "Shall we have sushi?"

She wrinkled her nose. "I thought we'd have pizza? It's been ages since I had a good, honest pizza. The ones at Wattle Tree Park always had fancy ingredients on them: spinach and sweet potato and strangely cooked chicken. Those are okay, but I'd kill for honest-to-god ham and pineapple." When I hesitated, she added, "Please? My shout."

I had almost a hundred dollars in my purse, most of it payment from Felice's somewhat bemused grandmother, but my income was sporadic. Of course, Mum's would be too if she wasn't careful. Still, I nodded my acceptance of her offer. She looked so proud of herself, and one time wouldn't hurt.

"Serenity called while you were out," Mum said as we crossed the old chess pit, passing a gaggle of gossiping office workers toting bags from a brand-name clothing store. There was an odd note in her voice but, when I glanced at her, her expression was pleasantly neutral. "She's found a new home for the shop."

"That's great news!" I grinned, thinking about my

comfortable old office out the back of Serenity's New Age Gifts. My visit to the Blackwoods had been a pleasant exception to my usual experience with house calls these past few months: more than I cared to consider had involved visiting houses that smelled of marijuana or stank so strongly of incense that my eyes watered. Sometimes both. I'd been growled at by an overprotective cattle dog, hit on by a stoner who thought I could give him dreams of his favourite supermodel—I could but didn't want to—and arrived to find no one home.

House calls sucked.

"About that..." Mum said. My grin faded at the hesitation in her voice. "Serenity said she wants to talk to you. I ... I don't think it's good news."

"Oh." My stomach swooped. That could only mean one thing: Serenity was cutting me loose. I couldn't blame her. Even though I hadn't held the matches, it had been my fault her shop had burned down. *Been* burned down. It still stung, though. When I'd worked with Serenity, she'd mothered me in a way my own mother rarely had.

Compressing my mouth into a grim line, I reached for my phone. "I'll call her."

Mum shook her head, nibbling her lip. "She's meeting us for dinner."

I didn't know whether to laugh or be shocked. It was sweet that Mum had arranged to be here so I wouldn't have to deal with the disappointment on my own. That was what I told myself ... although part of me squirmed inside at the idea of being sacked with my mother at the table. "At the pizza place?"

"Turns out she likes pizza too." Mum winked at me.

Serenity waited near the front of the café, wedged into a small booth. She filled the inside edge of the table, her generous frame seeming even larger in a flowing, tie-dyed dress. Serenity was huge: tall, and with broad shoulders and hips that would be well-suited to the football field. She smiled when she saw us, although I caught a hint of discomfort, too—and not from the seating arrangement, I was guessing. Suppressing a sigh, I smiled back and slid into a seat on one side of her. Mum sat opposite, picking up the menu with bright-eyed enthusiasm.

After the waiter took our orders, Serenity leaned back as far as the narrow space would allow. She twisted at the red serviette between her fingers until it tore, and I took a deep breath of warm air rich with the mingled scents of tomato and garlic, bracing myself for bad news. "Thanks for letting me gatecrash your dinner," she said.

"No worries," I replied, though I'd had very little to do with it. "How have you been?"

"Good." *Twist, twist.* "The insurance payout arrived, did I tell you? And there's this little shop in Griffith, recently redone and then vacated not long after. I could move straight in without having to do any refurbishments."

"That's great." I tried to cram as much enthusiasm into my voice as I could. She tipped her head to the side to regard me, a frown marring her forehead, and I decided to bite the bullet. "But what's the bad news?"

"Who said there was any...?" She stopped, shaking her head, and gave me a rueful smile. "I should know to just cut to the chase with you psychics."

"That's not how my power works, Serenity." I kept my voice gentle.

"Then how did you...?" she began. I put my hand out

and stilled her fidgeting fingers. Her serviette was half in shreds, fragments of thin red paper in a pile on the table's glossy surface. "Oh."

"So what is it?"

"The shop is smaller than my old one was." She heaved a sigh. "There's only one tiny storage room and the main storefront. I won't have room for my guided meditation class. Or for your office."

I didn't want my disappointment to show so I nodded, examining the central arrangement on the table to avoid meeting her gaze. *Salt and pepper shakers, container of sugar, serviettes, small plastic plant shaped like an olive tree...*

"I still want to try and come to some arrangement," she added hastily, engulfing my hand in one of hers. I looked up in surprise. "We can obviously put up a poster advertising your business, and if you have business cards printed I can stock them too. But I want to offer you a job working the shopfront. Eight hours a day if you want it. You know the customers and the work."

Relief flowed through me, cool as saline. Serenity wasn't trying to throw me out on my ear—she was trying to come up with a way to make the smaller shopfront work, to keep me involved. She wasn't angry at me for what had happened to her shop.

But a worm of doubt nibbled. Did I want to work fulltime as a shop assistant, even at a shop like Serenity's? What about my clients? I imagined the smug reaction of my uncle's widow, Lacey, to the news that my "dream therapy" business had failed. A high-powered lawyer, she already regarded me as the family's black sheep, only a step above my malingering, former hypersomniac mother. Of course,

I could still see clients of an evening, after shifts at the shop, but that sounded exhausting.

"How about four hours a day?" I suggested. "Please don't think I'm not grateful, but..."

"You have to look after your customers too." She leaned back in her chair until the seat squeaked a protest. "I understand."

"I could do the other four hours, if you're looking for someone." Mum's tone was casual as she plucked a straw-like sachet of sugar from its container and shook it, a tiny maraca. I stared at her, and she lifted her chin slightly. "Don't look at me like that. I know I need work, and it'd be good to have a reason to get out of the house."

"Sorry," I mumbled.

She grinned, the expression as sheepish as I felt. "It's alright. I know I've been a slugabed lately."

I nearly choked on my laughter.

Serenity's eyes twinkled as she looked between me and Mum. Finally, she cleared her throat and straightened the front of her dress as if she was preparing for a job interview ... which I supposed she was, only as the interviewer. "Do you have any previous retail experience, Davina?"

"Nothing in the last twenty years," Mum said. "I worked the counter at McDonald's before I got pregnant with Melaina." The idea of my mother in a fast food uniform made my mouth fall open with shock.

"Which means you wouldn't have any references...?"

"No." A blush flushed Mum's ears, and her cheek moved. Was she biting the inside of it? Still, she persisted. "I'm a fast learner, though."

Serenity's eyes widened as she took in Mum's embarrassed but proud demeanour. "Oh, lord, don't feel bad.

It just means to start with I'll have to roster you on at the same time as Melaina, or with me. Working a till isn't hard to learn, and you have something far more important than retail experience as far as I'm concerned."

"What's that?" I asked when Mum seemed too stunned to answer.

"Knowledge that there's more to this world than what there appears to be on the surface. You know there are spirits that haunt people's dreams, because you've experienced them. I'm not saying you have to believe every silly thing that other people do: faeries, unicorns and whatnot. But folks who've been touched by the supernatural are better at understanding those who believe in it. My customers don't want a doubting Thomas selling them incense. I can teach you how to reconcile the take at the end of the day, but I can't teach you to have an open mind and respect others' beliefs."

Tension flowed out of Mum; only when it was gone did I realise how stiff her posture had been. "I definitely have an open mind." Her grin faded a little. "At least, now Ollie's gone I suppose it's open." She glanced at me.

"I haven't tried going into your dreams since then." I shrugged. "I assume the protections he built are still there." But those protections weren't perfect; they'd been overcome first by Ikelos and then by me, my father and Leander, working together. If the walls were intact, the holes probably remained too. "Maybe I should—"

"Shh!" Serenity's voice was soft and emphatic as she reached over to squeeze my hand. I tipped my head to the side, noticing the direction of her gaze, up and over my shoulder. "Good evening, Constable Nelson," she said brightly.

Forewarned, I managed to control my expression as I turned to regard the senior constable who had investigated both Serenity's shop fire and, before that, Brad's blight-possessed assault on me. I blinked in surprise: he wasn't wearing his crisp police uniform but a pair of neat, dark jeans and a polo shirt. The clothes looked good on his tall frame, and the silver chain hanging around his neck, visible at the throat, made his steel-grey eyes gleam.

He smiled. "Please, call me David. It's Serenity, isn't it?" Despite the pleasantries, his eyes stayed cool, calculating, making me feel as if I'd done something wrong and he was trying to figure out what it was. Not all police officers made me feel that way; that power was all Nelson's. I suppressed a shudder.

Serenity nodded, holding out her hand for him to shake. He did so, leaning across the table to squeeze it briefly before releasing it. Was the flush of red at her throat a blush, or was she flustered?

"Have you reopened your shop yet?" he asked, standing uncomfortably close to me in the crowded café—close enough that I could smell his aftershave: a fresh, spicy scent. If it weren't for those eyes, I might have enjoyed the aroma. "You sold ... alternative goods, didn't you?"

The smile that twisted Serenity's lips was a little sour. "Yes. I'm hoping we'll reopen in the next month. Have you pressed charges against the man who burned it down yet? Ewan Wright?"

"That ... is more complicated." His gaze flickered to my face so quickly I would have missed it if I hadn't been studying him. "We have his fingerprints at the scene and evidence of an injury consistent with a glass wound, but the prosecutor is waiting on a court-ordered psychiatric

assessment."

She nodded. "So they told me. What about his involvement at Wattle Tree Park?"

"Unfortunately, there's not much we can do there." He shrugged, and this time the look he gave me was longer, more uncomfortable. "With Ms Armstrong—both Ms Armstrongs—" he nodded at my mother "—refusing blood tests, we have no way to know whether he really did drug any of the patients as they claim. The other comatose patient hasn't awoken, and his tox screen was clear."

I unclenched my jaw and looked towards the kitchen as though eager for my food. Did Brad know the police had taken a blood sample from his grandfather? Surely that sort of thing would need the family's permission … but, then, Belinda was the point of contact for the nursing home, not Brad. She might have agreed without Brad's involvement, or even his knowledge. I was sure he'd have mentioned it to me if he'd known.

"At the time, I'd had quite enough of needles," Mum said. "I'd make a different decision now, but I was delirious." She sat back in her chair and gave him a flinty, narrow-eyed glare. "Now, if you don't mind…?"

"Forgive me. I'm interrupting your meal." He raised an eyebrow as he regarded the table, bare of food, and the shredded serviette. "I just wanted to say hello." He looked at me a third time, finally addressing me directly. "How are you, Melaina?"

"Good." I tried to sound distracted rather than nervous. "You?"

"Fine. Are you still dating Mr Peterson?"

"What if I am?" I snapped. It wasn't smart, but his assumption that Brad was abusive and I was his battered girlfriend was infuriating. Understandable, given Nelson didn't know Brad had been possessed when he attacked me—but it still got under my skin.

"Melaina," Mum said, a quiet warning.

"I was just being polite." Nelson raised his open hands before him in a pacifying gesture. I didn't believe him for a second. He confirmed my suspicions when he added, "I've just been reviewing our records of the case and, when I saw you, I wondered."

"Which case?"

He raised his eyebrows and assumed an innocent expression. "Given the assault, the fire and the incident at the nursing home involved both you and Mr Peterson, I've been treating all three events as one case."

"That doesn't seem fair." I slid back along my seat towards Serenity. The smell of sandalwood incense that clung to her tickled my nose, but better that than being loomed over by Nelson. "Just because I had a run of bad luck…"

"There's no such thing as luck." Nelson's gaze darted towards the counter. "Ah, I believe my pizza is ready. Have a wonderful evening."

Before I could answer, he left, making his way across the café to the takeaway pizza counter. The fact he had an order to collect was somewhat reassuring. At least he hadn't actively come looking for me.

"He's such a Scorpio," Serenity muttered, sweeping the fragments of serviette into her hand and then slipping them into a pocket as if she'd done something wrong. "Observant, determined and suspicious. Definitely in the right line of work, that one."

"How do you know?" Mum asked, frowning at the

constable as he paid for his pizza. Perhaps she expected him to sprout a segmented tail with a poisonous tip.

"When he shook my hand, I saw the pendant at his throat," Serenity said. "Frankly, I'm surprised he believes in astrology at all. He doesn't seem the type. Still … Melaina, maybe you should tell him what really happened? It would get him off your back, and he could redirect his energy to pursuing actual criminals."

I shook my head. Nelson turned, pizza box in hand, and gave me a level look before heading for the door. I glanced hurriedly away. "Just because he wears an astrological symbol, that doesn't mean he wouldn't have me committed right alongside Ewan if I told him dream spirits did it. Besides, they don't have any proof we did anything wrong. And we were the victims, not Ewan. Why should I?"

Still, Serenity's words rang in my mind, filling me with doubt. *Observant, determined and suspicious.* Oh, goody.

Chapter Four

The next weekend my younger cousin, Justin, caught the bus over for a visit. Just shy of fourteen, he was desperate to grow up, get a car and move out of home. Although I felt his pain on the car front, part of me didn't understand why he was so keen to move out. His bedroom and study were larger than the lounge room in the flat I'd shared with Jen, and his house had a pool. On the other hand, having had the unique privilege of living with his mother, Lacey, during school holidays when I was a kid, the rest of me understood the urge. Living in a mansion wasn't everything.

Still, I fought to keep my expression polite as he complained about his mother. "Surely it's not that bad, Jat," I said, fixing him a plate of sandwiches. Jat was my nickname for him; the informality of it drove his mother wild. Standing on the other side of the kitchen bench with his back to the lounge room, he watched with keen eyes as I slathered on the Vegemite until the margarine

was barely a hint of yellow underneath. I liked Vegemite, but even my tongue curled at the thought of that much salty bitterness.

"She's even crankier than she used to be," Justin grumbled, leaning on the low counter. His Adidas sports gear looked freshly ironed and his hair was short around the sides and artfully messy on top. "Yesterday she grounded Olivia for rolling her eyes. Olivia was pissed. Mum was worse."

I bet. I'd felt Lacey's wrath before, most recently at Uncle Ian's wake, but never over a misdemeanour as minor as that. I handed Justin the plate.

"Thanks. Can I get a drink? Anyway, that's why she didn't come. She asked me to give you this as a house-warming present." I blinked, realising he meant his sister, not his mother, as he rummaged in a backpack for a moment, pulling out a small stack of folded linen coloured a pleasant minty green. "They're tea towels," he added unnecessarily as I unfolded one, smiling when I saw the clover pattern. I recognised them: they were one of Lacey's favourite sets. Still, they were good quality, and I doubted my uncle's widow would ever pop around and discover her daughter had given them away.

Besides, if Olivia was grounded, she'd hardly be able to go out and buy me something, would she?

"Thanks." I ran the top towel through the oven handle and then poured Justin a glass of milk. "Maybe you and Olivia should go easy on your mum," I suggested as I put the glass in front of him. "She's struggling after ... well, you know."

"She's not the only one," Justin muttered before taking a quick bite of the top sandwich. "She could go easy on us too. I mean, yeah, she lost her husband. But we lost our dad." His voice broke on the last word and he blinked rapidly, looking out the window like the view was much more fascinating than my washing, flapping in the wind.

I pretended not to notice, knowing sympathy would make him cry. He'd hate that. "I know. And you're right," I said. Looking for something to keep my hands busy, I put the spread in the pantry and wiped down the bench. "How is Olivia?"

Justin shrugged, taking a deep breath before turning back to face me. "She's been an A-grade cow lately. Barely comes out of her room. I think she broke up with her boyfriend. Remember Sam, from the funeral?"

I frowned. My impression of the man hadn't gone beyond black jeans and stubble. "Sort of?"

"Well, they had a huge fight. It was intense." He gesticulated with a crust. "Slamming doors, yelling..."

"The timing sucks. Poor Olivia."

"She's better off without him. The guy was a douche. Still, she's been bitchy as since it happened. It's not surprising her and Mum are fighting so much."

"How have you managed to avoid it?"

"I don't bite back." He grinned suddenly. "I rebel in sneakier ways. That reminds me, I got you a present too." He reached down into the backpack and pulled out a white paper bag about the size of a notebook, a silvery tree stencilled on the side. It was the logo for Neve's, a new-age shop in the city.

I tipped the object in the bag into my hand. It was a willow hoop, with dark yellow string weaving across the centre to form the distinct pattern of a spider web. Feathers and glossy beads dangled from it. A dreamcatcher—I

was familiar with them from working at Serenity's. "It's lovely," I said, running my finger over a silky feather. "And appropriate, since that's basically what I do for a living."

"Catch dreams?" He laughed, probably assuming I was joking, and I forced a grin, cursing silently. I hadn't explained to him the supernatural aspects of my job, worried that he'd tell Lacey. It was silly, but I didn't want to give her any more reasons to hate me than she already had. "Anyway, I thought you could use it to decorate your new office when you get one," he continued. "Just don't tell Serenity I got it at Neve's. I would've bought it from her shop, but..."

"Yeah. Don't worry, I won't tell her."

The sound of bare feet on the faux timber flooring drew our gaze towards the hallway leading to the bed-rooms. Jen appeared, dressed in jeans and a comfortable, somewhat crumpled jumper. "Hey, Jat," she said, smiling at him. He blushed. "When did you get here?"

"Maybe twenty minutes ago?"

"How did the game go?" She brushed a strand of blond hair behind her ear and came into the kitchen, crossing to our shiny new espresso machine and flicking it on. Her glasses reflected the red LED light that indicated the machine was warming up.

"Game?" Justin blinked, scratching the faint, some-what patchy stubble on his chin as if wishing he'd shaved.

"Yeah, you know? Game?" She gestured at him, taking in his soccer uniform. "I assume you played."

"Uh..."

"Jat pretended to be going to soccer practice so he could come over here," I said, glancing at him. His spine stiffened, and I grinned. "You did. I *knew* it."

"How'd you guess?" he said. I raised my eyebrows and crossed my arms, trying to look mysterious, but he wasn't buying it. "Seriously, how? If Mum notices, I'll be joining Olivia in the sin bin."

"You're too clean. I've never seen you look anything other than mud-stained and banged up after a game. Also, you hinted that my housewarming present was you rebelling. She doesn't want you coming over here, huh?"

"Well, she hasn't banned us from seeing you..."

"And you don't want to put the thought in her head?"

"Exactly!" He took a big bite of sandwich. Jen started the coffee machine, which grumbled to life, jingling the cutlery in the drying rack on the sink.

The vehemence with which Lacey had turned on me after Uncle David had died still stung. She'd insisted I no longer refer to her as my aunt, declaring I was wasn't her family. The fact I was her children's cousin didn't seem to matter to her. And she'd never even so much as called after Mum had seemingly had a miraculous recovery from her chronic hypersomnia.

Lacey probably believed Mum's illness had all been a scam, though I didn't know what she thought Mum had gained out of it given her inheritance—in the form of the trust fund—had been paying her accommodation for all these years. If it were a scam, Mum had only been scamming herself.

Justin seemed to sense the shift in my mood, because he finished his sandwich and sat back. "So how's work?"

"Good," I said, somewhat reflexively. More honestly, I added, "Annoying too. I still don't have an office to work out of. House calls suck."

"When's Serenity reopening?"

"Two weeks, but she won't have room for me to work from there." I sighed. I'd been trying to find another business that would let me sublet a small office, but there weren't too many independent shops that suited my line of work. Those few that did have the room already had their own resident kooks, as Brad would call them, his tongue in his cheek. Mostly.

"Why don't you just, you know, buy a place?"

"I'm not made of money," I said. Behind me, Jen's soft laugh mixed with the sound of coffee gurgling into a cup. I turned to face her, catching her devilish grin. "It's true!" I protested, my tone sharper than I'd intended.

"I know! I'm not either. You just sound like my mum did when I was a kid and asked for stuff I didn't need." Jen swallowed her amusement. "Sorry."

"Don't apologise. I *do* sound like your mum." From the corner of my eye, I saw Justin's face had settled into an embarrassed scowl. "It's alright, Jat." I took the empty plate and popped it in the sink. "Your idea would be the simplest, but I don't even have enough saved to pay the bond to rent a small space somewhere, let alone to buy something. And my work isn't the sort that convinces banks to give out business loans."

"So why not work from home? That's what Dad did, when he first started out in real estate. Mum told me."

My hand froze, halfway to the tap, as I turned the idea over in my mind. Finally, I shook my head. "It wouldn't work."

"Why not?" Jen said, regarding me over the top of her steaming coffee.

"We've only got the three bedrooms."

"So?"

"So..." I frowned. Was she suggesting I convert the single-car garage to a study? That would surprise me, given she owned the only car and detested scraping frost from her windshield in winter.

"You could use the dining room. Let's be honest, we're more of an 'eat in front of the TV' household."

Justin sighed enviously.

"But it has two doors. That would diminish the office vibe ... wouldn't it?" I walked through the open sliding door from the kitchen into the dining room, the others following. The pile of boxes had been removed, and the room was bare except for our vacuum cleaner and an empty indoor drying rack. The vertical blinds were open; sunlight streamed in the window, making a small rectangle on the carpet opposite the other door, which led to the lounge room. It was a decent-sized space, able to comfortably fit a six-seat dining table.

"You could buy a screen, pop it in front of the sliding door when you have customers," Jen said. "It just means we'd have to keep the lounge tidy. And find somewhere else to dry our bras."

Justin turned beet red, but still managed to look pleased that we were taking his suggestion seriously. He pointed to the blank wall opposite the lounge room door. "You could put the dreamcatcher there, so it's the first thing people see when they walk in."

Jen nodded enthusiastically. "And the chairs could go here and here." She pointed with her free hand. "Side table here, near the power point, for you to brew teas on, and—"

"Slow down," I said, laughing. "I have to ask Mum

first. She may not like a bunch of strangers coming into her home." The idea of working from home did have a certain appeal: no more house calls and fewer bus rides. But I was cautious too. Ewan had burned down Serenity's shop after I'd stumbled into a scheme his exiled Oneiroi master had hatched. The idea that people who might have blight infestations would be coming into our home, where Jen and my mother slept, worried me. Jen still flinched at the mention of blights, and Mum ... well, with my father gone, she was twice as vulnerable.

On the other hand, Ewan and the blights had managed to find our flat easily enough a few months ago by having Brad trail me home when he'd been possessed.

Still, I kept my reservations to myself. Jen would understand, but Justin didn't even know Brad had been the one to attack me, let alone that malevolent dream spirits were a factor in my business decisions. Hopefully, he'd never have to find out.

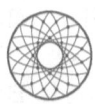

That night at dinner—eaten in the lounge room with the news on in the background—Jen prodded me into raising the idea of working from home with Mum. Together, they listened to my concerns about the risk to them. Then they dismissed them.

"At our previous place, you went crazy with the surface spray to stop nightmare beasties getting in. We can do that here too," Jen suggested, gesturing with a risotto-laden fork.

"That only works to stop the mara." I watched the clump of rice waving around, wondering whether it would give way and tumble into the couch crevices. "Because they use insects to manifest. Blights don't. They use people."

Jen shuddered, her face paling. "Don't remind me."

I felt a stab of guilt, but pressed on. "I can spray all the windows and doorframes, all the ways a bug could get in. But that won't stop someone from coming in here, all blight-possessed and crazy."

"From what you've told me," Mum said slowly, "people who are in the thrall of a blight are sleepwalkers. Like TV zombies. They can't talk or do much of anything. Surely we'd notice if one of them came to the door?"

"It's true." Jen sniggered. "Most doorknockers are only too happy to talk your ear off."

"Yes," I said, drawing out the word as I thought it over. "I mean, maybe. What if the blight was playing possum, being passive, and then took over once the person was inside the house?"

"Then we'd deal with it," Mum said. I stared at her, surprised by the hard edge to her voice.

"Davina's right," Jen said. "There are always more lamps I can belt people with. Besides, with Ikelos gone, whatever blights are out there should be just ... free-ranging, like angry, nightmare-eating chooks. They'd have no reason to target you specifically, right?"

I poked around in my risotto, avoiding pieces of chicken that suddenly didn't seem quite as appetising. "True. They don't seem to be very pack-minded. If I kick one out, the others have no reason to care. The only reason they got riled up when I evicted that one from Larry last winter was because Ikelos was driving them."

"There you go then," Jen said. Mum nodded, and I looked between them, realising the decision seemed to

have been made. "Monday's a public holiday so I don't have class. Why don't I drive you to the shops so we can buy the bits and pieces you need to set up the office?"

"Okay," I said, giving up. "Thanks."

Jen and I chatted about what I'd need to buy and how much delivery for the bulkier items might cost, while Mum listened quietly, half an eye on the television. She looked so much healthier than she had a few months ago. Her muscle tone was better, for a start: she was still slender, but no longer had the twiggy look of someone who had been bedridden for a long time. Her skin wasn't tanned, by any means, but it was no longer sickly either.

Maybe working from home would be a good thing. I could keep a closer eye on her, at least when she wasn't at work. But I would have to reinforce the protections around her dreaming mind before I risked a blight coming anywhere near her.

Her eyes narrowed as a news story caught her attention. I glanced at the screen in time to see a photo of a man with golden hair and pale eyes. Or, rather, it was a facial composite—the sort police use to represent someone they are looking for, based on the descriptions of an eye witness. The face looked familiar, but I couldn't place it.

Noticing our attention, Jen reached for the remote, turning it up so we could hear the story properly.

"—described as between 30 and 40 years old, around 180 centimetres tall, with a lean build, fair skin, short blond hair and blue eyes. Police would like to speak with anyone who recognises the man in the facefit."

The newsreader changed subjects, talking with pun-laden glee about an overturned cheese truck, and Jen turned the volume back down to a murmur, raising her eyebrows at us. "What'd he do?"

I shrugged, but Mum said, "Attacked someone. A stranger in Commonwealth Park, down by the lake." Her gaze turned to me in a way that made my stomach squirm with nerves. "The victim told police that his attacker seemed to be out of it. Drugged, like he was sleepwalking."

Oh.

"Do you know him?" Jen looked back at the television screen as if expecting the image to reappear.

"I think so," Mum said, her tone indicating that she wished she didn't. "The hair colour isn't quite right and his jaw is a little narrower, but I think ... That is, I'm pretty sure that was Daniel, one of the nurses from Wattle Tree Park."

Chapter Five

"We're assuming it's a blight, yes?" Mum asked.

The television was off. I'd taken the plates to the kitchen and made us all cups of tea—because nothing says "war conference" like Lady Grey. Mum and I sat on the three-seater lounge while Jen curled up on the two-seater.

"I am," I said.

"Me too," Jen replied in a quiet voice, raising her shoulder in a one-sided shrug. "The nursing home connection is too great a coincidence. The question is, what do we do about it?"

I clenched my jaw, slowly inhaling the warm, aromatic air drifting from my mug. If Daniel was possessed, I didn't want to just report him to the police. Like Brad months before, Daniel wouldn't be in control of his actions. I'd refused to give the police a statement back then, and that was when Brad had been a total stranger. I knew Daniel.

On the other hand, I was the only one Brad had hurt. I hadn't felt guilty about not helping the police because I'd been the sole victim. Now, though… "Did they say how badly injured the person he attacked is?"

Mum shook her head. "Not exactly, but I don't think the man's injuries are life-threatening. He's in a 'stable condition'—" she made air quotes "—in Canberra Hospital. If the injuries are bad they usually say 'serious condition'. Don't they?"

"He must be so scared." Jen's voice was soft, almost mournful. She tucked her feet under her as if cold and huddled into the couch, her shoulders drawn down.

"The victim?" Mum looked surprised. "I'm sure he was at the time, but—"

"Daniel."

I remembered how upset Brad had been, believing there was something wrong with him. No, upset wasn't strong enough a word. He'd been devastated: questioning his identity, his humanity. Thinking of the shy nurse, my heart ached.

"What do we do?" Jen asked again.

I rubbed my fingers over a fraying spot on the knee of my jeans. "If the blight is new I'll be able to kick it out, no worries, but…" I hesitated "…the victim. He will always wonder—"

"It's not Daniel's fault!" Jen's glasses flashed, catching the light as her face jerked up to glare at me. My own irritation flared and I sat up straighter in my seat, the sudden movement making the surface of my tea dance dangerously close to the lip of my mug.

"We don't have to decide whether to report him just yet," Mum said, patting the air in a soothing 'there there'

gesture. "We don't know for sure that it was Daniel who did this. And, even if he did, we don't know it was a blight. Let's figure those two things out first, and then decide from there."

After a moment, Jen and I both nodded. She gave me a rueful smile. "Sorry. It's just ... sometimes I have these nightmares where I dream that I've woken up and then I start attacking people, tearing at them with my ... my hands and teeth." Her lips paled as she pressed them together. "I feel so out of control. It's awful."

That type of dream was called a false awakening dream—but that was the sort of trivia I didn't think Jen would be interested in just now. "Why didn't you tell me?" I asked instead.

She shrugged. "I didn't want to seem needy, asking you to program my dreams all the time. You're not, like, Netflix for my brain."

The comparison startled a laugh out of me. "No, but I'm your friend. Of course I'll help. Tonight, before bed?"

"Sure!" Her smile faded. "About Daniel...?"

"I need to meet up with him. Five minutes alone will be enough for me to confirm whether he's got a blight hitching a ride." I sighed, glancing at Mum. "Don't take this the wrong way, but this would be a lot easier if you were still at the home. Then I'd have an excuse to visit."

She smiled, sipping her tea. "Why don't you get Brad to take you in to visit his grandfather? That wouldn't be so strange."

I remembered my boyfriend's comments the previous week about how he hated visiting the home. *He won't like that.* But it was the simplest solution. "I'll ask him."

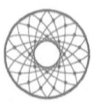

I was right: Brad didn't like the idea of going to the home. But he liked the idea of someone blight-possessed and violent having access to his grandfather even less, and agreed to the suggestion that we drop in to visit when I proposed it over a late breakfast at a café in Kingston the next day.

"We can go after this if you want. Just make sure he's there first," he said with a little sigh. "It'll look weird if we hang around, shift after shift, waiting for him to show up."

"How?"

He shrugged, drizzling maple syrup over crispy bacon in a way that gave me major food envy—I'd ordered eggs, corn fritters, fried tomatoes and wilted spinach on thick bread that was perfect for soaking up juices. It was delicious ... but it wasn't bacon-with-maple-syrup delicious. "Call and ask to speak to him. You don't have to say who it is."

"Good idea."

His eyes crinkled at the corners with amusement as he continued, "Now. Would you like a taste of my bacon or are you just going to stare at it all morning?"

I poked my tongue at him ... but I didn't say no either.

After breakfast, while Brad was paying the bill, I went out onto the leafy sidewalk to call the nursing home on my mobile, turning my back to the gentle breeze so it couldn't brush across the microphone. The call was picked up on the second ring. "Good morning, Wattle Tree Park. Can I help you?"

FALSE Awakening

I recognised the accented voice as belonging to Lien, the Vietnamese-born nurse who'd been on shift the night Brad and I had snuck into the home and confronted Ewan and Ikelos. She hadn't deserved to be knocked unconscious, even as gently as I'd done it. Guilt at the memory tightening my stomach, I made my voice raspy and deeper than normal when I asked her if I could speak to Daniel.

"I'm sorry, he isn't available. Is it something I can help with instead?"

"No, it's personal," I said, feeling a twinge of disappointment. Her answer was so general that I couldn't tell whether he was off-shift or just busy issuing medication or changing someone's bedding. *Damn her professionalism.* I tried again. "Could you ask him to call back when he's free?"

"We're not expecting to see him for several days." *Bingo!* "If you try his mobile number, you might be able to catch him." *D'oh.*

"Ah, I don't suppose you have his number there, do you?"

Her tone cooled. "I'm sorry, I can't give out that information."

"Of course not. Thanks for your help." I hung up before she could ask any more questions.

"I like it when you speak like that." Brad slid his hands around my waist. "Husky is sexy on you. I take it he's not there?"

"No. She said he's not expected for a few days." I slid the phone into the front pocket of my bag and then hooked an arm around his waist. He smelled good, like coffee and aftershave. "Maybe he called in sick."

"I would, in his shoes." Brad frowned. "In fact, I did. Still. Do you know his surname? His address might be in the phone book."

I racked my brain as we walked back to the car, embarrassed that I either couldn't remember or hadn't known it in the first place. "No, I don't think so."

"Belinda might," Brad said. "Let's drive back to mine and we'll see if she's there. She was going to the gym this morning, but she should be home by now. If so, we can look him up in the White Pages online."

Belinda was indeed home, her hair still damp from her post-workout shower. She sat on the couch in the lounge room, feet propped against the coffee table and a whirring laptop balanced on her lap. "Hey, guys." She glanced up, smiling, and then looked harder, examining her older brother's expression and then my own. "You look grim. What's up?"

"You know Daniel, the nurse at Wattle Tree Park?"

"The cute blond?" She grinned, eyes dancing, and Brad's expression darkened. "What? You're not my father. Cut the overprotective dad routine."

I laughed, and the corner of Brad's lips tightened in a grimace. "Sorry. Old habits."

"So what about Daniel?"

"We're trying to get in touch with him, but he hasn't been at work," I said. "Do you know his surname?"

"I can do better than that," she said, looking back at her laptop. "Why are you trying to get in touch with him, anyway?" she asked, fingers flying across the keys.

"Did you hear about that assault in Commonwealth Park on Friday night?"

"Yeah. Why...?" Her eyes opened wide. They were the

same colour as Brad's, the brown of a good-quality hot chocolate. "You don't think…? No. He wouldn't."

"And I wouldn't break into a stranger's flat and try to strangle her," Brad said, glancing at me. "But apparently one time I did just that."

"Oh no. Poor Daniel," she breathed. Belinda knew about blights, though she hadn't been as exposed as Brad had to the rest of my crazy world. Still, after Brad had attacked me, it had been Belinda who'd believed my talk of possession; she'd let me sneak into their home while he was sleeping so I could evict the blight.

"It's not definite." I sat beside her on the couch so I could peek at her computer screen. She had Facebook open and had typed a name into the search bar at the top: Daniel Gilchrist. A list of names opened underneath, but she clicked the one at the top, next to a profile picture of a sleek black motorbike with a pearlescent, Phantom-purple tank. I hadn't picked him for a motorbike person. "You're friends with him?"

"Facebook friends," Belinda clarified. "We don't hang or anything, but we chat sometimes. He's nice." She narrowed her eyes, scrolling through his wall. "He hasn't posted an update for a few days. Nothing to indicate he's on holidays or … wait." The screen stopped moving.

"What?" Brad sat on the other side of his sister, earning him an irritated look as the couch dipped.

"Look at this, from a week ago," Belinda said, steadying the laptop. "Posted at three in the morning."

I read the update, anxiety roiling in my gut. "Just had the worst nightmare. Last time I eat cheese before bed!" The laugh-till-you-cry emoticon filled me with dread.

"It's not a smoking gun, but…" Belinda drew out the

last word, looking at the more recent updates. A link to a review of a new superhero movie. A funny meme involving a cat. All seemingly innocuous. But Daniel was an active Facebook user, posting updates on average twice a day; to me, the three-day silence with no explanation was just as sinister as the comment about bad dreams.

"I need to see him. Do you have his number?"

"No. But I'll send him a message, ask him to give me a call." She opened a message window. "Uh. What do I write?"

"Give it here?" I asked. She slid the laptop to me. "This is Melaina, Davina Armstrong's daughter," I typed. "This might seem weird, but are you OK? If you've been sleep-walking and—" I hesitated "—other things, I can help. Call me."

I added my mobile number and hit enter. Daniel must have been online, because after a few seconds, a little tick and a "Seen" message appeared underneath my message. A bubble indicated he was typing back.

"Howd u know?"

"It's my job to know. Are you free this afternoon?"

There was a long pause after the tick appeared, but finally a reply came. "Yes."

Chapter Six

After some discussion, Brad and I agreed to Daniel's request that we go to his house rather than meeting out somewhere. At first it surprised me that Daniel was willing to have two almost-strangers over, especially almost-strangers connected to disruptions at his work. But if he believed he'd assaulted someone, he might not want to be around other people. His motivations didn't really matter to me; it was definitely more convenient to meet him somewhere private. Ousting blights was better done in a location with a bed … or at least a comfortable couch.

Daniel lived in an apartment in a trendy suburb maybe ten minutes' walk from the city—the sort of area Jen and I used to look at but could never afford. He must eat a lot of two-minute noodles to be able to pay the rent on a nurse's salary; even the one-bedroom apartments weren't cheap. A familiar motorbike was parked in the car spot assigned to his number.

This place is walking distance to Commonwealth Park. It'd be a bit of a hike, but doable. The thought tightened my jaw.

We trudged up the cheerily lit stairs to the second floor, listening to the muted sounds of people enjoying their Sunday afternoon: a football game, a Motown cover of a modern pop song, the rumbling bass of a movie soundtrack. Daniel's door looked the same as all the others but, behind it, his apartment was silent.

I knocked twice; my fingers had barely left the timber when the door cracked open and Daniel peered out, a safety chain bisecting his face. I gave him my most harmless smile. He nodded, shutting the door to release the chain before opening it again, hustling us into an apartment that was bright with afternoon sunlight and thick with the heady aroma of strong coffee. The recycling bin overflowed with cans of energy drink.

"This is my boyfriend, Brad," I said when Daniel looked at him askance. "He gave me a ride over."

"Pleased to meet you," Daniel muttered. He looked awful, his usually pleasant features made scruffy by several days' stubble. He shuffled back to the couch, a faded but comfortable three-seater, and sat down with a faint groan. He seemed to sink into his green hoodie, which was several sizes too big for the nurse's lean frame. I took a seat on the single-seat couch, while Brad crossed his arms and leaned against a small dining table piled high with the detritus of life.

"How long have you been sleepwalking?" I asked.

"Weeks." A tic jumped beneath one of Daniel's blood-shot eyes. "Weeks and weeks."

"And the nightmares?"

"They've been going on longer. But they're … getting worse. The last few days. Worse."

I glanced down, trying to get a look at his knuckles, to see if he'd been in a fight. The story about the attack hadn't mentioned a weapon; I assumed the victim had been beaten. But Daniel's fingers were hidden in the sleeves of the hoodie.

I'd have to ask. Dammit.

"Did you… Do you…" I grimaced. "After sleepwalking, have you ever found yourself anywhere completely unexpected? Down the street? Further?"

Daniel's gaze flicked to my face and his eyes narrowed, seemingly trying to bring me into focus. "Y-yes?"

"Commonwealth Park, maybe?" I tried to keep my tone gentle, but he sat up abruptly, arms wrapping around his torso as he leaned forward to stare at me.

I recoiled into my seat, and Brad took a step forward. "Steady on, mate. We're here to help."

"I don't remember being there," Daniel said, the words tumbling over themselves in his haste to speak them. "I don't ever remember walking anywhere. But…" He swallowed whatever he'd been about to say.

Brad finished it for him. "But you've been waking up in strange places." His hands were open and steady at his sides, like he was afraid of startling Daniel into flight. But I could see the tension in the line of his shoulders and I ached to go to him, wrap him in my arms. "Wearing clothes you don't remember putting on, with cuts and bruises you don't remember earning. Maybe with twigs in your hair, or leaves in your pocket? Maybe … maybe there's blood, but you can't find a corresponding injury?"

The look on Daniel's face broke my heart: fear, twisted

through with a wild, desperate hope. "How do you know?"

"Because it happened to me. It's not your fault. You're not going crazy. And Melaina can help." Brad nodded towards me, and I sat up straighter in my chair. Daniel certainly *looked* crazy—even more than Brad had when we'd first met. But at least Daniel wasn't trying to kill me. Not yet, anyway.

"What's happening to me?" Daniel whispered.

"Would you believe me if I said you were possessed?" I asked hopefully.

"No."

I sighed. No one ever did. "Well, I don't know what else to tell you, Daniel. I could try coming up with some psychobabble bullshit to make you feel better, but you've had more medical training than I ever did. You wouldn't buy it." Brad frowned at me. Daniel looked stunned. "Let's just say I'm here to help and leave it at that, yeah?"

"I'm an atheist," Daniel said, almost apologetically. "I don't believe in demons."

"It's not a demon. It's a largely intangible, malicious creature that feeds on your nightmares so it can take your body out for a joyride now and then. And it doesn't give a crap whether or not you believe in it."

"Let's say I accept what you're saying. What next? Holy water and chanting? Guided meditation?" His voice was sharp with bitterness.

"I just need you to go to sleep," I said. "I'll take care of the rest."

"*No.*" He stood abruptly, almost knocking into Brad in his haste to get to the tiny open-plan kitchen. "I can't sleep." Daniel picked up a coffee pot with shaking hands and poured its contents into a mug. Black coffee splashed

onto the bench, and he ran his finger through the puddle, sticking it in his mouth as if he couldn't waste even a drop of precious caffeine. "No sleeping," he said around his finger.

Brad gave me a helpless look and I stood. "Alright. Fine. No sleeping. We'll just talk. Come back to the couch." I was such a liar. But, fortunately, Daniel was either not very good at reading motivations or was too tired to see the truth, because he walked back over to the couch, brimming mug in one hand. He perched on the edge, perhaps worried he'd fall asleep if he got too comfortable. "When was the last time you slept?" I asked.

Daniel blinked, sipping his steaming coffee. "What day is it?"

"That long, huh?"

He gave me a wobbly grin. "Yeah."

"You're mad stubborn." I filled my tone with as much admiration as I could muster when all I felt was worry. He'd kill himself at this rate—and the more tired he got, the easier he was making it for the blight to take over. "Can you tell me about the dreams?"

His eyes widened. "No."

"Can't you remember them?" I glanced at the coffee mug. He'd freak if I moved to take it off him, but I didn't want to put him to sleep while he was holding that much hot liquid. The last thing either of us needed was a burn.

A shudder rippled through him. "I wish. No, I remember them too well. I just don't want to talk about them."

I held back a sigh by force of will. "Daniel, I want to help you, but you aren't making it easy."

"I don't want to focus on them. It makes them stronger." His gaze skittered away across the room, seemingly unable to focus on anything. "I know it sounds stupid."

"Not that stupid." For all I knew, it might even be true. "Alright, let's skip the details for now. Tell me about generalities. Do you get nightmares every night?"

"Every time I sleep. Even naps."

I leaned forward in my chair so our heads were closer together. He was in range of my power; I was thankful he was so tired, or he might remember the last time I'd rushed up to him, gotten this close. He'd passed out shortly afterwards. "Do you ever have normal dreams?"

"N-no. Not anymore." He didn't just sip the coffee; he slurped it. Good. He'd be done soon.

"What are you afraid of?" I murmured, stalling for time.

He looked at me, seeming surprised to find me so close. He inched back a little on the couch. Dammit. "That I'm losing my mind. That my subconscious is a thug on its way to becoming a serial killer. That I've hurt people."

"You're not going crazy," Brad said again. He had eased closer, and was now holding himself carefully still. Was he worried that the blight might take over and attack me, or that Daniel might flee? Either was plausible.

Daniel laughed, a harsh, broken sound. And he finished his coffee.

As soon as he set the cup down on the table next to the remote control, I leaned closer and exhaled onto his face. His eyes rolled back into his head and he slid sideways; together, Brad and I caught him, easing him back onto the couch so his head rested on one arm and his legs dangled over the other. Even in his sleep he looked anxious. Had the dreams started yet?

"I thought he'd never finish that." I indicated the coffee with a nod of my head.

"Is that what you were waiting for? I wondered." Brad picked up the mug, heading into the kitchen to place it in the sink. I heard a click as he turned off the coffee pot. "Dude's been mainlining caffeine for days. He needs a detox."

"Yeah." I opened the balcony door to let fresh air and traffic noise drift into the apartment. Then I settled back into my chair, looking at Daniel. "I like coffee, but the air's so thick with it I'm getting a headache."

Brad came back into the lounge, his brow furrowing as he took in my relaxed pose. "You're going in?"

I nodded. "I reckon his blight is about as established as yours was. I might be a while."

"I remember that fight." Brad had been present in the nightmare, albeit dreaming of himself as a small child. I doubted I'd see Daniel in his dream. He hadn't been asleep long enough. "You nearly got creamed."

He was right, but I set my jaw. "I was fine. Besides, I've been, um, working out. Doing lifts." I grinned. "I can fly now."

He snorted a laugh, but his amusement fled as quickly as it appeared. "I just wish I could help."

"You can help. Stay here—make sure the blight doesn't get him up and moving. Once it realises what I'm doing, it might try to hurt me on this end."

"I know," he said. "I just... I don't enjoy feeling useless. I wish you could bring me with you into his dream so I could help you kick its arse."

"Even if I could, I need you here," I said. But my mind spun at the suggestion. I'd never tried bringing a non-Oneiroi into another human's dreams. Could it even be done? I nibbled my lip, thinking it over. It might be worth experimenting with—but not here. Not now. "See you on the other side, lover."

Chapter Seven

$\mathcal{U}$sually when I stepped into someone's dreams just after they'd fallen asleep, I didn't arrive in an active dream so much as in a place of significance in their subconscious: a proto-dream of sorts. The kind of place they'd have recurring dreams about. As a lucid dreamer, I didn't have true recurring dreams—deliberately conjuring dreams of my favourite places didn't count. But I was familiar with the concept. Jen had told me that, usually, those dreams she remembered contained elements of her family home. Brad often dreamed of his grandparents' house, where he'd spent a lot of time as a child.

That was why, when I appeared in a brightly lit department store, I raised my eyebrows. *Huh. First job, maybe?* I stood in an aisle full of bags of confectionary: liquorice sticks, mixed lollies, chocolate drops. But everything was slightly off. When I focused on a rustling purple and yellow packet, trying to make out the brand name, the logo slid away from my gaze as if it didn't want to be nailed down. Price tags were illegible: smeared or written in gibberish characters. And when I looked between the packages I didn't see a backboard filled with mounting holes but sheer, impenetrable darkness.

The darkness gaped back at me.

With goosebumps shivering along the length of my forearms, I took a moment to prepare myself, sparing a thought and a shred of energy to conjure a set of trusty motorcycle leathers. I didn't have any such thing in the real world, but in dreams I'd found they served quite well as armour against the barbs on a blight's tentacles. A clear-faced, round helmet made me feel like an idiot but protected my eyes. I didn't know for certain that there was a blight here, but something was definitely not right. Even if it was just a creepy manifestation of Daniel's subconscious—even if he was indeed going crazy—it paid to be careful. Ephemera could still have teeth.

I crept towards the end of the aisle, leather squeaking faintly as I listened for the telltale bubbling hiss of a blight. Peering past a stand of round-bellied plastic animals stuffed with jellybeans, I saw a row of unattended registers to my left. To my right, clothes swayed in a breeze I couldn't feel. In front of me was the store's main entrance: the roller shutter was down, allowing only a vague impression of a darkened mall beyond.

Deserted apartment stores were bloody creepy. Even ones with the lights on. Still, this didn't look like a place a blight had trashed. Brad's had shredded the surface of his dream, tearing holes in walls and coating everything with a mess that would do a slimy *Ghostbusters* spectre proud. This store was creepy, sure, but trashed? No.

Like my thought made it happen, a corner of the store

went dark as one fluorescent light, then another, went out with a *pop* and a tinkle of glass on tile. "What the...?" I whispered, looking up.

That was when I spotted the blight.

It hung upside down from the ceiling, somewhere above the menswear section, like a deranged bat a few feet wide and made of smog. Its tentacles were jammed deep into the rectangular ceiling tiles; the tiles themselves were slick with an oily coating of blight ichor that dripped downwards, spattering across a garish display of novelty ties that hurt my eyes.

"Gross," I said, my voice somewhat muffled behind the helmet's faceplate. The blight turned, rotating slowly until its stained yellow eyes glared down at me.

"*Oneeiiiiroi,*" the creature hissed.

"I was talking about those ties, but you're gross too. You look like an evil Christmas ornament up there, you know." I gathered power around my hands, threads of blue-white lightning encircling my wrists and licking down my fingers. The fine hairs on the back of my hands stood on end, tickling until I had to resist the urge to scratch them. I forced my back straight and my shoulders square so the blight wouldn't see my energy flagging, draining into the lightning.

With a shriek so high it hurt my ears, the blight yanked downwards, its tentacles tearing ceiling tiles free to smash to the floor. One tile, three, five. Then dozens. Tiles shattered around me and jellybeans scattered like marbles. Fluorescent lights exploded, plunging the store into gloom. By the glow of my lightning charge, I darted towards a service desk, diving under the counter hatch. Huddling in my leathers and helmet, I barely fit.

I stared at the rain of tile fragments as it slowed, and then stopped. Each was coated on one side with blight ichor, as if the entire ceiling cavity had been filled with the blight's contamination.

This blight hadn't destroyed the surface of the dream. It had rotted its very bones.

I couldn't see more than a dozen feet in front of me. The light curling around my hands wavered and danced. Maintaining it was eroding my reserves of energy. Normally if I ran out, I'd be thrown out of a person's dream and into a deep sleep of my own, where I could recover. No big deal. With a blight on the prowl, though? I shuddered.

Breathing as quietly as I could, I tried to hear the blight over the distant tinkle and crash of merchandise tumbling to the ground. But it was futile. The creature could float. Unless it spoke, I wouldn't hear it until it was on top of me.

I couldn't stay here. At least, if I saw it coming, I could fight it.

Gritting my teeth, I stood, shouldering the hatch up. It flipped over, slamming against the counter. I flung my hands into the air, shooting the stored lightning towards what was left of the ceiling, willing the roof to catch fire. The bolt exploded against something above me with a sizzling, spitting sound like bacon in a frying pan. I stared upwards, mouth falling open.

Hidden beneath the tiles had been a second ceiling, a mass of flesh and writhing tentacles that glistened wetly. Tongues of fire ignited by my strike curled among them, cooking them. I tasted acid as bile rose in my throat.

Wailing, the blight descended on me like an asteroid

on a hapless dinosaur. I leapt to the side, smashing my hip against the counter, and held my hands out in front of me to protect myself from the lashing tentacles. They snared around the leather sheathing my forearms, winding tight as the creature attempted to yank me off balance. I braced myself, knees bent to lower my centre of gravity. Still, my boots skidded on the tiles, dragging me centimetre by centimetre closer to the creature's volcanic maw.

I yanked my arms backward and one pulled free, a few broken tentacles still embedded in the leather. They twitched spasmodically. I glanced around, looking for a weapon. A toppled stand of DVDs was just out of reach—but, even if it weren't, the corrugated cardboard was too flimsy to be of use. Nothing else was close.

Taking a deep breath, I hauled backwards, reeling the blight in towards me by the tentacles still wrapped around my left arm. The leather tore, and barbs bit into my skin. Pain flared. I imagined a long-bladed dagger, wickedly sharp, into my other hand. My strength flagged. I couldn't keep this up for much longer.

Bracing the dagger's hilt against my torso, I gave one final yank on the tentacles, pulling the blight's roiling, gaseous body onto the glittering steel. The cloud's smoky surface gave and, as my hand reached the edge of the cloud, the blade bit into something more solid underneath.

I sent a blast of energy from my hand, through the dagger, and into the creature. Behind me, ghostly wings flared, throwing my shadow to the ground before me.

For one long moment, the blight and I stared at each other as the power grew inside its core. Its eyes were bright with hatred ... hatred that morphed into terror as it realised what I had done. The roiling flickers of light in the cloud grew brighter. Frenetic.

I turned my face away just as the creature exploded.

The blast knocked me back, shoving me into the counter again. I rolled over the top. My helmet cracked against something as I fell, its plastic exterior shattering like an egg but protecting my skull. I didn't feel particularly lucky, though. Blood pooled beneath me, flowing from the slash in my throbbing arm, and my ears rung from the blight's final screech. I ached all over, and if my leathers had been real they'd be beyond saving, covered in gore and scorched by flame. But it was done. I yanked the helmet off and ran a hand through my hair, feeling the tender spot on my head with a wince. The helmet was a mess. *Lucky this is just a dream, or I'd have a huge egg tomorrow.*

The sound of a second blight's hiss turned my blood to ice in my veins.

I whipped my head up to look over the counter, swallowing bile as a wave of dizziness washed over me. The second blight was smaller, barely the size of a football as it scooted towards me from the appliance section. A baby. Its tentacles had yet to develop barbs, instead being covered with fine, prickly hairs. I could easily beat it if I weren't already battered and weary.

It took almost all my remaining energy to blast it from the air, leaving a steaming, blobby corpse. The dregs of power I had left were all that kept me tethered to Daniel's dream. No more changing the dreamscape for me.

When I heard a third blight, and a fourth, I bit back a sob. *What's happening?* Above me, the roiling mass in the ceiling burbled a laugh. The realisation hit me like a blow, and I gasped. It was a breeder blight. Not as well developed

as the one in Brad's grandfather. Not as strong. Maybe a juvenile itself. But it was still able to produce baby blights. The flames I'd cast into it were flickering and dying, doused by its slime, and I couldn't make any more.

I struggled against despair as my boots crunched in tile shards, sticky jellybeans and a viscous grey substance I didn't want to examine too closely. The breeder blight might be young, but it was still stronger than me. The two new blights shot towards me, tentacles whipping around underneath them like those of a jellyfish. Above, the breeder blight didn't seem able to move, but an expanding pustule on its belly contained flickers of lightning. Yet another blight, almost ready to tear free of its revolting parent.

I couldn't win this fight. If I fled into my own consciousness, would the blights follow me? I realised with a sickening certainty that they would

"Melaina! Over here!"

Chapter Eight

I spun on my heel at the voice, seeing the familiar, winged shape of my childhood friend standing in the manchester section. Leander wore tight pine-green leather armour and his four moth wings flared at his back, their soft grey reflecting the dying firelight until they glowed orange themselves.

Under other circumstances, the tightness of his armour would've had me rolling my eyes. But, right then, relief washed over me. I'd never been so glad to see the Oneiroi in my life.

Holding my bleeding arm against my side, I stumbled towards Leander, every muscle aching, my head throbbing in time with my racing heartbeat. One of the baby blights lunged at me, screaming, and I flinched away ... only to see it explode in a cloud of gore as a silver-hued bolt of energy slammed into it. When I reached Leander, panting, he gave me a wide grin even as his gaze took in my wounds. "You're poisoned." He shot another bolt over

my shoulder. Another blight screeched and died. "That should give us enough time to deal with it."

"What?" I stared down at my wounded arm, struggling to comprehend his words.

"Hold still. This might sting a little."

I bit my lip to keep back a yelp of pain as his strong hands tore the shredded leather from my arm. Smoky black tendrils threaded under my skin from the place where the barbs had punctured my forearm. My head swam. "Oh, shit."

Jaw clenched, Leander gripped my hand in his and placed his other hand on the inside of my elbow. Slowly, and with a solemn expression, he ran it down my arm. As his palm crossed over the first of the black lines, a hiss arose. It sounded like a blight bellowing its defiance. Agony shafted through me and I screamed, trying to yank free, but Leander's other hand held me in a grip as firm as iron. I stared in horror as threads of smoke slipped out from between his fingers, as gritty as sand from a soot-stained beach. The blight had ... had *infected* me through its barbs.

It was hard to tell in the dim light, but when the pain receded my arm looked as good as new. Leander released me and wiped his hand clean on a beach towel, wrinkling his nose. Then he brushed his fingers through my hair, healing the swelling bruise with a thought. Compared to the first pain, I barely noticed.

"You said it *might* sting," I croaked, flexing my fingers. His grip had left them feeling achy.

He peered past me, looking around and then up at the breeder blight. The ceiling had fallen back into shadow, the last of my flames extinguished, and Leander sent a ball of silver energy to hover high in the air. The cool glow revealed that several more pustules were swelling, ready to burst. "I may have understated the truth a little," he admitted.

You think? Still, I didn't have the energy to be grouchy at him. "Well, thank you."

He glanced at me, surprise in the roundness of his green eyes. "You're welcome. Now, why are you going up against a breeder blight on your own?"

"I didn't know it was here." I cast around for a weapon, but we were surrounded by bedding and towels. I didn't think a blight would hold still while I smothered it with a pillow. "This is Daniel's dream. He's a nurse at Wattle Tree Park."

Leander's eyes narrowed and his wings twitched with irritation. "Not the nurse who was working with Ikelos?"

"No, that was Ewan. Daniel's another one. He's one of the good guys." I studied Leander, looking for signs of exhaustion in the set of his shoulders. There were none. "Are you good to take this thing on or do we need help?"

"On my own?"

My pride smarted to admit it, but what choice did I have? "I'm tapped out. You said you'd bring other Oneiroi back with you." I looked around, half expecting Oneiroi to appear like a flight of avenging angels who'd traded their feathers for chitin.

"That's ... complicated." His gaze slid away from mine, and I narrowed my eyes. "But the upshot is that they aren't here."

"You promised!"

"Is now really the time to fight about it?" Leander shot another silver bolt at the ceiling. I turned in time to see

it vaporise a newly hatched blight tumbling from a bursting pustule. "To answer your question, no, I don't have enough raw power to take this thing out."

My heart sunk to my boots, and I absently rubbed the healed skin of my arm with my other hand. Daniel was relying on me ... and the breeder was too dangerous to leave wandering around in his skin. What would I do with him? Keep him unconscious in his apartment until I could get the other Oneiroi to show up? Someone would come looking for him eventually, and then what? I imagined what the suspicious-eyed Constable Nelson would say if I told him I'd abducted Daniel for the public good.

"So," Leander continued, drawing my attention back to him, "any bright ideas?" I frowned at him and he shrugged. "Last time I saw you, you gave me a lecture about trying to brute force my way through problems. Aren't you the one who is good at using a small amount of power to get a big result in a dream, while I'm the wasteful Oneiroi?"

A blush warmed my throat at his words as I remembered my tirade. I'd called both him and my father lazy. But he was right. "Accept the dreamer's paradigm, then work with it," I said, recalling my advice to them.

"Right." He looked around. "What is there in a ... whatever this place is that we can use?"

"It's a department store." I looked at the shelves around me. Pillows, towels and bathmats weren't going to be of any use. Neither would clothes, no matter how garish, and the only weapons would be in the toy section—but I didn't think foam bullets were going to cut it. "Let's head to the sports department. They sell camping accessories. Maybe we can find some gas tanks or something."

"Great." The leather of Leander's armour squeaked softly as he rolled his shoulders. "Where's that?"

"I ... don't know."

He stepped behind me. "May I?" Before I realised what he was doing, he'd hooked his arms around me, under my arms and up to grip my shoulders firmly. I squeaked as the aisle lurched and began to recede; air rushed across my face.

Leander flew. Not in a sedate Supergirl-style way, hand out and body steady, but in a stomach-churning lift and drop as his wings pumped, carrying us up over the aisles. My feet dangled close to the dusty tops of the shelves as I swallowed a rush of adrenalin and looked around, squinting through the gloom. A crooked sign, smeared with goo from the falling ceiling tiles, gave me the clue I needed. "Over there ... oh god, *Leander*." This last was a gasp as he dove in the direction my finger pointed. For a heart-stopping moment I was sure we were going to collide head-first with a stack of camping chairs. Gritty air full of tile shards and who knew what else whipped around my face, and I scrunched my eyes shut and tensed all over, anticipating the snap of bone against aluminium and canvas.

Leander's steadying hold kept my knees from buckling when we touched down delicately in the middle of the aisle. I opened my eyes and he nodded, stepping away. The light was so dim in this corner of the store that his face was little more than a pale oval. Still, I caught the hint of a smile.

When he created a tiny ball of light so we could see properly, he'd managed to straighten his features. I pretended I hadn't noticed.

It wasn't much of a camping department. Maybe this store had been in an inner city somewhere, or maybe this section hadn't featured prominently in Daniel's past. I studied the shelves; the labels on the various cans and boxes shifted like oil on water, refusing to stay still. "Dammit!"

"What's the matter?"

"I can't read the labels to see which of these are flammable."

Wings held aloft so they wouldn't drag in the muck, Leander squatted. He placed a hand palm-down on the floor, closing his eyes. I stared as he shimmered with the same silver glow that infused his attacks. The light shivered over his skin like an aura, flaring in time with his heartbeat. Finally it faded, and he looked up at me, satisfaction quirking one corner of his lips. "How about now?"

I stared at the shelves. They seemed realer, somehow. More solid, less capricious. The sense that something was staring out from between the merchandise, waiting to attack, had faded, and the writing had stabilised, the packaging growing familiar. I expected if I compared it to a real-world sample of the same product the details would be wrong, but it was close enough for our purposes. "Wow."

"Thank you," Leander said, standing slowly.

"What did you do?"

"I strengthened the effect of the dreamer's memory on the dream."

"You can do that?" I tried to keep the stunned awe out of my voice, but—if his cocky grin was anything to go by—wasn't successful.

A pair of gas stoves were on display partway along the aisle. Nearby were a half dozen boxes of butane gas cans, but no bigger gas cylinders of the sort I'd hoped for. Leander followed my disappointed gaze.

"The contents of those cans are flammable. But they won't go very far."

He strode over to the cylinders, collecting them in his arms and turning back to me. But I'd already caught sight of another promising find: a display of firelighters, paraffin cubes that the packaging claimed burned odourless and smokeless. A grim smile tugged at my lips as I scooped up the boxes, looking around for something to hold them. A trolley abandoned at the end of the opposite aisle caught my eye and I strode over, dumping the boxes with a clatter. "Put them in here."

Soon we'd almost filled the trolley with every highly flammable object we could find: several one litre bottles of methylated spirits from the cleaning aisle, an entire pallet of bug bombs, even a shelf of hairspray. The breeder blight released several more offspring, which Leander destroyed with an almost offhanded air, leaving the huge, blubbering creature to screech its protests as we gathered the means to destroy it. I would've felt sorry for it, trapped upside down in the ceiling like the parasite it was, if I hadn't known it was gradually spreading its corruption throughout the store, conquering Daniel's subconscious mind.

Leander studied me from the other side of the trolley. I could see the shadows of fatigue under his eyes, which shocked me. Leander *never* looked tired. Cocky and self-assured? Yes. But tired? No. Not even when Ikelos had bound him with barbed wire. Despite his relaxed manner, increasing the hold of Daniel's memory over the dream

and destroying so many blights was draining him. And he was too proud to admit it.

I clenched my jaw and took a breath. I'd wanted to look for matches and maybe some reams of paper, but we didn't have time. Another blight was about to hatch. "Alright." I pulled several packets of nails down and tossed them onto the top of the trolley with a sick feeling. I'd seen enough news stories to know real-world lunatics packed their bombs with shards, to cause additional damage. "Can you get this up there, and then explode it?" I glanced at the nails. "From a d—"

The floor erupted beneath us.

Tentacles, each as thick as one of Leander's well-muscled thighs, smashed through the floor. The blight hadn't been as helpless as I'd assumed ... and corruption hadn't been the only thing it had been spreading. My cheek burned as a shard of floor tile sliced it, blood welling. The trolley tipped and I ignored the pain, lunging forward to steady it before its contents spilled into the sticky darkness below. Leander leaned over and gripped the frame, placing one hand on either side, his fingers brushing against mine as I let go. His grim gaze held mine for a moment, and then his wings pumped. Air washed over me as he lifted the overstuffed trolley into the air, towards the central body mass of the blight.

For a second I felt relief as he carried the improvised bomb above the thrashing tentacles. Then one of those tentacles slid around my waist, barbs as long as my palm tearing through the scorched armour of my motorcycle leathers. I gasped and prised at them with bare hands, trying to wiggle free but succeeding only in cutting my palms. Above me, the muscles in Leander's back worked as he strained to haul the trolley upwards, ignoring the now-free baby blight buzzing around him like an oversized mosquito. He was dragging the bomb up there with brute force. Pain caused my vision to blur, but not before I realised he was going to ignite the trolley's contents *while he was holding it*. The damned fool Oneiroi had no idea what would happen.

The tentacle dragged me towards the jagged hole in the floor. I didn't look down, not wanting to see what awaited me. The wet smacking sound and the putrid smell were bad enough. Sweat beaded on my brow and I set my jaw against the pain, blinking to clear my vision, staring up at Leander.

He drove the end of the trolley into the breeder blight's wet mass, leaning against the handle to brace it there as he conjured a spark in one hand.

The spark descended towards the makeshift bomb.

I cried out, using the last of my energy to fling a shield, a wall of force, between Leander and the trolley.

Fire and exploding chunks of meat raining down around me. My vision blackened, and I tumbled out of the dream.

Chapter Nine

*A*wareness crept over me and I groaned, trying to crawl back into the deep, dreamless state in which I'd been floating. I didn't *want* to be awake. Awake was hurting from head to toe, with a skull that pounded and a mouth that tasted like something unbearable had crawled in there to nap. Or die. Maybe both.

Movement thundered nearby, and I cracked an eyelid to see a familiar face leaning over me. Brad. Relief and concern warred across his features, widening his eyes and tightening his lips. I wanted to kiss him. It hurt to move.

"Here." He held out a teaspoon. I cracked opened my mouth—even my jaws ached, dammit—and he slid the spoon inside. I'd expected medicine of some kind, but the warm, rich sweetness of honey exploded on my tongue. I swallowed and he offered another, dripping a little bit onto my chin in his haste. His finger was warm as he wiped it away. "I know you prefer caramels," he said as he gave me a third spoonful, "but I figured this was easier to swallow."

Soon the energy seeped into my limbs, replacing what I'd burned in Daniel's dream. My muscles still protested when I sat up, but at least the joint-crunching pain had faded to something tolerable.

Sadly for me, this wasn't the first time I'd awoken in a stranger's bed after a run-in with a blight. The previous time it had been Brad's bed, before we'd started dating. "Where are we? Daniel's place?" I croaked. The furniture was unfamiliar, the curtains covered in tiny white flowers. Sunset seeped through the gaps.

"Yeah," he said. I glanced again at the flowers. Brad settled beside me with a weary sigh, and I leaned against him.

"How is he?"

"Fine," Brad said. "He's been up for a couple of hours now. I gave him some of the caramels from your bag and he picked right up."

I studied the fatigue straining my boyfriend's face. His stubble was thicker than it had been when we'd arrived at Daniel's that afternoon. But wasn't it sunset? That didn't make sense. "How long have I been out?"

"All night," he said. "It's dawn. I phoned your mum to let her know where we were. I should ring her back. Jen was all set to charge across here with her stethoscope or whatever, but I told her I'd call an ambulance if you got worse."

I blinked. I could imagine Jen doing just that.

I felt Brad's absence after he stood, listening to the muffled sound of his and Daniel's conversation. I didn't remember a single dream of my own after I'd been thrown out of Daniel's nightmare.

"Leander!" The name escaped my lips in a gasp as I recalled my desperate attempt to shield the Oneiroi from the trolley's exploding contents. Had I managed to save him? The recollection of those nails on top of the top of the load tightened my throat. They would have shredded his wings like confetti. I stumbled out of the bedroom and across to the open door of the bathroom, bracing myself against a sink cluttered with men's toiletries to stare into the mirror.

My reflection stared at me, face pale and blue eyes wild. My hair was sweat-stained and stuck up in all directions, the blue streak in my fringe vivid against my pale skin. But, right then, I didn't care. "Leander, are you there? *Leander.* Talk to me."

When my reflection shimmered and then faded from view, my knees buckled with relief. Leander smiled back at me, looking healthier and more alert than either Brad or I did. "Good morning, Melaina," he said, brushing invisible specks of dirt from the front of his green armour. It wasn't even scratched. "You look awful."

"Thanks. I feel like a million bucks," I said dryly, nudging the bathroom door closed with my bare toes before Daniel wandered up the hall to see what I was doing. The bathroom tiles were cold against the soles of my feet. "You're looking pretty good for someone who blew himself up."

The grin slipped a little, and he placed his hands at his sides, bowing in my direction. If the mirror had been a camera, his hair would've brushed against it. He seemed close enough for me to reach through and tousle those golden-brown locks. "Your intervention meant I only got a little singed."

"You look alright now...?"

He shrugged in response to the question in my voice. "After I cleaned up the blight taint from your Daniel's dream, I rested for a couple of hours."

"He's not *my* Daniel," I said, a knot of tension I hadn't realised I was carrying uncoiling in my belly. "So he's good to go? I won't have to go back in there...?" I fidgeted with the cans of deodorant and shaving cream, not wanting to make eye contact with the Oneiroi. I didn't want him to see how much the dream had frightened me. That final terror and sense of helplessness as the blight had dragged me towards it, the feeling of its barbs biting into me ... I shuddered at the memory.

"No. I took care of it." His voice was gentle, and I looked up, surprised. "Paid a quick visit to your dreams too. To make sure no blights followed you home and that you weren't reinfected."

My fingers curled on the edge of the basin. A flare of annoyance that I hadn't noticed him was quickly smothered by gratitude that he'd thought to check. "And did they? Was I?"

"No. You're fine."

"Good. Okay. Thank you."

Leander paused, and I wondered what he was waiting for. "You, ah, haven't asked me about your father."

Oh shit. Mum would kill me. I really *was* exhausted. "I haven't had my coffee yet," I mumbled. "Is he alright?"

"He's still alive, if that's what you mean. The Morpheus imprisoned him."

The idea that he might not be alive hadn't even occurred to me and, even though my father's and my relationship had never been a typical one, I still felt like a terrible

daughter—if not to him then to my mother. I was sure she'd have thought of it. Worried about it. "For how long?"

Leander's wings drooped. "Thirty years. I'm sorry. I did try to speak in his defence, but..."

"I'm guessing the Oneiroi justice system doesn't include a mechanism for appeals," I said.

Leander shook his head. "There's more."

"What?"

"The Morpheus wants to meet you."

"Me? Why?" As far as I knew, I hadn't broken any Oneiroi laws. Sure, my existence was a little ... unorthodox, but I fought blights, mara and other dream-based bad guys that mucked up Erebus for the Oneiroi. They should be giving me a medal.

My stomach sank as I realised what it had to be. "It's about Ikelos, isn't it? The Morpheus's brother?"

Ikelos had been in exile when I'd killed him, but that didn't mean the Morpheus, king of the Oneiroi, wouldn't take offence.

"I don't know. He said it was about your father, but..." Leander shrugged. "Melaina? He's made meeting with you a condition of his sending anyone to help with Brad's grandfather. If you don't agree to the meeting, he won't let the Oneiroi clean up that breeder blight. Including me."

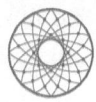

I'd tried to keep my voice down while I told Leander exactly what I thought of being blackmailed, but Daniel still looked at me sideways when I came out of the bathroom, hair damp and a trickle of tepid water trailing down the back of my neck. I hadn't wanted to shower at Daniel's, especially given the stall was in line-of-sight of the mirror, so I'd settled for dunking my head under the tap.

"You better?" I asked the nurse. I knew I should try to be polite, but my clothes were dirty and rumpled, and I wanted to brush my teeth.

"Pretty ragged," he said, rolling his head from side to side as though trying to stretch out a kink. He was still wearing the oversized green hoodie, but now the hood was back it suited him a little better. "The couch isn't the most comfortable place to sleep. But, on the other hand, I actually slept, so I feel about a thousand times better than I did. Did you...? Am I...?"

"Your sleepwalking days are through. For now, at least. Next time, I'd suggest giving me a call when you're still at the horrific nightmare stage, rather than waiting until you start waking up on the wrong side of town."

His skin blanched grey, the blond stubble stark against it, and I instantly regretted my flippancy. "*Next time?*" he squeaked.

"If. I meant *if* there's a next time."

Brad stepped up beside me, sliding an arm around my shoulder and kissing my temple. It did little to ease my chagrin. "What Melaina's being too polite to say is that my grandfather is patient zero. He's at the nursing home."

"I thought you looked familiar. Your grandfather's the sleeper?" Daniel's ears reddened. "The comatose patient, I mean?"

"Yeah." If Brad hadn't heard the staff's nickname for his grandfather before, he didn't let it show. "He's the source of your infestation. Infection, I mean."

"No, you mean my possession. Right?"

"Now he believes us," I muttered, and Daniel raised

his eyebrows. "I know, I know," I said. "It sounded ridiculous, you're a rational man, and you required proof. Now you have it."

Daniel's laugh was tired, but the amusement crinkling the corners of his eyes seemed genuine. "Yeah, pretty much. Tell me, though: if Mr Peterson is patient zero, what can I do to limit infection? I don't want to go through this again, and I don't want anyone else to either."

"The blights—that's what the spirits are called—well, they spread via microscopic larvae. They could be as small as skin cells, even. So I guess all the things you'd normally do to stop a cold from spreading? Washing your hands a lot?"

"Are they airborne?"

"Not that I know of." I shrugged.

"That's something." Daniel's eyes grew distant for a moment. "I'll see what I can do. But not today. I need a shower and another twenty-four hours' sleep."

His words so closely mirrored what I was thinking that I grinned. "I hear you."

Daniel smiled back. But Brad's next words killed our good humour. "There's one more thing you need to consider, Daniel. The man who was assaulted in Commonwealth Park."

"I..." The nurse seemed to deflate, slumping back against the dining table. A small stack of junk mail toppled over, sliding to the floor. He didn't notice. "Do you think it was me?"

Brad shrugged, but his grim expression told a different story. "The facefit looked enough like you that Melaina's mother figured it out. And it matches the timing of one of your blackouts, right?"

Daniel slid his long sleeves up and stared at his hands. The knuckles of his right hand were covered in grazes. My stomach turned to ice; it definitely looked as if he'd been in a fight. "But I don't remember doing it," he said softly.

I remembered my earlier thought that reporting Daniel might be the right thing to do, for the victim's sake. Looking at him now and knowing for certain that the assault hadn't been his fault, I wasn't so sure. Possession wouldn't hold up as a defence in court. He could argue he'd had some sort of psychotic break, but if he had no previous history of mental illness... "They might go easier on you if you turned yourself in," I said, uncertainty furrowing my brow. "If you told them you'd been sick and couldn't remember, but you thought you might have done it. Maybe?"

"Maybe." Daniel stared at his hands for a long moment. I glanced at Brad, who shrugged back. He was clearly going to leave the decision to Daniel. "Will you report me if I don't?"

I shook my head, catching my bottom lip between my teeth. In some ways, it would be better if Daniel didn't turn himself in. Now he knew about Brad's grandfather, he could do a lot of good, trying to prevent further accidental blight infestations until I could unravel the mess with the Oneiroi and get the old man cleansed. But I didn't want to say anything either way. Daniel needed to decide for himself.

"We should go," I said to Brad, who nodded, turning to get his keys. "Um. Where are my boots?"

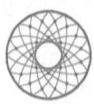

When Brad and I got home, I was too tired to go shopping with Jen for my new office supplies. Thankfully it was a public holiday, so he and I spent a good portion of the day either napping or vegetating in front of the television. Mum and Jen were in and out, so Brad and I even managed to sneak a little "couple time" together, feeling like a pair of giggling teenagers waiting for a disapproving parent to leave the house.

Afterwards, we watched the news channel for a while. I didn't want to admit it out loud, but I was looking for signs of more blight infestations. I didn't see any new ones, but I flinched every time I heard about the assault in Commonwealth Park. Until recently, I hadn't had many interactions with the police, and I'd always thought of myself as a law-abiding sort of person. Before Brad and I had broken into the nursing home, the worst thing I'd done was graffiti the back of the toilet door in high school. Rebecca, the girl I'd written about, had totally had it coming.

Besides, we hadn't *actually* broken into the home. Not really. Lien had let us in. I *had* knocked a whole bunch of people unconscious though. Was putting a person to sleep with magic against their will actually illegal? It might be, depending on how broadly worded the law was. I didn't know.

When Brad stood to swap one superhero DVD for another, I frowned at the shadowed television screen. Had that hint of movement been his shadow, or was Leander lurking? But when Brad bent over the DVD player, the movement was gone.

I groaned, stretching along the couch. "I'm still annoyed at Leander for not bringing the other Oneiroi with him."

The spot where Brad had been sitting was warm, and I sprawled across it with a sigh.

"He's just the messenger." Brad dropped the disc into the tray with a clatter. "I'm annoyed at the boss Oneiroi guy. The king or whatever. I would have thought dealing with a breeder blight would be his top priority. Didn't you say he was meant to keep the nightmare spirits under control?"

"Yeah, apparently they pollute Erebus for everyone else."

He walked back to the couch, lifting my legs and sliding underneath before draping them across his knees. "When's the meeting?"

I shrugged, a lopsided gesture given my awkward position. "The Morpheus has to come to me, given I can't flitter from dream to dream like a full Oneiroi. Weeks, maybe."

"Bet that annoys him." Brad huffed a laugh.

"Yeah," I said sourly. "He'll be super-pleased when he gets here."

"Hey." Brad massaged one of my calves with his free hand as he fished for the remote down the side of the seat cushion. "Don't forget you haven't done anything wrong."

"Except kill his brother that one time," I pointed out.

"Yeah, but his brother started it," Brad said, flashing me a grin.

I laughed. "I'll make sure to tell the Morpheus that."

Chapter Ten

Serenity's new shop opened a fortnight later. Serenity, Mum and I worked all weekend to stock the shelves, and by the time the store opened on the Monday we were exhausted and looking forward to not having to lug boxes. Gemstones are *really* heavy in bulk. Despite Serenity taking out a radio ad campaign and emailing her newsletter subscribers, we weren't expecting it to be a busy day—Monday wasn't one for high retail turnover. The only reason both Mum and I were rostered on was so I could show her the ropes, and by opening on a Monday she had a few days to get up to speed before late-night shopping on Friday.

Serenity practically glowed as she flipped the sign over on the glass door, humming something unrecognisable under her breath. Mum looked apprehensive, as if she expected a flood of people to pour through the entrance as soon as we opened.

"You'll be fine," I murmured to her before saying more

loudly, "I still think you should've named it *Serenity's New New Age Gifts.*"

"It is funny," Serenity said in a tone of voice that suggested she was humouring me, "but I just want to put the fire behind me." She ran her gaze over the shelves before nudging a stack of tarot cards on its display holder so that the gorgeous, gold-hued cover art caught the light. "Onward and upward. I'll be in the back, going over invoices. Call me if you need me."

We didn't need her, but that didn't stop her from popping out to see how we were going every time the bell over the door tinkled. She set a bowl of colourful, wrapped lollies by the register, and we encouraged the few customers we had to take a handful. Mum rang up each sale. By the time lunch came around, she was confident enough with the register that I was able to go out to get us all salad rolls, coffee and a celebratory box of custard tarts. The scent of vanilla and freshly roasted coffee made my mouth water and my stomach growl as I strode back up the shady sidewalk towards Serenity's.

My grip tightened on the cardboard drink tray, the bag crunching between the fingers of my other hand, when I saw the police car parked in front of the shop. My first thought was of Daniel, and guilt killed my appetite. But surely not. It had been two weeks; the nurse had returned to work rather than turning himself in, and there'd been no sign that any of the staff at Wattle Tree Park had connected his unexpected illness with the assault on the news.

The other cause for concern, Ewan, was still in the mental health unit at the Canberra Hospital ... and, even if he hadn't been, he wasn't so unstable that he'd set fire

to the shop again. Not during the day, at least, while we were in it to stop him. No, it was far more likely that the police had stopped by the shops to go to a café or to get some of the excellent coffee I'd just bought, and that they'd parked out the front of Serenity's because that had been the only vacant spot.

Telling myself I was being paranoid, I strode up to the shop door, nudging it open with my hip and sliding through.

Constable Nelson stood by the herbal teas. He was in uniform this time. If he was wearing that Scorpio pendant Serenity had spotted, there was no sign of it beneath the shirt's crisp blue collar.

I glanced at Mum, setting the tray of coffees beside the register. "Yours is on the end," I murmured, giving her a questioning look and indicating Nelson with a faint tilt of my head. She shrugged back at me. "I'll be back in a sec," I said, taking the food to Serenity in the tiny office. I wanted to hide out there; instead, I squared my shoulders and marched into the shopfront, heading over to the police officer. He was scrutinising the back of a packet of tea, a frown puckering his brows. "Can I help you with anything?"

"Maybe," he said in a distracted tone, peering at the tiny writing. "I'm wondering what you'd recommend for someone who's having trouble sleeping."

My eyes rounded and my mouth gaped. I clenched my jaw as I fought to wipe the shock from my face. But Nelson was now studying me intently, and I was sure he'd caught the flare of surprise. I managed to croak out, "Is it for you, or for someone else?"

"Oh, Melaina, hello," he said, although I didn't believe

for a second that he hadn't noticed who he was talking to. "Let's say it's for me." Even though his eyes were lined with what could be fatigue, I didn't believe that either.

I took a breath and stiffened my spine. I wouldn't let him get to me. "Well, it depends what sort of trouble you've been having," I said. "If you're having difficulty relaxing before bed, for example, I'd recommend a tea containing chamomile and valerian. This brand—" I brushed a box with a fingertip "—also contains peppermint, which is useful if you've got a bit of an upset stomach that's keeping you awake. These ones have orange blossoms, and this one over here contains apple."

"What's the benefit of that?" He didn't even look at the boxes as I pointed to them.

"It smells nice?" I bit off the words. He didn't care about the tea. He was after something else. *So much for not letting him get to me.* "This one over here has lemon balm, lavender and jasmine and may promote good dreams, if you're having issues with nightmares."

He regarded me for a moment before turning back to the teas. "What would you recommend for a person who sleeps fine once they are asleep but who has trouble drifting off? Shift-workers, say?" I opened my mouth to reply, but before I could say anything he added, "Like nurses? Or security guards?"

Ice crept over my face as I considered his words. *He knows. But how?* When Brad and I had gone to Wattle Tree Park, Lien wasn't the only one I'd given a dose of my sleepy-time magic. There'd been the security guard at the gate outside. I reached almost blindly for the first box of tea I'd described, shoving it into his open hand. "I'd go for this one. Though valerian isn't recommended

FALSE *Awakening*

if you have liver disease."

"Thank you for your help," he said, following me as I scurried back to the register.

Mum saw my harried expression and scowled at the police officer. I tried to hush her with a gesture, but she ignored me. "Shouldn't you be out arresting criminals? Or building a case against that Ewan man for drugging me and bashing my daughter's boyfriend on the head?" she asked Nelson. Her tone was light but the paper bag crackled with her sharp movements as she bagged the tea.

"I'm on lunch." He sounded unruffled as he pulled a credit card out of his wallet. "But it's funny you should mention Ewan. I went out to see him at the hospital yesterday, and he told me some interesting things." His gaze slid back to mine, and the cold feeling spread from my face to sheathe the rest of my body, leaving me clammy. I picked up my takeaway coffee; the corrugated cardboard scalded my icy fingers, but I didn't care. "Did you know Wattle Tree Park has security cameras?" Nelson continued. "Not all over, unfortunately, but they cover the outside perimeter quite well. I gather the management had them installed after a couple of patients with dementia wandered off."

"That's why it's the most expensive nursing home in Canberra," Mum said brightly, processing Nelson's payment. But her eyes flashed with fury. "They take good care of their patients. Mostly."

Nausea churned my stomach, and my mouth went dry. The cameras. I remembered noticing the one above the guard's outpost that night, but there hadn't been any way to avoid it. In the intervening months, given nothing had come of it, I'd begun to believe no one had thought to check. I had no doubt now that Nelson, worded up by Ewan, had finally reviewed the footage. What had he seen? The guard leaning forward towards me, and then lowering his face to his arms and beginning to snore?

I jumped when the bell over the door jingled and a second police officer—not one I recognised—walked in. She was holding a plastic bag, and the smell of hot lemongrass and ginger wafted in behind her. "Hey, David, you almost done?" she said, eyeing the brown paper bag with Serenity's logo on it, probably wondering what her straight-laced colleague could possibly be buying from a hippy shop like ours.

"Yup." Nelson took the credit card and receipt from Mum with a polite smile. Like it was an afterthought, he took one of my business cards from the little stand beside the register. My fingers twitched with the urge to snatch it off him. "Thank you, ladies. It's been a pleasure."

"Have a wonderful afternoon," Mum trilled. When the door swung shut, she added, "you nosy bastard."

I leaned against the wall behind the counter, trying to get my thoughts in order. I still felt dizzy from the shock and wanted nothing more than for Nelson to leave me alone, but still... "He's just doing his job," I said weakly, taking a deep breath of the steam threading through the hole in the plastic lid covering my coffee. Dissatisfied, I pulled the lid off and took another breath.

"Well, I wish he would do it somewhere else."

"Me too." I sighed. "But the person I want to punch in the nose is Ewan. He tipped Nelson off, told him to check the home's camera footage. At least, that's what Nelson was implying." I explained to Mum how Brad and I had gotten into the home that night, and realisation

dawned in her eyes, concern on its heels.

"So that's what he was on about. You think he, what, suspects you used a chemical to subdue the guard?"

"Well, he sure as hell doesn't believe I used herbal tea," I said, dropping my voice as the bell rang and a couple of teenage girls in long-skirted private school uniforms poked their heads in, eyes bright with curiosity.

Once they'd chosen their purchases—a book of Wiccan spells and a rose quartz pendant that made me suspect someone was looking to score a date for an end-of-year formal—I slipped out the back to eat my roll and think over my options. Wiping her fingers clean on a serviette, Serenity went out onto the floor to relieve Mum so she could eat too. By the time Mum joined me, I was scrolling through my Facebook page on Serenity's computer. There was an event invitation from Olivia for her eighteenth birthday party on Saturday. It was being held at her house in one of Canberra's flashiest suburbs, Red Hill. I wondered whether her mother knew she'd invited us, but shrugged, hitting accept. I'd worry about it later. Then I hunted for Daniel's name in the list of Belinda's friends.

"I need to see Ewan," I said, sending Daniel a friend request. Hopefully the other nurse would be able to give me some suggestions on how best to approach visiting the mental health unit.

"Is that such a good idea? He'll mention it to Nelson, who'll be even more suspicious. Going out there might even be what Nelson is after, hinting to you that Ewan warned him."

I shrugged, logging out of my account and joining Mum. "Nelson's already suspicious. And it's possible Ewan picked up his own blight infection while he was helping Ikelos infect people with them. Maybe that's what's driving his behaviour?" I didn't believe it, not really. It seemed more likely that he was pursuing me out of a desire to avenge his deceased Oneiroi master. But I'd given Daniel the benefit of the doubt. Shouldn't I do the same with Ewan?

Chapter Eleven

*D*aniel gave me a run-down on the mental health unit's rules and visiting hours; he'd been in to visit his former colleague a couple of times since Ewan had been admitted. I didn't have the heart to tell Daniel that Ewan had been at least indirectly responsible for his recent possession. Instead, I thanked him for the advice, deflecting his questions about why I wanted to see the other nurse. He knew we weren't exactly on the best of terms.

The next day, after an early lunch, Jen drove me in to the hospital. Ostensibly, she'd offered so I wouldn't have to catch the bus, but I knew she was also concerned at the idea of me going alone. She worked her jaw as we approached the unit, and I wondered if I should have made some excuse and refused her offer. Maybe waited until the weekend, when Brad could come with me? We could have gone before Olivia's party. Unlike Daniel, Jen was very well aware that Ewan had been behind her blight infestation and, in her case, there hadn't been any "indirectly" about it. He'd infected her food when they went on a date. I still felt guilty for setting them up.

The mental health unit was separate from the main hospital. "At least it's close to the carpark," I said, smoothing the front of my shirt down and wondering whether I should have dressed more conservatively as we approached the low, sprawling façade of the structure. It had a modern vibe; rectangles of various sizes in muted colours covered the outside wall.

"It looks like an architect barfed all over some kid's building blocks." Jen pursed her lips, looking back the way we'd come. "Though the multistorey carpark is so ugly it makes this place look good."

I laughed a little nervously as we entered the building and reported to reception. The nurse on duty didn't bat an eyelid at my dark jeans, nose piercing, band T-shirt or heavy boots. She did notice the way we gawked at the high ceilings and the light-filled space; the interior was much nicer than the exterior. "Is this your first time visiting?" she said.

We nodded.

"And who are you here to visit?"

"Ewan Wright. He's in the low-dependency wing."

"Is he expecting you?"

I shook my head, and she pointed to a couple of low, uncomfortable-looking couches. "Please take a seat while I see whether Mr Wright is accepting visitors today."

We did as instructed. "Accepting visitors? Fancy," I muttered to Jen as we sank onto the low couch. Daniel had mentioned that the other nurse may not agree to see us, but I was hoping Ewan's curiosity would overcome his reluctance. Or, failing that, maybe his hatred of me

would be enough to make him want to see me. I hoped the staff had quick reflexes in the event that he attempted to avenge Ikelos.

"It makes sense," Jen said, pulling out her phone. "They are trying to create a safe space here. If patients can't control who drops in, that wouldn't be very safe."

"Yeah." I crossed one leg over the other knee and tapped the side of my boot. Jen began to play a game with the sound off. I didn't own a smart phone, but I didn't think a game would be able to distract me from my nerves anyway.

After a long enough period of time that I worried Ewan had refused to see us, a smiling nurse came over and gestured for us to follow her. She led us into a big, open space with huge windows overlooking a sunny courtyard. The walls were white with green and yellow accents that reminded me of dandelions. Other people moved around: nurses in their uniforms and visitors or patients dressed in street clothes. Ewan waited for us in the centre of the space, sitting at a table with two single-seat couches on each side. The chairs were low enough that his long frame looked gangly, his knees bent and his elbows resting awkwardly on the arms of his seat. He was dressed in baggy jeans and a striped shirt. A jumper was draped across the couch beside him as if he was claiming the space for a friend.

Taking the hint that he didn't want either of us to get too close, Jen and I sat on the other side of the table. "Hi," I said, feeling awkward as I sank into the squishy chair.

"Hello, Melaina." He blinked a couple of times, his gaze sliding across to my friend. "Jenny."

Jen's eyes narrowed but she didn't reply.

Ewan frowned; he'd probably hoped for a bigger reaction. "How are you feeling? Sleeping well?" he asked, running a hand over his hair, which had been cut short. The blond streak that had made him look like a skunk had been trimmed away so that his hair was now a solid, dark brown. The colour suited him better, as much as I hated to admit it.

"Just fine, thanks." Jen took off her glasses and cleaned them on the hem of her shirt. Since I'd started providing Netflix for her brain, as she'd put it, the statement was even true. She hadn't had a nightmare about being possessed in a couple of weeks. "No thanks to you," she added, not meeting his gaze, and Ewan smiled. I'd noted in the past that he was cute when he smiled, but now the expression tightened something in my chest—and not in a good way. Maybe it was the tic that jumped beside his eye, or the way the smile was perilously close to being a smirk.

"I was bestowing an honour on you," he said. "I chose you to be the host for something greater. Something holy. I can't pay you a greater compliment than that."

"Ugh." Jen slid her glasses back on with such force that I winced. "Because the only purpose of a woman is to breed, right?"

"That's not the *only* purpose." He licked his lips as he ran his gaze down her body. She stiffened in her seat and he grinned, meeting her gaze again. "Besides, I didn't just choose women. I'm not sexist."

"And now Ikelos is gone, what are you playing at?" I spoke quickly, before my friend leapt across the low table to punch him in the nose. Nelson would have a field day if that happened.

Ewan blinked again, that tiny muscle beside his eye

twitching like a dying spider. "The psychologists here assure me he never existed to start with. They tell me he was a ... a product of my psychosis. I'm on little tablets, four times a day. They make me sleepy. Like your mother. How is your mother?"

"Not that sleepy anymore," I snapped. A passing nurse glanced over, and I lowered my voice. "You didn't answer my question, though. Are you trying to get me in trouble with the police?"

"I didn't answer? Imagine that," he said. I opened my mouth to object, and he waved me off. "What am I trying to do? Why, Melaina, I'm trying to help that nice police officer understand what happened that night. He's very concerned. He also has the kind of personality that can't stand a riddle. And now I appreciate that my behaviour was wrong, I want to try and make amends to society." He placed a hand over his heart, his expression so nauseatingly earnest that *I* wanted to punch him in the nose.

"Make amends to society, my arse," I said. Jen put her hand on my arm, but I barely noticed. "You're trying to punish me for burning your master in a river of lava."

The rage that flashed across his face was the first genuine expression I'd seen from him since we'd arrived. It flared in his eyes and bared his teeth in a silent snarl. The couch seat squeaked a protest as his fingers dug into the arms. The emotion was so strong I slid back in my chair ... but, before I could brace for an attack, he took a deep breath and the fury melted away, leaving only faint amusement in its place. All he said was, "The master that never existed."

Do you really believe that? Ikelos had most definitely existed. He'd forced my mother into a coma so he could take over her mind. He'd tortured my father for information and had bound Leander with barbed vines that had cut his wings to shreds. I stared at Ewan like I could bore into his brain with my gaze alone, determine whether he was telling the truth. He stared back, the hint of a sneer curling his top lip to reveal a glimpse of faintly stained teeth.

When the silence had stretched on for a couple of minutes, I decided to change tack. "How have *you* been sleeping, Ewan? Any bad dreams?"

"The usual." His gaze slid away from my face to the arm of the chair, where his fingers still pressed into the fabric. His eyes widened with surprise, as if he'd just noticed his reaction, and he loosened his grip. "I'm not possessed, if that's what you're asking."

"How do you know you're not?"

"Because there's no such thing as blights," Ewan replied brightly. He twitched with a spasm. A side-effect of the medication? But when he glanced back up at me, a new, steely determination glittered in his eyes. Something else had changed in his expression, too, though I couldn't put my finger on what it was. "If you come any closer to me, Melaina Armstrong, I *will* defend myself." His voice was low, almost a growl, and his hands curled into fists. "Even if it means they increase my medication until I'm a drooling mess and remove my privileges. I won't have you putting me to sleep again. I won't have you invading my mind."

Jen stood, grabbing my arm and dragging me to my feet. She hooked her arm through mine, either to restrain me or to support herself. Maybe both. "Funny how you don't want your own mind invaded, but you were happy enough for mine to be."

"Yes." Ewan regarded her with a cold expression. "Funny."

It wasn't until we were leaving the unit, emerging into warm spring air that did little to ease the chill inside me, that I realised what it was in Ewan's expression that had changed.

The tic beside his eye had disappeared.

Chapter Twelve

*B*rad, Mum and I clambered out of Brad's car onto the wide, but nevertheless vehicle-choked, street. The distant rumble of thunder was barely audible over the closer wails of a pop diva letting loose on a stereo that had to be too loud for the neighbours' comfort. *I hope for Olivia's sake that it doesn't rain.* I narrowed my eyes at the looming clouds on the southern horizon, hugging the leather jacket I'd borrowed—okay, acquisitioned—from Brad around me.

Mum shifted her bag on her shoulder, looking towards the giant, glass-and-concrete monstrosity that had been her brother's house. After Uncle Ian and his wife bought it a few years ago, she'd visited a handful of times—mostly on Christmas Day when he collected her from the home. But she still examined it with a wrinkled nose.

"I know, right?" I kept my tone light to hide my vague sense of anxiety. This would be the first time I'd seen Lacey since Uncle Ian's wake, when she'd effectively

disowned me. *This party could get super awkward.* "It's very … beige."

"I don't mind it too much," Brad said. "I mean, the bones are there. It has a good floorplan if you're looking for a mansion, and the gardens are nice. I'd go for a brick finish though. Rendered concrete isn't my thing."

Mum looked between us, raising her eyebrows. "I don't disagree," she said, "but I was wondering what's going on with that song." We were closer now, and the music had a cheerful beat that set my feet to tapping. If Olivia was still pining after her ex-boyfriend, the upbeat music she'd chosen didn't show it. "That girl's voice is … weird."

I began to laugh. It was a little mean, but I couldn't help it. She sounded just like one of the old ladies from the nursing home where she'd spent most of the last twenty-odd years. "You're showing your age, Mum."

"What?" She frowned at me.

"It's called auto-tune." Brad gave me a reproachful look. "They use it on a lot of songs, to correct vocal imperfections or achieve different creative effects."

"But … that's *cheating*," Mum spluttered.

"The kids and their music." I giggled.

Mum swatted at me, and I danced backwards. "Stop it, you. I know I said we had TV in the nursing home, but choosing shows was a democratic process, and I was rather outnumbered by people who weren't interested in watching *Rage*."

"Okay, okay," I said, swallowing my laughter. Like I was being punished by the universe, the giggles caught in my throat, turning into coughs. Brad patted me on the back while Mum lifted her chin and tried to look haughty. "Sorry," I croaked.

"I forgive you."

The house's glass-paned double doors were open, and several teenagers sat at the top of the long flight of stairs, talking loudly. They weren't much younger than me—two or three years at most. But I felt the difference keenly. It wasn't so much the age gap, I realised as we stepped past them and into the entry hall. It was that Olivia's friends were mostly children of privilege. Uncle Ian had sent his daughter and son to the best private schools in Canberra, and their friends either had rich parents or were the children of diplomats. Perhaps both. I'd wager none of them had ever lived in a tiny, shabby flat of the sort I'd shared with Jen, or that they ever would.

"Melaina!" a familiar voice called. I turned to see Justin standing in the open dining room, halogen down-lights making his hair glow. Platters of fancy canapes covered the glass-topped table, although the guests gathered around it were still drinking from plastic cups. "Down here, quick." He darted down a side corridor, speaking over his shoulder. "Hi, Aunt Davina. Brad."

"Hi," Mum said, sounding bemused as we followed my cousin to his room. The door was ajar, and covered in a huge sign printed in a Celtic-type script. It read, "No admittance, especially on party business".

"Nice," Brad said, nodding at the sign.

"I'm even more of a hermit than Bilbo," Justin said, flashing Brad a grin. "I'm hiding out in here. You know, if you need to retreat at any point."

"Retreat?" I asked.

"From Olivia and her lame-o friends?" The smile vanished, and his eyes no longer sparkled. "Or from Mum?"

"Ah." I was unable to help the glance I threw over my

shoulder. "Does she know we're coming?"

"Yeah," Justin said. "She checked the event on Facebook. Freaked when she saw how many people were coming, so she's in a mood. And I think she'll be even more moody when..." His glance slid from my face to Mum's before jerking back to me.

"Oh goody."

"Yeah." Justin slipped through his door. "Like I said. Retreat."

"Gotcha. Thanks, Jat," I said, grinding my teeth. It wasn't my fault my grandfather's inheritance had named me the executor of Mum's trust fund in the event of Uncle Ian's death. Mum, on the other hand, wasn't quite as undeserving of Lacey's wrath... *In a way, Lacey is right in thinking Mum's condition was self-inflicted. Mum only returned to normal when Ollie left. But it wasn't a scam; it was love.* Would my solicitor aunt regard love as a solid defence?

Shaking my head, I decided not to worry about it. "Let's go find Olivia," I said, slipping my hand into Brad's. "If only so we can wish her happy birthday before her mother throws us out."

"Surely she won't," Brad said as we walked down the corridor, past the closed door to Olivia's room, and into the family room. The timber floor clunked under my boots, felt more than heard given how close we stood to the stereo. I stopped before a pair of laughing teenage girls with hair dyed bright colours: one was pink, and the other shaded from green at the roots to blue at the tips, colours that melded in an aqua band around her ears. It must have cost a fortune to maintain.

"Love the hair," I said loudly, giving them a thumb's

up so they couldn't misunderstand. They regarded the streak of blue in my fringe, their smiles growing brighter. I couldn't tell if they were pleased to see a hair-dying kindred spirit, or laughing at me for the home dye job. I didn't much care either way. One of the joys of finishing high school was that I no longer had to put up with that crap. "Where's Olivia?"

"In the garden," the pink-haired girl yelled.

"By the pool, I think?" the other one added, flicking her hair back from her face and smiling.

"Thanks," I said, leading the way out the double doors and into the entertaining area. A shining, stainless steel barbeque and an outdoor setting occupied the porch area. Off-white pavers reflected yet more downlights, making the space glow despite the fading light of the setting sun. Tall hedges lined the space, lit by solar lights. *It's very pretty*, I admitted to myself, *though it'd be better with twenty or thirty less people.*

"Over there." Brad pointed to our right.

Sure enough, Olivia was near the pool. It was too cold to swim, and no one had braved the water yet. I wondered how long it would be until someone was pushed—or fell—in.

Olivia looked fabulous, her glossy brown hair caught in a complicated do that framed her face with loose ringlets. Her dress was slinky and a bright emerald green, cut low in front, gathered at the waist to flatter her curves, and flowing around her feet. I felt underdressed in my dark blue jeans and black satin tank top—especially as the latter was mostly hidden by Brad's jacket. Still, everyone looked underdressed compared to Olivia. She was stunning.

"Melaina," Olivia squealed. I blinked, surprised as she threw her arms around me, kissing the air next to my cheek. She wasn't usually so affectionate with me, and I wondered how much she'd had to drink. Quite a few of her nearby friends bore clear plastic cups holding liquids ranging from an earthy spirit-brown to vivid blues and pinks that I doubted were soft drinks, but I couldn't smell alcohol on her breath. "I'm so glad you came," she said. "And hi, Aunt Davina. It's so funny to see you outside that stinky old home." Mum smiled back, although she was a little wide-eyed. Olivia turned her gaze to Brad. "Remind me, Melaina, who's your handsome older man?"

"Brad." I hooked an arm around his waist and pulled him closer. "Though he's not that much older. Only seven years."

"Seven years is *way* older." Olivia rolled her eyes and then winked at us. "It's totally hot."

I smiled, glad she seemed to be over the heartbreak of her relationship with Sam ending. Either she'd decided she didn't care, she'd already found a new boyfriend, or her and Sam had gotten back together. I hoped it was the first option. I'd done rebound relationships before. They sucked.

"We all pitched in to buy you this." Mum reached into her bag, pulling out a small jewellery box tied with a blue ribbon. I'd found one that didn't have Serenity's store logo on it, even though we'd bought the piece at the shop. I didn't want to be that blatant about the fact we'd used a staff discount

"Oh, you shouldn't have," Olivia said politely, untying the ribbon.

When she lifted the silver ring from its cushion, an

expression of genuine delight transformed her face until it seemed to glow, her eyes widening and her lips parting in a gasp. Serenity hadn't had much in the way of jewellery a mainstream girl like my cousin would appreciate, but the ring, with its delicate silver butterfly wings set with cubic zirconias, was elegant and feminine without being too new-age spiritual. I held my breath as Olivia slid the ring on—Justin had been my partner in crime in getting her ring size, but I was still nervous. Thankfully, it fit perfectly, the butterfly wings spreading out along the band where it arced across the top of her finger, like they were hugging her.

"Oh, it's wonderful," Olivia said, her voice barely above a whisper. I realised with shock that the glitter in her eyes wasn't just from the reflected lights. "So perfect. Thank you." She sniffled.

"They aren't real diamonds," I blurted, flustered by the strength of her reaction. I usually gave her art supplies; she'd never reacted like this to those.

"I don't care. It's still lovely." She lowered her voice. "The best present I've received all day. And, given Mum gave me this, you should know how much I love it." Her finger brushed a yellow-gold pendant hanging at her throat, glittering red and white with stones I was sure were rubies and diamonds. *Wow.* "It doesn't even go with my dress," Olivia added, feigning a pout. At least, I assumed she was feigning. "She knew I was wearing green."

"Ah, well." Mum patted Olivia on the shoulder. "Perhaps she bought the necklace before you decided what dress to wear?"

"Maybe." Olivia held her hand up to regard the ring. "This doesn't match my pendant. Maybe I should take

it off?"

I thought she meant the ring and was stunned when she reached back to unclasp the expensive necklace. But Mum moved to stop Olivia's hand. "Leave it," she said gently. "Your mother would be upset if you took it off. Besides, it's your party. You can clash if you want to."

Olivia exploded into peals of laughter, kissing Mum on the cheek before dancing away, hand extended so she could admire her gift. She left a tiny smudge of lipstick behind, and I was suddenly grateful for the air kiss I'd received.

"I wonder where your aunt is?" Brad craned his head to scan the crowd.

"In the kitchen, maybe?" Mum suggested. "Or she might have gone out to get away from the noise and crowds."

"And leave the place defenceless?" I snorted. "Not likely." Thunder grumbled as if to underline my words—although the sound was fainter than before, the storm cell moving away to the east.

After a moment, Brad nodded back the way we'd come. "She's on the balcony. See?"

I narrowed my eyes against the glare of the lights, examining the balcony that overlooked the barbeque area. Its ubiquitous beige concrete managed to look foreboding in the shadow of the brightly lit courtyard below. And sure enough, leaning on the wall and regarding us with her face in shadow, was my cousins' mother, Lacey.

Seeing us watching her, she raised her hand and beckoned, a sharp gesture.

Or maybe the storm is upstairs.

Chapter Thirteen

Mum and I climbed the stairs to Lacey's study, while Brad stayed downstairs, probably sensing this was a family situation he was better off staying out of. I wished I was down there with him, but I refused to abandon Mum to Lacey's wrath.

The study had a mixed purpose: part office, part miniature gym. Lacey's computer sat on an expensive desk against one wall, while the opposite wall was covered with bookshelves heavy with legal texts. A single metal filing cabinet sat nestled in the far corner, near the glass doors that led out onto the balcony. A treadmill and a rowing machine took up the floor in the middle of the room, and I wondered if Lacey ever got annoyed at having to step around them to reach the bookshelf. Maybe the books were just for show? But no, she was far too pragmatic to waste shelf-space on unnecessary things.

Unless you counted the exercise equipment, the only seat in the room was a leather computer chair that wouldn't

look out of place on the set of a science fiction television show, given all the levers and dials clustered beneath the seat. Lacey sat in that chair, calm and in control.

"It's good to see you, Lacey," my mother said, shoes clicking lightly on the floorboards as she stepped inside the room. "I sent you a condolence card after I recovered from my illness. Did you, ah … did you get it?"

"Possibly." Lacey's voice was cool. Her knee-length spotted navy dress was probably worth more than Jen's car. It was definitely worth more than anything I owned.

"Oh." Mum's shoulders drooped at the lack of warmth in Lacey's tone, but she persevered. "I haven't had the chance to say it before now, but I'm sorry for your loss."

My uncle's widow raised elegant eyebrows and paused, seeming to consider what to say, what response would be the most cutting. I didn't give her a chance. "The polite thing to do would be to say you're sorry for Mum's loss too." I leaned against the doorjamb and folded my arms. "She lost her brother, and was too ill to get to the funeral."

"Melaina…" Mum said, her voice containing a note of warning, "don't speak to your aunt that way."

I jutted my chin out. "Sorry, Mum, but last time I was here she pretty much disowned me."

"I did no such thing." Lacey reclined in the chair a little. "I told you not to call me aunt anymore, since we're not actually related. But you're still my children's cousin."

I ground my teeth together but refrained from snapping at her. I'd had to point that fact out to her at the time, and she'd seemed … angry about it. But maybe I was being unfair? She *had* just buried her husband when she'd said it.

"You seem well, Davina," Lacey said, looking Mum up

and down. "It's amazing how those doctors were able to cure your condition after all this time."

"Yes." Mum's fingers twisted together.

"And all you had to do was actually let them treat you. It's a shame it took twenty years for you to agree."

"I had my reasons."

"Yes, well." Lacey brushed a speck of dirt off her skirt. "I suppose we all like a sleep-in. But you might have considered your daughter. We had to raise her for you."

Nope, I'm not being unfair. Lacey's a bitch.

Mum's face flushed and her eyes opened wide, as if Lacey had slapped her. When she spoke, her voice trembled. "I know you've never liked me," she said, lifting her chin, "and, frankly, Lacey, I've always considered you the least compassionate person I've ever met. But I'm fond of your children and, for their sake if no one else's, I'm hoping we can bury the hatchet."

Lacey opened her mouth and I wondered if she was going to suggest where Mum might like to bury her hatchet, but before she could speak we heard a heavy tread on the stair. "Lacey?" a vaguely familiar voice said. "Are you up here?"

My mouth fell open when Thomas appeared at the top of the stairs. I'd only ever met the tall, fair man at my uncle's funeral and the subsequent wake, but he'd ... made an impression.

Brad suspected Thomas was my biological father. Although Mum had always called Ollie my dad, Brad had reasoned that Mum had probably made a baby in the old-fashioned way. My Oneiroi traits could have developed based on my proximity to Ollie, who was holed up in Mum's mind the entire time she was pregnant with me.

Brad's theory made more sense to me than the notion that Mum had managed to have a baby to Ollie, a creature of pure spirit, but I'd never been as sure as Brad was that Thomas was my real father ... even if his eyes were the same pale shade of blue as my own.

Still, the way those eyes opened wide when they settled on me made Brad's theory seem plausible. When he saw Mum and blanched, I grew even more certain. Mum also seemed flustered, glancing at him and then away, biting her lip.

"Uh, Lacey?" Thomas forced a smile as he stopped in the hallway beside me. He was so close I was able to catch the tangy scent of his cologne and, beneath that, the rich aroma of red wine. "Come back to the games room. The kids can entertain themselves for a while without your supervision, and the others are wondering where you went."

Lacey examined Mum and for a long moment before standing. "Very well." She didn't glance us as she swept past, heels striking the floorboards with each stride like she was trying to punch a hole in them. I wasn't sure how to interpret her angry departure; we hadn't been invited to the adult part of the party, but we hadn't been thrown out either—which I'd assumed had been her reason for calling us up here. Was it a truce, at least for now? Or was she simply too embarrassed to attack Mum further in front of Uncle Ian's best friend?

Thomas turned to go. I glanced between him and Mum, realising she wasn't going to say anything. "Excuse me," I said before he could escape. He turned back, looking as if he'd rather play football with a hive of bees than join us in the study. "I wanted to thank you for what you said about me at my uncle's funeral."

Thomas cleared his throat uncomfortably. "Yes. Well. He often spoke fondly of you."

"Really?" My ex-aunt wasn't the only one who could do the sceptical eyebrow raise, and I employed it now. "I always thought he didn't approve of me. What with the nose piercing and the dropping out of university."

Thomas looked like he wanted to sink through the floor, melting into a puddle and seeping through the cracks in the timbers. *I'm such a people person.* I sighed. "I'm going to cut to the chase here." I stepped around Thomas, shutting the door to the stairs. It was only made of slatted timber but, given the volume of the music below, I doubted anyone would be able to eavesdrop, even if they stood right on the other side. "Are you my father?"

Mum coughed, looking as if she'd swallowed her tongue as she sank into Lacey's chair. Thomas's fair skin turned an interesting shade of scarlet, cheeks flaming. "Uh. I. Uh," he spluttered.

"Look," I said, putting my hands on my hips, "you don't have to worry anymore. Uncle Ian can't disembowel you for sleeping with his kid sister. I'm twenty-one, so no one is about to claim child support. And if my maths is correct, Mum was legal when she got pregnant with me, so even if Lacey wanted to press charges, there'd be no grounds." With each point I listed, he flinched, looking a little more embarrassed. A little more shame-faced.

"You don't think much of me, do you?" Thomas said, his voice so quiet I barely heard him.

"I don't even know you," I murmured. His answer was as good as a yes. He *was* my father. My heart leapt ... but then a thought occurred to me and it plummeted

into my belly just as fast, leaving the latter churning. It was a rough day to be one of my internal organs.

"I have one question, though." Steeling myself, I leaned in towards him, staring him in the eye. There *was* one thing he needed to worry about—one thing I'd left off my list. "Uncle Ian always assumed Mum had been raped and that it gave her PTSD. He believed that caused her condition."

My voice dropped to a whisper as I fought to keep from letting my rage and fear show. Did I really want to know the answer to the next question? *No, I don't.* But I asked it anyway.

"Was she?"

"No!" Thomas and Mum said together, their voices equally vehement, equally horrified.

Mum leapt to her feet. "Sweetheart," she said, moving past Thomas to ease one of my hands from where it fisted against my hip, "how could you even think that?"

"Oh, I don't know?" I said. "Maybe it was because Uncle Ian told me my father was a monster but not to worry, the Armstrong family genes would stop me from going off the rails?" I'd meant the words to come out in a jocular way, as if they hadn't bothered me. But they had, and my voice rasped with pain. He'd made that declaration during the same discussion in which he'd demanded I blackmail my mother into accepting treatment for her hypersomnia. *Dammit.* I swallowed hard.

"Oh, honey," Mum breathed, tears glittering in her eyes. Her hazel eyes: a warmer colour than mine. Than Thomas's.

"It wasn't... It was consensual." Thomas stood just out of arm's reach, keeping a safe distance from us, but his expression was pained and guilty. "We'd been drinking and started fooling around. One thing led to another, and..."

"I came onto him," Mum added, glancing at Thomas almost shyly. "I thought he was handsome, and—"

I held up my hand. "No oversharing!"

"Okay." Mischief twinkled in Mum's eyes, fading as she continued, "Needless to say, your uncle was wrong. Why didn't you just ask me?"

I shrugged, looking down. At first, I'd thought Ollie was my father and, although my uncle's opinion that I was genetically compromised had hurt, I'd been able to brush it off, thinking I knew the truth. And after Brad had explained his theory about Thomas... "I didn't want to upset you."

Mum's mouth turned down and she brushed the hair out of my eyes with a tender gesture that made my throat tighten.

"I am sorry I wasn't there for you, you know," Thomas said, his face seeming to beg me to believe him. "At first I was scared. I was still at uni, and was as afraid of the responsibility as I was of Ian, um, disembowelling me. Later, after Ian and Lacey took you in, it seemed like it would cause too much disruption in your life. I got married, you know, but my wife ... well, we couldn't have children." I blinked. I hadn't even considered the idea that I might have half-siblings running around. He ran a hand through his hair; the smattering of silver at his temples glittered against the pale blond. "Part of me has always regretted that I wasn't a braver person."

"Oh." He would have been around my age when he found out Mum was pregnant; I tried to imagine how I'd

react in his shoes. Would I own up and risk social censure, giving up everything to raise a child? I liked to think I would, that I'd save the child from being shipped off to boarding school and ignored. But I wasn't so sure. "Oh," I repeated.

Thomas cleared his throat again. It seemed to be a nervous habit. "If you wanted to ... that is, if I ... well. I'd have to talk to my wife first, but if you wanted to get to know each other, maybe...?" He trailed off, shifting from foot to foot.

"I..." Did I want that? It was too much to wrap my head around right then. "Can I have time to think about it?"

"Sure." Thomas nodded, and I tried not to feel hurt at the relief on his face. "If you ever want to get in touch, you can get my number from Lacey. Or—" he grimaced, seeming to recall the scene he'd walked in on just a few minutes before "—maybe from Olivia or Justin. That might be better."

I nodded, not saying anything else as he gave us a small smile and opened the door, escaping back downstairs.

"I was serious before," Mum said as soon as he'd disappeared from view. "Why didn't you ask me? I feel awful, that you believed Ian's ridiculous theory."

"By the time I started thinking it might be true, you were in your coma." I sighed, examining my boots. One of the laces was fraying into purple fuzz. "And afterwards, Ollie was gone. I ... I didn't think you'd like me suggesting he wasn't really my dad."

"But he *is* your dad," Mum said, again brushing the hair away from my eyes. I hadn't realised it was so messy. "Think of it like adoption. Yes, Thomas is your biological father, and I'm sorry I didn't tell you that sooner. But

Ollie is your true dad."

I looked towards the glass doors leading out to the balcony. The curtains were open, but I couldn't see the night beyond, only the reflection of me and Mum, standing in the study's wide doorway.

Mum's comparison wasn't perfect, of course: pretty much any adoptive father would be more involved in a child's life than Ollie had ever been in mine. Sure, he'd taken an interest, but only ever a passive one. I'd never even spoken to him until Mum's coma, when he'd needed my help to save her from Ikelos.

Still, I didn't say what I was thinking. Pointing out to her what a bad father Ollie had been would be cruel, especially when she was trying so hard to be brave. To be normal.

Movement on the stairs made me jump, and I hastily wiped the corner of my eye with the back of a hand, not wanting Lacey to see my moment of weakness. But it wasn't Lacey; it was Brad. "Is everything okay?" He stepped forward, sliding an arm around my waist. I leaned into him, soaking up the comfort he offered, using it to make myself strong again. "I saw Lacey and Thomas come downstairs...?" he said.

"Yeah, you were right, you big smarty pants," I grumbled into his shirt. "Thomas is my biological father."

"Oh." Brad paused before adding, "That must have been awkward."

"No kidding." I laughed softly. Behind me, Mum chuckled. "This party blows," I said. "Let's go home and have pizza or something."

As we turned towards the stairs, I caught another glimpse of our reflections in the balcony door: me, nestled

under Brad's arm, with Mum on my other side. The image made me smile.

But the smile dropped away when Leander suddenly obscured the picture. He was dressed in the same leather armour he'd worn when I last saw him, but something looked different. He looked ... solemn. Even when we'd faced down the breeder blight he hadn't looked solemn. "Melaina," he called, waving me over.

I didn't think he'd ever tried to talk to me when other people had been present. Glare at me, sure, or pull faces, but not talk. "What is it?" I slid out of Brad's grip and strode across the room. When I stubbed my toe on the rowing machine and stumbled, Leander didn't even crack a smile. *It must be serious.* I glanced at Mum and Brad; they were looking between me and the glass, their expressions somewhere between puzzlement and concern. I must look crazy to them, talking to my reflection. They both knew about the Oneiroi, but...

Leander's next words drove the thought right from my mind. "It's the Morpheus. He's arrived and he wants to meet you. Tonight."

Chapter Fourteen

"I don't like this." Brad folded his arms, watching as I brushed my teeth.

I'd changed into a pair of yoga pants and a baggy T-shirt, and was preparing myself as if for a normal night's sleep. "I'll be fine," I said after I'd rinsed. I tried to project confidence, but he looked sceptical. "I will," I insisted.

"I'll be there," Leander reassured me from the mirror. Really, couldn't I get a moment's peace? I gave him the barest nod, not wanting to talk to him and shut Brad out of the conversation. Then I slid past my boyfriend into the hallway.

Mum hovered by my bedroom door, wringing her hands. Everyone's anxiety was starting to get to me. "Will you … if you see your father...?"

"I won't," I told her gently. "Leander said he's in prison. But I'll ask after him. I promise."

"Right. Okay." She hesitated a moment and then turned, striding up the corridor towards the kitchen. I pretended

not to notice the way her shoulders shook.

Jen was sitting on my bed; unlike the others, her face was calm. "We'll stay with you," she said, standing to give me a hug. "If you're gone for too long, I can make sure your body's looked after." She waggled her eyebrows and grinned. Though the attempt at humour seemed half-hearted, I appreciated it.

"Do you have access to a drip?"

"Sure." She grinned. "Though it's the catheter you ought to be worried about."

My eyes widened. I wasn't sure what bothered me more: the idea of my best friend hooking me up to a catheter, or the idea of wetting myself if I was unconscious too long. I put as much determination into my voice as I could. "I'll make sure I'm back before that's necessary."

"Please do." Jen looked towards the door. "I'll be back in a minute." She hustled after Mum.

Brad's mouth curled down as I climbed under the sheets, settling my head against the pillow. My hair was damp from my shower. "I'll be fine," I said again.

He nodded, a sour twist to his lips. "I know you will. It's like I told you when you went into Daniel's dream: I just hate feeling useless. I want to be able to help."

"You're not useless," I said. "I need you to stop Jen from intubating me or whatever." He laughed, but the expression didn't reach his eyes. "Seriously, Brad, I'll be okay. I haven't broken any Oneiroi laws or anything." *That I know of.* "He just wants to talk. And then I'll be able to get your grandfather the help he needs." I hesitated, and then added, "How about you talk to Jen while I'm out, see whether she'd be interested in an experiment?"

"What experiment?" he said. The fact he didn't turn

my comment into some sort of teasing innuendo showed me more than anything that he wasn't in a joking mood.

"We'll see whether I can bring you into another person's dream, like you suggested. It might be useful."

He brightened a little. "Okay. Yeah, I'll ask."

"Goodnight, Brad," I said.

He leaned over and kissed my forehead. "Pleasant dreams, Melaina."

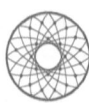

Leander was there before my dream had a chance to coalesce. Mist swirled, parting to give glimpses of a half-formed dream. Sunlight. The rich aroma of coffee. A fragment of birdsong. In the moments it had taken me to fall asleep, the Oneiroi had changed clothes, switching from the dark green armour to something more subdued. It still appeared to be made of a supple, form-fitting leather that allowed him to move, but it was the same dove-grey colour as his wings. By contrast, his honey-coloured skin seemed even warmer and his eyes, gold-flecked green, were like a sun-dappled forest clearing. His hair, shoulder-length and normally free-flowing, was tied back into a short ponytail at the base of his skull. The style strengthened his face somehow, made him seem more ... mature.

A teasing comment about his vanity leapt to my lips, but died when I saw the sombre look in his eyes. "Is it that bad?"

"Bad? No. Not exactly." He looked down at my clothes and raised an eyebrow. My dream self had appeared wearing the clothes in which I'd fallen asleep.

"You got here too fast." I frowned, transforming the garments into my usual motorcycle leathers, minus the helmet. "Better?"

"Um. Would you consider a—" he saw my scowl and seemed to change what he'd been about to say "—ah, something more formal?"

"You're wearing armour. Why can't I?"

"I'm a member of the Morpheus's Hawks," Leander said. I raised an eyebrow at the unfamiliar term and he added, "His hunters. It affords me certain luxuries, such as going armed and armoured in his presence. And you're asking him a favour, remember?"

I eyed Leander; if he was armed, I couldn't see any hint of the weapon. "Fine," I said with a sigh. "What does an Oneiroi civilian wear?"

"Whatever they wish; this is the world of dreams, after all."

"But you just said—"

"Just make it less military. You want to look competent, but not like you're challenging him."

I regarded him, turning the thought over in my mind. Respectful, competent and unthreatening? I'd assumed Leander was about to suggest I wear a dress, but I didn't want to wear something I'd be uncomfortable in, something that would restrict my movement. Also, in a realm where the denizens could fly and gravity was sometimes optional, I didn't want to risk people being able to look up my skirts.

Smirking to myself as I decided on a compromise, I replaced the jacket with a sleeveless A-line dress that fell to my knees. It was a cobalt blue, the same colour as the streak in my fringe, but was made of the same supple leather as Leander's armour. To soften it further, I added glittering blue stones around the hem. The leather motorcycle pants became heavy black tights.

At my thought, a thick band of twisted wire snaked around my throat and another encircled each of my wrists. They resembled a collar and cuffs, suitably sub-servient, but I made them strong enough to blunt the force of strikes against my neck and arms if I got into a fight. Finally, staring down at my feet, I decided to keep the boots unchanged. *All the better to stomp you with, my dear.* The thought was giddy with nerves.

"Better." Leander smiled and held out his hand to me. A gemstone glittered on his middle finger: a bright sapphire set in a silver band. Had that been there before, or was he copying my style? "Shall we?"

"Are we going somewhere?" I couldn't flit between dreams like a true Oneiroi. My access was limited to my own dreams or those of someone in the same room as me. That was the whole reason the Morpheus had needed to come to me in the first place.

"Not exactly," he said. "But I need to prepare for the court's arrival, and it's easier to change your dream if you let me do it."

"Wait, what?" I took a step backwards, narrowing my eyes at him. "He's bringing his whole court here? I don't want lots of Oneiroi in my head. I'm barely comfortable having you here."

"Melaina..." His hand dropped back to his side.

"I'm serious," I said with a scowl. "I don't want dozens or hundreds of spirits invading my dreams. I'll go mad!"

Leander's eyes were pleading. "The Morpheus's court moves from dream to dream all the time, as various

dreamers enter and leave Erebus. We don't drive people mad. If they remember anything at all, it's that they had a particularly colourful dream, full of butterflies and magic."

"No."

"But—"

"*No.* The difference is that I'd know they were here. I wouldn't forget about it." I shuddered. "It's creepy."

Leander's shoulders drooped. Was he simply disappointed, or had I hurt his feelings? Before I could think of a way to ask that wouldn't make it worse, he nodded. "Alright. How about this—we'll make a dome on the edge of your dream, something that looks out onto the blackness. Most of the court can stay out there, but they'll be able to see in."

"They won't be able to influence my dream? Read my thoughts?"

"I'm standing right here beside you and *I* can't read your thoughts," Leander said. Then he grinned, stretching in a way I was sure was intended to show off the muscles beneath all that tight-fitting leather. "More's the pity."

I refused to be distracted, to let him fluster me. "You didn't answer my question."

"They won't be able to influence your dreams *or* read your thoughts," he said. "Even if they could, I wouldn't let them."

I regarded him. A few months ago, I wouldn't have trusted him. But he'd redeemed himself in my eyes, bending the rules and holding off arresting Ollie until after we'd saved Mum. And he *seemed* earnest. Besides, what choice did I have? I held out my hand, and Leander took it. His fingers curled around my mine, warm and reassuring.

Then he changed my dream.

What the Oneiroi called Erebus had two parts: the shifting dreams, and the formless void in which they floated, tiny glowing suns in the blanket of space. The void was not just blackness, as Leander had called it, but a place where there was no ground or sky, no up or down— a lot like I imagined true space might be if it weren't freezing and airless. The Oneiroi were nearly powerless in the void ... but I was completely powerless. Like them, I couldn't change it because there was no dream-stuff to manipulate; unlike them, I couldn't navigate it because I didn't have true Oneiroi wings. The only way to see it from within a dream was to break my way through the dream's outer wall. It wasn't something I normally chose to do. All that looming darkness gave me the willies.

But Leander did it now. The mists swirled around us in one final burst of frenetic activity, and then fell away. Where the fragments of dream had lurked was now a circular room that resembled the top of an observatory, except someone had stripped out all that pesky instrumentation and replaced it with a low-backed throne on a raised dais. The floor was inlaid timber in a spiralling pattern, like the heart of a seashell, and the domed ceiling wasn't made of arching steel but of translucent glass the colour of ashes. A strip of clear glass ran from the base opposite the throne to the dome's top, mirroring the opening through which a telescope would peer.

"When have you ever seen an observatory?" I asked, gazing around in wonder at the delicate stonework, the almost hypnotic pattern in the floor.

"I spent a few weeks in an astronomer's dreams once," Leander said. "She liked to stargaze."

"She, eh?"

"Yes," he said blandly, folding his hands behind his back, beneath the shadow of his wings, and turning to face the throne. "He's coming." The words prickled along my skin, and I spun, staring.

The Morpheus didn't enter through a door or via the huge ceiling above. Instead, the air around the throne shimmered for a moment … and then he was there.

Sometimes I still had nightmares, albeit short-lived ones, about Ikelos, with his Monarch butterfly wings and the thick, dark lines that covered his skin, encircling it like someone had bound him in heavy knots. In my dreams, the tattoos shifted and his eyes burned with flames the colour of the lava that had swallowed him at the end. So the first sight of his brother made me gasp, feeling as if all the oxygen had gone out of the room.

The Morpheus appeared to be in his mid-twenties, though he had to be much older: he'd been the one to send Leander to spy on me when I was a child. He had the same inky black hair as his brother, but his fell down his back in loose, glossy waves. He wore a tunic and pants in a steel blue colour that accentuated those magnificent orange-and-black wings. Bracers in some dull material encircled his wrists, and a simple circlet of the same material sat on his brow. Like Ikelos, he also had tattoos twisting in sleeves down his bare arms and across his bare feet; however, unlike Ikelos's tattoos, which had been solid black and somehow angular, the corded patterns the Morpheus wore had lighter highlights and were more sinuous. They drew the eye, and I would have continued to stare at them if Leander hadn't shifted beside me, clearing his throat. I glanced at him and he nodded towards the seated Oneiroi.

"Um." I bowed awkwardly, the leather of my dress rustling. "Pleased to meet you, your Majesty."

"Melaina," the seated man said. I'd expected his voice to be resonant, magical somehow; after all, the Ancient Greeks had believed Morpheus to be not a position but a god, the god of dreams, son of Sleep and nephew of Death. And the Morpheus's voice was pleasant enough, I supposed, but—like Leander's—it sounded human. More human than Ikelos's had, at any rate. The rogue Oneiroi's voice had penetrated my mother's dream, crawling into every corner, even when he spoke softly. Did the difference have something to do with the fact the Morpheus hadn't seized control of my mind? Was he reining in his power out of respect, or so he wouldn't shatter my little human brain? It seemed wiser not to ask.

"Thank you for agreeing to meet with me," the Morpheus continued, nodding.

I didn't have much of a choice. But I kept the observation to myself. Go, me. "You're welcome. What do you … that is, what can I do for you?"

"You know, I gather, that we have been most curious about you since your Oneiroi abilities manifested when you were a child?"

I nodded, glancing at Leander. He hadn't moved, and his impassive expression and downturned eyes gave nothing away. Even his wings, usually so expressive, hung still behind him.

"How do you think he did it?" The Morpheus leaned forward. "How did your father manage to create you?"

"He didn't, not really," I said.

The Morpheus raised perfectly sculpted eyebrows. He

had a strong, elegant face that wouldn't have been out of place in a fashion magazine if it weren't for the tattoos coiling around his hairline. "What do you mean?"

I hesitated. The confirmation that Thomas was my biological father was still too fresh, and I didn't know how I felt about it yet. Still, I had to answer. "I have a human father. He is a normal man, as far as I can tell."

"Then how do you think you have received the gift of Oneiroi magic? There is the power of dreams in you. I can see the shadow of it." He gestured with a hand, the motion somehow tracing the shape of my body without seeming sleazy. He regarded me more as a curiosity, a puzzle to be solved; people didn't have sleazy thoughts about puzzles. Most people, anyway.

"Osmosis," I said. He raised his eyebrows, seeming to invite further explanation, so I added, "Ollie was in my mother's dreams while she was pregnant with me."

The Morpheus narrowed eyes that had the same dusky orange irises as Ikelos's. They seemed to look right through me, to sense my discomfort. "Oneiroi have gone into the dreams of pregnant women before," he said. "Many times."

"Yes," I said with a nod, "but he was there the *entire* time she was pregnant with me. He didn't leave once. I'd wager that's not something your people usually do." What was he looking for? I was sure my father—Ollie—would have already told him this.

"And why do you think he did that?" the Morpheus asked.

"He loved her. They wanted to be together."

"She knew he was there? She wanted him to stay?"

I hesitated, unnerved by the sudden intensity in his voice. Would Ollie be in even more trouble if they thought he'd moved into Mum's mind against her will? Finally, I nodded again. "Is that significant?"

"It is very unusual for a dreaming human to know that an Oneiroi is in her thoughts. Ollie must have been careless."

"I've always known..."

"You are part Oneiroi," the Morpheus pointed out, "by osmosis." Was that a hint of a smile crinkling around his eyes?

"Well, yes, but I'm also a lucid dreamer. So is Mum."

"Ah." The man sat back slightly, his butterfly wings flapping gently. "That would explain it. Lucid dreamers have always been harder to deceive."

"Deceive?"

"To hide from. We aren't used to being subtle. It's so rarely necessary, as Erebus is too great a thing for a human mind to comprehend. That is why most of them forget it so quickly, lest they go mad. It is possible you were only able to absorb some part of Ollie's power by virtue of your mother's ability." He cocked his head, his gaze growing distant.

After several heartbeats of silence, I frowned, glancing at Leander. "So if Mum wasn't a lucid dreamer, Ollie being in her mind for that long might not have affected me?" I asked my friend, keeping my voice quiet.

Beside me, Leander nodded, his gaze remaining on the floor. "Though if she weren't, he'd have had no reason to hang around for that long," he murmured.

"He loves her," I said, affronted on Mum's behalf.

"Yes, because of who she is. Being a lucid dreamer is part of that. Could you fall in love with someone who forgot you every time she awoke?"

"I..." I nibbled my lip, thinking it over. He had a point. But the entire thing was academic. I didn't really care about how I'd come to be born. What I wanted to ask was whether the Morpheus would agree to help Brad's grandfather and where Ollie was, whether he was alright.

The youthful Oneiroi king was regarding me again, a faint frown creasing that perfect forehead. Beside me, Leander's wings quivered with tension.

A blush heated my cheeks. "Sorry, Your Majesty. Did you say something?"

"Tell me what happened with my brother."

I took a slow breath, ordering my thoughts. I could get myself into a lot of trouble if I wasn't careful, and I was all too aware that I didn't know the rules of this society. "He found out about me," I said slowly. "He was using the breeder blight in Brad's grandfather, the one I asked for help with, to make himself an army of blights." The Morpheus nodded; the news didn't surprise him. Encouraged, I continued, "He had a human who was working with him, a nurse named Ewan, who had access to the breeder blight. He was deliberately infecting people visiting patients and other visitors to the home. I encountered one of the blights in the dreams of a client of mine, and it figured out I was part Oneiroi when I evicted it. Ikelos then sent a blight-possessed human and some mara to try and kill me."

The Morpheus's jaw tightened and I hesitated, my heart in my throat. When he was angry, the Oneiroi king looked a lot like his brother; I recalled the fury on Ikelos's face as he'd hunted me down in my mother's hijacked dream. He'd intended to torture me for the secret of how I'd come to be—and, if Ollie and Leander hadn't distracted him, he would have been successful. Would the Morpheus torture me too, if I displeased him?

The Oneiroi king gestured for me to continue, and I wrapped my hands in the folds of my skirt to hide their trembling. "Ikelos figured out Mum was the key to it all, I guess, because he forced his way into Mum's dream and threw Ollie out." I hesitated. "Ollie agreed to surrender to Leander in exchange for his help with saving Mum." The full story was that Leander had captured Ollie, and then I'd captured Leander. I'd pretty much forced the two to work together ... but I didn't think Leander would thank me for sharing that with his king. I continued quickly, before the Morpheus asked any questions. "Anyway, we figured out how to get into Mum's dream, which had originally been fortified by Ollie. Ikelos had ... done something to Mum. Put her to sleep somehow, so she couldn't resist him. I found and freed her, and together we, ah..." There was no nice way to say it.

"You threw Ikelos into a lava flow."

I nodded, raising my chin. I wouldn't look guilty. I wasn't a child in the schoolyard, being chastised for being rough with the other kids. "It was self-defence. He'd already hurt Mum, Ollie and Leander, and he was trying to hurt me. He was so powerful. And I don't think we could've reasoned with him."

"You couldn't have." The Morpheus ran a hand through his hair in a surprisingly human gesture of frustration. "Believe me, I've tried."

I blinked, opening my mouth to ask, but Leander inhaled sharply. When I looked at him, he shook his head, glancing towards the arcing pane of clear glass above our heads. I looked up, and my eyes widened as I

took in the several dozen Oneiroi who hovered in the void outside, peering in at us. There were both men and women, many of them outlandish, all of them lovely, floating on wings patterned in a manner similar to different species of moth. *Don't embarrass the king in front of his subjects. Right.*

"So," I said instead, "am I in some kind of trouble here, Your Majesty?"

"Trouble? No. What made you think that?"

I gestured from him to me. "You came a long way to talk to me, and I'm sure Leander could have told you everything I did."

"Ah, but Leander can only tell me what he saw. I needed to hear the truth from your own lips." He tapped the fingers of one hand against the bracer on the opposite wrist, drawing my gaze. The bracers' matt grey and white seemed to swirl together. They didn't look like metal, more like … bone. I shivered. "Thank you for being so forthcoming," the Morpheus added. "I believe we are done here. I will send a score of Oneiroi to deal with Ikelos's breeder blight, so it cannot produce more offspring to trouble you."

"Thanks." Relief flowed through me. I'd made it through the weirdest interview of my life, even including Nelson's interrogations of me. Although we weren't quite done yet. "Can I ask you a question?"

"I can't free Ollie, if that is what you want to ask me," the Morpheus said. "He broke our laws and has to serve out the duration of his sentence."

"What laws did he break?" He raised an eyebrow, and I added quickly, "I'm not trying to be rude. I don't know your laws."

"Grievously tampering with a human. Revealing his nature to a human without permission. Refusing a summons by his liege."

My heart sank. I couldn't argue with any of those points, not really. Although I hadn't really suffered as a result of Ollie's tampering and it had probably been inadvertent, the fact he'd done *something* to me was obvious. "I don't suppose the fact Mum's a lucid dreamer counts as a mitigating circumstance for the second crime, does it? You said they—we—are difficult to deceive."

"No. He should have tried harder."

Icy dread slashed through me. I'd revealed myself to Brad and Jen. Best keep that fact to myself, lest the Morpheus try to punish me too. Did he believe I fell under his jurisdiction? Did I? "Okay," I said. "It's just that Mum will want me to ask. Is he well? Can I see him?"

"I'm afraid that's impossible. His prison is on the other side of the world." The king's stern expression softened a little. "But he has not been harmed. And thirty years isn't such a long time. Your mother will see him again one day."

I released my breath in a slow, trembling gasp. His words reassured me about something I'd been too afraid to ask: they weren't going to do anything to Mum for knowing about the Oneiroi. Still, I doubted she'd regard thirty years as a short time. She'd be in her seventies by the time Ollie was released.

"We will deal with the breeder blight while we are here," the Morpheus said, growing indistinct as the dream faded around me. "Farewell, Melaina."

Chapter Fifteen

I woke slowly, arching my back into a stretch beneath the sheets. I was alone in the bed, and for a moment I luxuriated in having the space to myself ... before the strangeness of being alone sunk in.

I sat abruptly, looking around the room, which was bathed in glorious mid-morning light. A depression in the doona beside me indicated someone had been lying there at some point, and a fold-out camping chair hogged the space beside the bed. Mum, Jen and Brad: they'd been keeping watch over me. Where were they? I wasn't hooked up to a catheter or a drip, to my great relief, though I did have a rather urgent need to pee. The clock said it was just after ten in the morning. I clambered across the bed to get around the chair, sliding my feet into my slippers.

After taking care of necessities, I brushed my teeth quickly, the sound of voices, quiet but intense, catching my ear from the other end of the house.

Walking up the hall, I saw Brad and Jen standing before the open front door, their arms crossed and expressions grim. With a sinking feeling, I knew who would be on the other side of the door before I rounded the corner. David Nelson. Despite being in uniform, he seemed to be alone. So he probably wasn't here to arrest me for something. Was he? Surely he'd bring a colleague for that?

"Ah, Melaina." Although he looked tired, his eyes shadowed as if he was at the end of a long shift, his gaze was still sharp as it took in my yoga pants and sleep-rumpled T-shirt. I wished I'd taken the time to get dressed. "Did I wake you?"

"No," I said, stepping between my boyfriend and my best friend. Brad placed a hand on my arm, and I couldn't tell whether it was in reassurance or warning.

"It didn't occur to me that you'd be asleep this late," Nelson said, glancing at his watch.

"It's a Sunday," I said, hoping I was right. Surely I hadn't slept for more than a day?

He didn't bat an eyelid, so I guessed I must be. "Sleeping in must run in the family, I suppose."

"I guess." I narrowed my eyes at him. *He's trying to goad me.* "What can I do for you?"

He pulled a notebook and pen out of one of his many pockets. "I went out to visit Ewan this morning. He said you dropped by on Tuesday."

"So?"

"What was the reason for your visit?"

"Why do you think?" I scowled. I was *so* not in the mood for this. I hadn't even had a coffee yet ... though I may have been putting too much faith in the restorative

powers of caffeine if I thought that would make this easier. "After you popped by the shop and insinuated he'd been making up stories about me, I wanted to ask him what his game was."

"Making up stories?"

I put my hands on my hips and did my best to ignore the fact I was in fluffy bunny slippers. "Yeah." Beside me, Jen made an uncomfortable noise in the back of her throat.

"He merely suggested I review the home's security footage if I wanted to know what really happened that night," Nelson said. "The footage doesn't lie."

On my other side, Brad shuffled his feet, glancing at me. I sighed. He and Jen were right; I shouldn't be antagonising the constable any further if I could avoid it. I covered Brad's hand with mine, giving it a reassuring squeeze. "What do you think 'really happened'?" I asked in a more neutral tone.

Nelson blinked, regarding me with those silver-grey eyes. "You knocked that guard out somehow, and two nurses."

Two nurses? It was true, of course, but Ewan had been awake and raving by the time the police had arrived. He'd no doubt told Nelson what I'd done, but the fact the constable was taking the word of a suspected arsonist over mine wasn't soothing. "And did he say how I did that, hypothetically? A strong pot of chamomile tea, or a ray gun, or..."

"You tell me." Nelson poised his pen, ready to jot down my answer.

"I have no idea," I lied, adding quickly, "but even if I could knock them out, why would I? That's what I don't get about all this. What possible motivation do you think I could have for randomly attacking people?"

"Not randomly. Mr Peterson here claimed Ewan was drugging your mother and his grandfather. Perhaps you believed the rest of the staff were in on it. Perhaps you were seeking revenge." His expression softened, and his voice turned sympathetic. "I can understand how that would be the case. Your poor, vulnerable mother."

Damn, he's good. Better at this than me. My head began to ache, and I rubbed my forehead. "He was. But I wasn't seeking revenge. We went to confront Ewan and he attacked us. I don't know, maybe he knocked Lien out."

The sympathy dropped away. "But not the security guard."

I shrugged, pressing my lips together. That damned footage. I couldn't argue with it. Nerves fizzed down my spine; I felt sure the astute constable could sense my agitation.

"Your story is full of holes, Melaina." Nelson snapped his notebook closed without writing a word. The sharp sound made me jump. "Things will go easier for you if you tell me the truth now, rather than waiting for me to dig it up on my own. And I *will* find it."

"That's quite enough." Brad stepped forward. "Unless you're planning on arresting Melaina, we're done here. Please don't approach her again unless her lawyer is present, or we'll complain to the department about your harassment." With his jaw tight, he shut the door in Nelson's face.

We waited in the entryway, silent, watching out the side window as Nelson slid into his car—a metallic blue sedan, not a police cruiser—and started the engine. Then

I spoke quietly. "I don't have a lawyer, Brad."

"You will by the end of tomorrow," he said firmly. "I'm going to get you one. The way he's behaving is not okay."

"I can't afford it."

He shook his head. "I'll pay." I opened my mouth to protest, and he put a finger against my lips. "I was there that night, same as you. If he builds a case against you, I'm sure I'll get charged with something too."

"Is this more of your enlightened self-interest?"

"Of course," Brad said, a twinkle in his eye as he bent his head to kiss me. His lips tasted of the coffee I wished I'd had, and for a moment I lost myself in the embrace … before Jen, standing on my other side, made retching noises.

"Jen!"

"Sorry." She feigned wiping her mouth. "But you two are grossing me out."

"Then don't watch," Brad replied, pulling me close to him again. I started to move forward … but then I saw my mother, standing in the doorway to the kitchen with her heart in her eyes, and any desire I had to snuggle fell away.

"You're up," she said, brushing her long hair back from her face. She'd clearly just woken up herself. She was on the afternoon shift at Serenity's. "How … how did it go?"

"It could've been worse." I stepped forward to give her a quick hug. "I didn't see him," I said as Brad and Jen moved past us, heading for the kitchen and giving us a moment of privacy. "Apparently he's fine, but he's imprisoned overseas somewhere."

"How does that even work?" She sniffled a little as she

stepped back. Her eyes shone with tears, but her cheeks were dry. "How do you imprison a spirit in a world made of dreams?"

"I don't know." I tried to smile, though the expression felt weak and ill-fitting. "I didn't ask."

"Is he going to take care of my granddad?" Brad asked as we walked into the kitchen. He stood beside the coffee machine, gazing at his hands as he prepared to make me a cup. That he'd thought to do so without me having to ask warmed me to my toes.

"Yup," I said, sliding onto a stool and leaning my elbows on the kitchen bench. "For all I know, they're getting rid of the breeder blight now. The Morpheus seemed keen to get it over with."

"You weren't invited?" Jen raised an eyebrow at me from over the open fridge door.

"No. I'm kind of grateful, though." I didn't elaborate, but Jen saw my shudder and nodded. Her lips pressed together as she closed the fridge, holding a carton of eggs and a half-empty packet of ham. "The Morpheus brought his entire court with him," I added. "He doesn't need my help."

"I guess we'll know it's done when Grandad wakes up," Brad said over the watery hiss of the coffee machine as he steamed some milk. "*If* he wakes up."

"I'm sure he will," Jen said stoutly. I wasn't so confident. His grandfather's car accident and coma had pre-dated the blight infestation; they were what had landed him in the home and in Ewan's so-called care, where he'd been infected.

I knew Brad shared my lack of confidence, but he smiled a thanks at my friend for her words.

"What were they like? The Oneiroi?" Mum asked, sitting beside me. I was sure she was looking for a distraction, and I was happy to oblige, filling the three of them in on what had happened during my meeting with the Morpheus while Brad finished making a round of drinks and Jen fixed us all some scrambled eggs. The smell of toasting bread and coffee soon filled the little kitchen, and I relaxed, content to be with my favourite people.

"So you were right," Jen said when I was done, scraping eggs onto a plate. "It was about Ikelos."

I curled my fingers around my mug. "He was pretty interested in the whole lucid dreamer thing too. But yeah, mostly Ikelos, I think."

"I can see why." She gesticulated with a wooden spoon. "I mean, he presumably exiled his brother for a reason. And then Ikelos started building himself a blight army, and no one ever does that because they're looking to kiss and make up. The Morpheus would want to be sure Ikelos was dead."

"Did he say that?" Mum asked, taking a plate from Jen with a grateful smile. The rest of us followed her out to the lounge room and sat, plates on our knees.

"Say what?" Jen frowned, taking a mouthful of coffee before placing her cup on a side table.

Mum nodded towards me. "Did the Morpheus actually say Ikelos is dead?"

I shook my head slowly, thinking the conversation over. "He asked me what happened, so I told him. He didn't really say much of anything about it, just thanked me for cooperating."

"He should've given you a medal," Jen murmured.

"I was thinking the exact same thing the other day."

I grinned at her.

"And did he seem particularly sad? Relieved?" Mum pressed.

"No. More ... frustrated. He was pretty hard to read, though. I don't think he liked that Ikelos was using nightmare spirits against me. Leander told me once that the Morpheus is a bit of an environmentalist. He doesn't like blights and mara messing up Erebus for the Oneiroi."

"Messing it up?" Jen said.

"You know. Filling it with creepy clowns and spiders, that sort of thing. What's this about, Mum?""

"I don't know for sure, but..." Mum pushed a piece of toast around on her plate with her fork.

"But?"

It was Brad who replied, his brow creased with worry. "The Morpheus thinks Ikelos is still alive."

"What?" I gasped, sitting up straighter. My plate tilted precariously on my lap; Brad reached to steady it. "He can't be. We threw him into lava. No one survives that!"

"Tell that to Darth Vader," Brad said.

"Yeah, but this isn't the movies. It's real life!" I realised how stupid that sounded and bit my lip. "Dream life. Whatever. Besides, I haven't seen any indication that Ikelos is still directing the blights. They could be infecting people through natural exposure. Free ranging, like angry nightmare chickens."

"He might be licking his wounds somewhere. Recovering," Mum said.

"Having a cybernetic suit thing made," Jen said with a small laugh, glancing at Brad. He grinned back. I took a deep breath and tried to let their humour thaw some of the ice flowing through my veins at the thought that

Ikelos might be out there somewhere, waiting. Plotting his revenge.

"It's just a theory." Mum looked up. "I remember what we did to him. But it's not like we ever saw a body..."

An uncomfortable silence fell, as I turned over their words in my mind. Did Oneiroi even leave bodies? I'd never seen a dead one. They could be hurt by things in dreams. Leander's wings had been torn by the ephemeral barbed wire Ikelos had conjured. That meant they could be killed—though, given their instant ability to change a dreamscape, it was very unlikely to happen unless they were being opposed by another Oneiroi. I'd opposed Ikelos that day, stopped him from seizing control of Mum's dream to save himself. I was sure of it.

Wasn't I?

Chapter Sixteen

"Where shall we do this?" I looked between Brad and Jen. The former looked excited, the latter curious and anxious in equal measure. Jen had agreed to Brad's suggestion that we see whether my powers extended to bringing one person into another's dream, but now I wondered whether she was regretting it, at least a little. I knew I was—I had no idea where to even begin, and I didn't want to disappoint Brad. But I'd promised him I'd try, so here we were.

"In the lounge room?" Jen suggested, running her hands down the front of her T-shirt. She'd changed into comfortable clothes once we'd decided to give our little experiment a go. So had Brad, swapping his jeans for a pair of winter-weight pyjama pants that he'd left here.

I was still in yoga pants. Fresh ones, though.

"Your bedroom would make more sense," I said. She blushed and I hurried to add, "Or mine. You know. Whatever."

"It's too early for bed," Jen said as we filed into the lounge room. Afternoon sun streaked through the open blinds, bathing the room with slatted golden light. The door to my office was open, the doorway framing Jat's dreamcatcher perfectly. I even had a desk sitting beneath it on the far wall, though I'd yet to save up for a computer. It was the first thing I was going to buy when I had the money. Too many customers contacted me via email, and I hated that they had to wait for a reply.

"Well, yeah." I turned away from the office to face my boyfriend and best friend. Brad's eyes were bright, while Jen shuffled from foot to foot. "But we aren't planning on staying asleep. It shouldn't take more than a few minutes to know whether it's going to work or not. Half an hour at most."

"If it would make Jen more comfortable, I'm happy to do it here," Brad said, and I bit my lip to hold in the inappropriate giggle at his words. Anyone would think we were planning something a little kinky. Maybe that was why Jen was so keen to stay out of the bedroom? Was the idea of lying on a bed with the two of us that weird?

On reflection, maybe she was right.

"Okay," I said. "But if anyone gets a crick in their neck, it's not my fault."

"Understood." Brad grinned, placing his phone, wallet and keys in a neat little stack on the coffee table. Jen nodded, some of the tension easing from her shoulders.

We settled in, Brad and Jen sitting on either side of me and arranging our colourful cushions around them until they were comfortable. I leaned over Brad first, kissing his lips lightly. "Nighty night?" he said, and I nodded. Then I put him under, puffing gently on his face. His breathing slowed instantly to the even, deep rhythm of sleep.

"That's kinda freaky to watch." Jen looked a little pale. "I've never seen the process from the outside before."

"I had a breath mint, at least, so you won't get heinous coffee breath," I teased, trying to lighten the mood. "And I don't have to kiss you first."

She rolled her eyes. "I know that, Netflix girl."

I glanced at Brad, who was out for the count. I'd picked him to go first deliberately. "Look, are you sure you want to try this? You seem pretty wound up."

"It's just…" She looked down, examining a glittering ring on her pinkie finger. A rose quartz gemstone winked as she moved her hand in the sunlight, motes of dust dancing around us. "Well, I've never had someone other than you in my dreams. I like Brad, but this is a big deal for me. Dreams are … they can be private, you know?" She looked up at me, her eyes begging for understanding.

"Is that what you're worried about?"

She nodded, twisting the ring around.

"Do you want me to bring you into Brad's dream instead?"

She glanced at him, her expression thoughtful, and then shook her head. "No, it's okay. Just…"

"I won't let your dream take any embarrassing turns while Brad's there." *Assuming we can even get this to work.* "Scout's honour."

"Thanks." She reached out to squeeze my hand. Her fingers were cool in mine. "I know it's silly."

"No, it's not. I should've thought of it sooner. I mean, I wasn't exactly wild about having the Morpheus in my head."

Jen smiled weakly. "At least I know you guys." She adjusted her ponytail so it hung beside one ear rather

than down the back of her neck. Then she slid her glasses off, leaning forward to place them on the coffee table. "If your mum comes home and we're all passed out on the couch, is she going to freak?" She fluffed the cushion behind her one last time.

"Nah, I warned her before she left for work." I turned towards Jen, propping myself against the arm of the chair. I could see why she was a little uncomfortable. Being this close to both her and Brad felt intimate. I preferred guys—but, if I didn't, Jen would definitely be my type. As it was, sitting between them, I felt … safe. Bolstered by their trust. "Are you ready?"

"Hit me," Jen said, closing her eyes as I leaned over her.

"See you on the flip side."

Within heartbeats, her slow breathing joined Brad's, a tiny almost-snore escaping her parted lips as her head lolled to one side. *We should've done this lying down*, I thought again as I took their hands in mine. *Too late now.*

I closed my eyes and, breathing out in a sigh, entered Erebus.

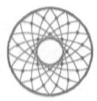

I stepped into Jen's dream first. She wasn't there—my power forced a person to skip the light sleep stage when they drifted off, but didn't usually shove them straight into active dreaming. Her proto-dream this time was of a library, with mazes of book-lined corridors lit by swinging lampshades. It might have been creepy except for the delicious smell of leather bindings, dust and, more faintly, ink, adhesive and a flowery, nutty smell that I thought might be old paper.

I made my way into the dream, winding my way through the labyrinthine corridors, farther away from the light, until I found a small side chamber. Heavy slate tiles covered the floor and the walls were of bare stone. A single window looked out onto a dark sky, studded all around with stars.

No, not stars. Dreaming minds. The raw void of Erebus.

Feeling a surge of the nervousness I'd kept hidden from Brad and Jen, I pushed the window open and leaned out. The atmosphere outside seemed warmer than the cool air of the stone-lined library halls, insulated as they were, but I knew from experience that the void's temperature was neither warm nor cold, as if it matched the temperature of my dreaming mind. What temperature that would be, I had no idea. But it felt like a mild spring day ... if the spring day was completely still, pitch black and directionless.

Okay, not *that* much like a mild spring day.

My power to find a dream amidst the apparent chaos of the void was tied to physical proximity. Unlike an Oneiroi, I couldn't hop from mind to mind. But I was right beside both Brad and Jen, and I somehow knew, with absolute certainty, that the star below me and to my right, the one with the faintly greenish glow, was Brad's mind.

Now, how do I...?

"What are you doing?" The voice came from just behind me.

I jumped, my fingernails biting into the timber windowsill and my heart leaping into my throat. "Don't sneak up on me," I scolded Leander even as I turned to face him.

He stood in the middle of the room. His dove-grey wings seemed to fill the small space, and his clothes were, for him, unusually casual and modern: neat jeans and a collared shirt with the top two buttons undone so I could catch a glimpse of his sculpted chest. His feet were bare, as usual, which was probably why I hadn't heard him coming. Either that or he'd just materialised in that spot.

"Sorry," he said with a grin, not at all repentant.

"What if I'd fallen?"

"I would have caught you." His gaze slid past me to look out on Erebus.

"Still, I'd rather not risk it, thanks." The idea of tumbling out that window, spiralling away into nothingness, tightened my stomach. Not wanting to show it, I put my hands on my hips. "Am I in trouble? Does the Morpheus want to see me again?"

"No," Leander said, a question in his voice. "I just saw you in Jen's dream. Is she having nightmares again?"

"Not recently." I eyed him. "Is that really why you're here?"

"Well, when I saw you looking out onto the void…" He paused, his own hands going on his hips in a mirror of mine. "What? Can't I just drop by to say hello?"

"You never have before." I turned back to look out the window. Brad's dream hadn't moved—at least, not relative to our position. For all I knew, we were all spinning through space together, like an arm of the galaxy.

"Well, I also wanted to let you know we're done with the breeder blight."

Already? That was fast. But then I realised the odd note in Leander's reply had been hurt, and guilt was a sudden stab in my chest. Leander *had* saved my bacon with Daniel's blight three weeks before. Sure, he'd had another reason for showing up then too, but still. I took a deep breath and reminded myself that, while he had been spying on me for all those years in an effort to find my father, he had also become my friend. "Sorry," I mumbled, not turning back to him. "I didn't mean to be crotchety."

"It's alright." Leander came to stand beside me. His left wings, the primary and the hindwing, hung down behind me. Although they didn't touch me, I could sense their presence, like the warmth of another's hand an inch away from your skin. "I know what a moody thing you can be sometimes," he added.

I elbowed him in the ribs, and he chuckled. "Did Mr Peterson—Brad's grandfather—did he wake up?" I asked.

Leander shook his head, his gaze growing distant as he regarded the void before us. "I don't think so. I can still sense his dreaming mind. It's ... well, now the breeder blight's gone, it's..."

"What?" I looked up at him, surprised at how close he was. His mouth was turned down at the corners and his brows were puckered in the middle.

"His dreams are formless, like his mind has been hollowed out. I think whatever damage put him in the coma in the first place is still there. I've seen it before."

"Oh," I said quietly. Brad hadn't been expecting miracles, but he must have hoped he'd get his grandfather back. "Do I need to clean up the muck from the blight? Otherwise he might get reinfected, right?"

"It's taken care of."

I nodded, feeling a surge of gratitude that I wouldn't have to wade through a formless dreamscape, cleaning up slime. Guilt followed on gratitude's heels and I

sighed, deciding to change the subject before I got maudlin. "So the reason I'm here is that I'm conducting an experiment."

"Oh? In Jen's dream?" Leander raised his eyebrows, the gold flecks in his irises dancing with amusement. "Tell me more."

"Not like that." The tips of my ears burned with sudden embarrassment. "It was Brad's idea, actually."

"I'll bet."

"Not like that," I repeated. "He suggested that, if I could bring him into someone else's dream, he might be able to help me fight blights and things."

Leander snorted. "No offence to your boyfriend, but he's not really equipped for it."

I shrugged. "I know. But an extra pair of hands would've been helpful in Daniel's dream. We could've collected what we needed even faster. Let's be honest, by the time you arrived I was pretty much a regular human myself."

"You could never be a regular human," Leander said, his voice gentle.

Suddenly uncomfortable, I took a half-step away from him. "I meant that—"

"I know what you mean. It's okay." He waved my explanation away and I relaxed.

"Besides," I said, "maybe he could contribute some extra energy to me if I needed it. It wouldn't be ideal, but..." I shrugged.

"It doesn't work that way," Leander said. "We can bring one human into another's dreams, but it costs you energy, not the other way around."

"Oh." My shoulders drooped. Brad would be disappointed.

"Also," Leander added, "I don't think this is something you could do."

"But you just said...?"

"That's his dream over there, right?" He pointed to the green-tinged star, and I nodded. "To bring him over here, an Oneiroi would have to fly over there and drag him back."

I grimaced, eying Leander's wings with a familiar surge of jealousy. "Ah."

"Still," he said with a grin, "this is a great opportunity for me to meet your boyfriend and your best friend at the same time." He placed his hands on the window frame and launched himself forward, air from his wings buffeting me as they thrust downwards, just missing my bare arms.

"Isn't revealing your nature to a human without permission illegal?" I called after Leander. If he heard me, he gave no indication, kiting through the void towards Brad's dream like an eagle riding a thermal. What was he playing at?

That thought was nothing compared to the sudden anxiety I felt at the idea of Leander and Brad meeting. Face to face. Was this how teenage girls felt, introducing their boyfriend to their father for the first time? Or was it more how a teenage girl felt, introducing her boyfriend to her hot, winged childhood friend?

Hot? Where the hell had that come from? Flustered, I transformed my yoga pants and shapeless T-shirt into something closer to my usual streetwear: jeans, form-fitting tee, leather boots. No way could I face this meeting in my pyjamas.

Chapter Seventeen

"Melaina?" The voice came from behind me. I whirled, my heart leaping back into my throat—and then felt silly when I saw Jen standing there, wearing a knee-length aqua sundress covered in bright yellow flowers and looking confused. Of course she'd shown up. It was *her* dream. "Is it time to study?" She looked down at her empty arms. "I … seem to have lost my books."

"We're seeing if I can bring Brad into your dream. Remember?"

"Oh." She rubbed her forehead, seeming to struggle through the fog of the dream, but after a moment the baffled frown fled and she gave me a sharp look. "I forgot. How strange."

"Not that strange. You're not a freaky lucid dreamer like me."

"You're not freaky," she said. I snorted with disbelief, and she gave me a sideways grin. "Okay, maybe a tiny bit freaky." She examined her clothes, probably checking them for suitability for guests. She gave them a tiny, approving nod before regarding her bare feet. "Can I have some shoes? These tiles are cold."

"Sure." Brushing her arm with my fingers so the change didn't cost me anything, I conjured her a pair of strappy sandals the same colour as the dress. A yellow fabric sunflower adorned each one.

"You're better than a gold credit card at the mall," she said with a laugh, smoothing the front of her skirt.

"If only I could take this stuff out into the real world." I sighed, turning to look back out the window. Leander had disappeared from view, presumably into the green star that was Brad's dreaming mind. The idea made me want to squirm with discomfort. "Leander's gone to get Brad. I can't do it. No wings."

"Leander?" Jen crossed to my side and peered out the window. "I've always wanted to see what he looks like."

"He's annoying," I groused, "but kind of cute, if insects are your thing."

She raised her eyebrows at me archly. "Worried?"

"A little," I said. I was about to say more, but the appearance of Leander, carrying something—no, some-one—across the void made the words stick in my throat. The person was a small boy with a shock of dark hair. As they came closer I saw his eyes were closed, but I knew they'd be a chocolatey brown. I'd met pre-pubescent Brad in his dreams once before. Last time it had been in a dream version of his grandmother's house ... which I'd then burned to the ground in a gas explosion. Oops.

"Is that a tiny Brad?" Jen squealed as Leander came to hover before the window.

"Yeah," I said, pulling her back by the arm so the

Oneiroi could land on the sill, ducking his head as he stepped through.

"Here." Leander handed the sleeping child to me. I breathed a quiet sigh of relief. This would be awkward enough as it was without Brad waking in Leander's arms. "I decided to take the miniature version."

"Well, why wouldn't you?" Jen stepped forward, holding out her hand for Leander to shake. "Much more portable."

"You must be Jen." Leander bent forward to kiss the back of her hand. "Delighted to meet you. Melaina talks about you all the time."

"Really?" Jen's eyes sparkled and a blush shaded her cheeks a pretty red.

"Of course. When we're not busy fighting nightmare demons, that is."

"Naturally. Who has time to chat mid-combat?"

Half listening to their banter, I turned, placing the sleepy child on his feet and holding him upright as he swayed, his eyelids fluttering. Brad made an impossibly cute kid. "Wake up," I whispered, sending a surge of energy into him, imagining him fully grown and in adult clothes rather than the cartoon T-shirt and high-waisted jeans that would've been all the rage in the nineties. The effect was rather strange to watch; as his eyes opened to regard me, his face lost the softness of youth and he grew taller. The fabric twisted and changed into slacks and a white collared shirt. I hadn't consciously chosen those clothes, but Brad looked hot in business attire. I staggered, unbalanced by my hands on his sides as his weight shifted.

"Steady." Leander caught me by the elbow and gave me a bright smile. Behind him, Jen looked him up and down, examining his wings with wide eyes.

"Where are we?" Brad said sleepily, rubbing his forehead.

"Jen's dream."

"Jen's..." His hands dropped to his sides, and he gave me a relieved hug. "It worked! I knew you could do it."

"Not so much," I said, indicating Leander with a nod and a grimace. "It turns out it is possible to bring one person into another's dream, but only a full-blooded Oneiroi can do it. It's a wing thing. Brad, this is Leander. Leander, this is my boyfriend, Brad."

"Pleased to meet you." Brad held out his free hand as Jen had done, keeping the other hooked around my waist.

Thankfully, Leander didn't kiss Brad's hand, just shook it. "And you." The look the Oneiroi gave Brad was appraising, his eyes narrowed and his normally cheerful lips pressed together in a flat line.

Jen broke the awkward silence. "I thought you'd be more insect-y."

"Insect-y?" Leander's smile was back.

"Yeah, you know. Antennae, bug eyes—that sort of thing."

Leander laughed. "No, we look human. For the most part." He flexed his wings the same way another man might flex his muscles. Jen ducked as one of his hind-wings brushed her shoulder.

"Shall we go somewhere with a little more space?" I said, trying to keep from laughing. "If you're going to keep flapping those things around, we need more headroom."

"Right you are," Leander said, not the least bit embarrassed. "My lady?" He held out his hand to Jen. After a

brief hesitation, she took it and, without another word, Leander changed her dream.

I'd expected Leander to completely rewrite the dream to something outdoorsy; he'd done that to me more than once. But he surprised me by moving us within the existing dream. We appeared in the middle of a high-ceilinged reading room. Tables stood in rows along each side of a central aisle, each with a pair of blue-shaded reading lamps angled downwards. Arched windows lined the walls, sunlight pouring through, and the ceiling above rose to a dome. I raised my eyebrows at Jen. "Awesome library."

"Too much study, I guess," she said with a shrug.

Brad, who'd materialised several tables down from us, crossed to my side with a glare at the Oneiroi, pulling out a chair and seating himself. Feeling daring even though there wasn't a librarian in sight to scold me, I sat on the table beside him, my knee against his shoulder. I was sure Leander had deliberately moved Brad away from me in transit. Was he *trying* to make my life hard?

Jen leaned against a table and crossed her arms as she regarded Leander. "Can I ask you a question?"

"Sure." He adopted the same casual pose as her, leaning against a table across the aisle from hers.

"Is Ikelos still alive?"

Leander stiffened, his eyes widening and his wings jerking with surprise. One of them knocked a lamp to the side. I cringed as it teetered on the edge of the table, but Leander twisted around, steadying it before it could crash to the floor.

"I take it that's a yes?" Jen said.

"It's a no," Leander said, struggling to look calm even

as his fingers tightened against the tabletop. "Or, rather, it's an I don't know. Why do you ask?"

"Melaina told us about meeting the Morpheus," she said. Leander glanced at me and I gave him an apologetic shrug. "He seemed very interested in what happened to his brother," Jen continued. "We think maybe he doesn't believe Ikelos died."

"I don't know what the Morpheus thinks," Leander said. "He doesn't confide in me."

"But you suspect we're right, don't you?"

"I … have wondered, yes."

"Well, crap," Jen muttered. Leander nodded in agreement.

"What does this mean for Melaina?" Brad asked, seeming to forget his irritation at the Oneiroi in the face of a more pressing concern. "If Ikelos is still alive, will he come after her?"

Leander's gaze flicked to meet mine, and I read the answer in his sombre regard before he spoke it aloud. "He might." A chill ran down my spine and I inched closer to Brad, seeking comfort in his warmth. "But he probably won't," Leander added hurriedly. "The exile from court came with some very specific terms—that he disappear and not make a fuss. Breeding blights obviously puts him in contravention of those. The Morpheus won't let him roam free, not now he knows. If Ikelos has realised his brother was here, he'll have left the city. Maybe the country. He always did prefer the Mediterranean." He gave me a soft smile that I suspected was meant to be reassuring. But something he'd said niggled at me. After a moment, I figured it out.

"Was?"

"Pardon?" He blinked at me.

"You said 'his brother *was* here'. Has the Morpheus gone already?"

Leander nodded. "But don't worry, you won't be alone. He left me and a few others in the area, just in case."

Brad stood, his eyes narrowing. "What about my grandad, moth boy? He promised—"

"It's all taken care of," Leander interrupted. I glared at him, and he added in a softer tone, "Though I regret to inform you that your grandfather is still in a coma. It … doesn't look good."

"Oh." Brad looked down the length of the reading room, blinking hard. "Excuse me." He strode away, the sound of his shoes striking the tiled floor echoing in the empty space.

"Crap," I murmured, standing to follow him. "I should've told him straight away."

Leander caught my arm before I could follow Brad. "Can I talk to you for a second?"

"But…" I looked from my boyfriend's retreating back, stiff with tension, to Leander's furrowed brow. "Alright, but make it quick."

Leander led me several tables away and then waved his hand. A shimmer appeared in the air around us, like hot air above a summer road, and both Jen and Brad froze. "I paused the dream."

"You can do that? Freeze non-ephemera?" I stared at him. "That would've been useful when we were fighting those blights, you know."

"I can't do it for long, or when someone or something is actively resisting me," he said. Then he took a deep breath, as if bracing for something. *Uh-oh.* "Remember how the Morpheus said that an Oneiroi revealing his or her nature to a human is against our laws?"

I folded my arms. "Yes. But I figured that horse has bolted, as far as Mum, Brad and Jen go. They've known about me for ages." *Though I did tell them about the Morpheus, and now Leander knows it.* He worked for the Morpheus. Would he have to tell his ruler what I'd done? I realised I was biting my lip and forced myself to stop.

"You're fine. You're only half Oneiroi. Our laws don't apply to you."

I raised an eyebrow, wishing he'd told me that before I'd met the Morpheus—it would have saved me a lot of stress. "What about you, though? Do you have some sort of 'Morpheus's Hawk' loophole?"

He shook his head, grimacing.

"Then why on earth did you stick around once I told you what I was doing?"

"Because you needed my help to bring Brad across here," he said, his gaze sliding away from mine to the shelves behind me.

"That excuse is pretty feeble," I said gently. "I didn't need him here for anything important."

"I know," he replied, the corner of his mouth quirking in a rueful half-smile. "That's why I'd rather not need to use it. If you do run into one of the other Oneiroi, please don't mention that I met Brad and Jen."

A slow grin spread across my face. "What's in it for me?"

"Hey!" Leander's eyes widened and he put a hand to his chest, feigning shock. "After all I've done for you?"

"I'm teasing. Of course I won't tell."

"Thank you." He turned back to Jen and Brad, raising

his hand as though to end a spell.

"Wait." I caught his hand before he could gesture, and he turned back towards me. "Do you really think Ikelos is alive? Honestly?"

"Honestly?" He regarded me, his eyes shadowed. "Yes, I do. We're not that easy to kill."

Lava is easy? I swallowed hard around a sudden tightness in my throat. "And do you really believe he left the city?"

Leander shook his head. "Leaving would be the smart thing to do, but he's always been reckless. That's what got him into trouble in the first place. He was the younger brother but tried to take the throne."

"Oh." I stared down at my boots. "Well, thanks for hanging around, I guess. At the very least, there are bound to be more free-range blights that need dealing with."

"Melaina." The seriousness of his tone drew my gaze back to his face. "I won't let anything happen to you. I promise." He squeezed my hand before releasing it and turning back to the others and completing the gesture he'd been about to do. "Now go, comfort your boyfriend," he said, his voice carefree once more.

Chapter Eighteen

"Are you okay?" I eyed Brad as he rolled his head from side to side as if trying to stretch out a kink.

"Yeah." He rinsed our coffee cups, leaving them upside down on the drain board. "I just have a crick in my neck." He glanced sideways at me, smiling faintly. "And no, I'm not blaming you."

I felt surprisingly well after our impromptu nap on the couch. Of course, I'd awoken with my head pillowed against Jen's shoulder, which may have had something to do with it. "Do you want me to give you a massage? Or a *massage*?" I raised an eyebrow. Jen had left half an hour before to go to the library—the real one this time—which meant we had the house to ourselves. I'd vacuumed while Brad was showering, and put a load of towels on the line, so I could relax without feeling guilty. And I knew exactly how I wanted to relax.

"Actually, I'm thinking I might get changed and head home," Brad replied with a sigh. "See if the nursing home

has called."

Shame clenched at my gut, and I rounded the bench to give him a hug. Here I was, thinking about sex when he'd just been told his grandfather might never wake after all. "I'm sorry."

"For what? You didn't make my grandfather crash his car all those years ago." Brad's breath tickled my ear as he drew me close.

"For being insensitive. I'm an idiot."

"You're not." He rested his cheek against my hair and I took a deep breath, filling my lungs with the spicy scent of his aftershave. "Maybe he'd prefer it this way," Brad continued. "I don't know that he'd even want to wake up, you know?"

"Yeah," I said softly. Brad suspected his grandfather's crash had been deliberate, a grisly attempt to join his wife after she'd passed away. I'd seen Mum struggle with Ollie's absence. How would she have reacted if he'd been executed rather than imprisoned? I swallowed the lump in my throat, shoving the thought away. "That has to hurt."

"It did at first, but I'm used to it now. Anyway, maybe there … there might have been some change. Maybe Leander's wrong?"

"Maybe." I winced as I heard the dubious tone in my voice. *Way to go, Melaina.* Thankfully, Brad didn't ask me to elaborate on my thoughts. I didn't want to have to tell him what Leander had said: that his grandfather's dreams had been hollowed out. The phrase made me think of the crumpled, sad skin of a kiwi fruit after the flesh had been eaten. Brad didn't need that mental image.

Keeping his arms around my waist, Brad took half a

step back, leaning against the sink. A wan smile crept onto his face. "So Leander has a crush on you," he teased.

My stomach swooped. "What? No!"

"He does. I'd bet a pile of money on it."

"Are you thinking of the way he treated you before?" I asked. Brad nodded, and I wrinkled my nose. "I've known him since I was a kid. He's just overprotective. He doesn't think anyone is good enough for me. It's nothing personal."

Brad tipped his head to the side, looking down at me. "You really believe that, don't you?"

"I ... yes?" I did, didn't it? But several memories flooded my mind: Leander, coming to my rescue on more than one occasion. Him fighting blights for me. Fighting *Ikelos* for me. His offhanded comments about me being special, or remarkable. "Maybe?" My cheeks felt hot as I stared back at Brad.

"Now she gets it," he said, his smile growing bigger. "I saw the way he looked at you today, Melaina. That's not brotherly affection."

"Even if you're right, it doesn't matter." My words tumbled over one another in their rush to be spoken. "I'm with you."

"I know," he said easily, kissing the tip of my nose.

The light tone brought me up short. "It doesn't bother you?" I frowned at him. "You're not jealous?"

He shrugged, the gesture tightening his hands around my waist. "Why would I be jealous? He's in Erebus, I'm here, and never the twain shall meet, Jen's dream notwithstanding. And I can't see that ever happening again."

"But I can spend time with him when you're not there..."

FALSE *Awakening*

"I know. But I trust you." He laughed, a soft, self-deprecating sound. "I went through a jealous phase when I was in my teens, but I'm not that insecure little boy anymore. Besides, Leander might get to spend time with you in here—" he tapped my temple lightly "—but I get to spend it with you in the real world, where it matters." His hand dropped to my shoulder and then slid down the length of my arm. Goosebumps rose in its wake.

"That's a very mature perspective," I murmured, my gaze dropping from his eyes to his lips, so soft and dusky red.

"I am nothing if not mature." His fingers tightened, one on my wrist and the other on my other hip.

"And I do prefer my men tangible."

"Do you now?" he rumbled, his pupils dilating. Warmth blossomed in my belly at the want in that look. "That's reassuring."

"I know, right?" I leaned into him, kissing him lightly. "I know you said you wanted to go," I murmured against his lips. They were as soft as they looked.

"I did…"

"I can't tempt you to stay a little longer?" I kissed from the corner of his mouth back in a line to his ear. "Even fifteen minutes?" I whispered, before catching the lobe between my teeth.

He gasped a laugh, drawing me tight against his chest. "Fifteen minutes? Give me more credit than that."

"Is that a yes?" I mumbled.

"You know I'm powerless to resist you."

Our lips crashed together, tongues tangling in a sinuous dance. Desire flared in me, brighter than the late afternoon sun haloing Brad's hair, filling the warm brown strands with flecks of gold. My hands ran down his sides, seeking the smoothness of his skin through his T-shirt and pyjama pants. A questing finger found the elastic of boxer shorts underneath. It was too much to hope he'd gone commando under the circumstances ... but still, this was much, *much* better than jeans.

Brad seemed to feel the same way if the low growl in his throat was any indication. Although my T-shirt fell past my waist, my yoga pants didn't leave a lot to the imagination—not when questing hands were involved.

A sudden thought brought me up short with a disappointed gasp.

"What is it?" Brad pulled back to regard me. His lips were swollen from my kisses, which made me want to taste them all over again.

"We ran out of condoms, remember?" I groaned, thumping my head against his chest. Maybe he could run to the store? Did he have time?

He laughed; I felt the sound as a vibration through my forehead as much as I heard it with my ears. "I've got a spare in my wallet."

"I love you," I said, kissing him again.

We stumbled together out to the lounge and Brad knocked his phone and keys aside in his haste to grab his wallet. I shifted from foot to foot as he dropped several receipts onto the coffee table, but after what seemed to my horny mind like an eternity he brandished the foil wrapper, holding it up like a trophy.

"Good job," I breathed, reaching for him again. Together we fell onto the couch, cushions tumbling aside. I stripped Brad's T-shirt off even as I straddled him, balling the fabric and tossing it to the floor. His hands reached for

my shirt but I swatted them aside, leaning to run my tongue from the side of his throat down to one of his now-bared nipples.

He groaned and I felt him through the layers of fabric—his pants, my shirt. He was hard as rock where he pressed against my stomach. I nibbled and teased his nipple until it stood proud before turning my attention to the other one. He took advantage of my distraction to slide a hand up the back of my shirt, unclasping my bra, pressing the small of my back down so I lay flush along his body. I wriggled against him and he flexed his hips in return. "I want you so badly," he said, his voice low and husky.

His nipple caught between my teeth, I peered up at his face, expecting to see his eyes closed. But he was studying me with a half-lidded gaze. "Do you now?" I murmured, shifting so I could reach my hands into the waistband of his pants, working both them and his boxers off. His shaft sprang free of the fabric and he lay, completely naked, on my couch. The thought of taking this to the bedroom crossed my mind, but that seemed impossibly far away, and the idea of having him right here drove me almost wild with a naughty thrill of anticipation. *Not the bedroom.* I shook off the loose bra and shirt, and Brad sat upright to help me with my pants. I would have moved back onto him but he held me away with his hands on my hips, running his gaze along the length of me. Maybe I should have felt self-conscious, but the desire burning in his eyes lifted me up, made me feel like a goddess.

"Lie back." He steered me so it was my turn to recline, my butt hanging slightly over the edge of the couch cushion. He shoved the coffee table so it sat against the television unit, out of the way, and knelt between my thighs, licking his lips, a slow and deliberate gesture that banished the vague sense of awkwardness I felt at my position. "I want you to scream for me," he whispered, before lowering himself down to taste me.

I gasped, eyes closing as I lost myself to the sensation of his strong, hot mouth pressing against me, one of his hands running along the inside of my thigh before joining his tongue in a probing dance.

I was already slick and hot with want, and the climax came swiftly—almost too swiftly—smashing into me. Distantly, I felt my toes curl into the carpet, my fingers into the cushion beside me. Through my eyelashes, I saw that Brad's eyes were once again fixed on my face, drinking in my expression. When the paroxysm of pleasure began to fade, I expected him to pull away ... but he stayed where he was, continuing to make gentle movements against my oversensitive core that left me writhing. "Brad," I gasped.

He lifted his face slightly away, though his fingers stayed where they were, pulsing inside me. "Yes?" he asked innocently, his lips so close to me that even his breath made me quiver. "Is there something you'd like?"

"I..." His tongue darted out again, pressing against me firmly, making me squirm. "Oh god, yes." Again he lapped against me, sending tendrils of intense pleasure shooting through me, starbursts exploding from a firework. "*Brad!*"

He took one final taste, heavy satisfaction in his expression, and knelt, retrieving the condom from where it had tumbled to the floor. I watched, still caught up in

a blissful aftermath of pleasure that left me floating, as he donned it and shuffled between my thighs. I arched my back towards him, but he rubbed himself against the outside of me with a wicked glint in his eye. "Tell me you want me."

"If you don't take me, I'm giving you nightmares for a week," I growled, reaching out to bury my hands in his hair, trying to draw him down onto me. Into me. "Right now!"

"That'll do," he said with a laugh, his hands lifting my hips, angling them just so. Then he drove inside me, burying himself in a quick thrust all the way to the hilt. I moaned, unashamed, as he filled me, waiting there for a brief moment before drawing back and slamming into me again. And again.

Sometimes our lovemaking was gentle, sweet. This wasn't one of those times. This was raw, filled with hot, urgent need, and a fleeting part of me wondered, as I dug my fingers into his back and bit at his throat, whether a part of Brad was jealous of Leander after all? Whether this was him claiming me, out here in this world where Leander could never go? If it was, I didn't care. Brad was mine as much as I was his.

As if to prove the point to myself, I pushed him back, steering him down until he lay on the carpet, and straddled him again, riding him, driving him into me until another orgasm shuddered through me and I did scream, a hoarse animal sound. Brad clenched me in a grip hard enough to bruise, thrusting upwards into my quivering body until I felt him vibrate and tremble with his own orgasm.

I collapsed against him, sweaty and tingling.

"Holy shit," he breathed. "That was intense."

"Why?" I replied, kissing his throat. A hickey was already starting to blossom there. "Did I do something?"

He laughed breathlessly at the question, possibly remembering the first time he'd said the same thing to me in similar circumstances, and drew my head down to rest on his shoulder. His heart raced in his chest, and his hands brushed along my ribs as I fought to slow my own racing pulse. "I love you too," Brad murmured in my ear.

I lifted my chin to study his face, remembering my blurted declaration of love when he'd told me about the condom. It wasn't the first time I'd told him how I felt, or that he'd told me, but declarations of love between us were still new enough that the words sent a happy thrill through me. "You better," I said. My grin was lazy as I rolled off him onto the carpet. My knee smacked into the coffee table. *Ugh.* Maybe we should have gone up to the bedroom after all.

"Or you'll give me nightmares for a week?" he said with a laugh, pushing himself to his feet and turning away to remove the condom.

"Damn straight." I admired his departing backside as I groped for my bra and shirt.

It wasn't until I was pulling on my yoga pants that I saw it, through the blinds. A metallic blue sedan, parked under the tree across the street.

Nelson's car.

Chapter Nineteen

I must have sworn because Brad came back into the room, frowning. "Put some clothes on." I shoved some hastily snatched fabric at him. "We're being watched."

"What?"

"Nelson," I spat, pointing at the offending car. My hand shook with fury. "That's his car, I'm sure of it. He's *spying* on me. I'm going to wring his bloody neck."

I started towards the front door, but Brad grabbed my arm awkwardly, his other hand holding his crumpled pyjama pants in front of his groin. "Hold your horses," he said. "Just wait."

"He's been there the whole time," I said, though I didn't know that for sure. Had the constable left after we'd sent him packing from our doorstep that morning? Surely he hadn't just parked across the street; Mum or Jen would have noticed when they'd left the house. Still, the idea summoned cold sweat to prickle my palms. "We just had sex, and the blinds were open, and he's probably got binoculars in there or something. Our shagging is now part of a criminal investigation!" My voice was shrill in my own ears, my panic and indignation bleeding through.

"It's okay. We were on the couch the whole time. Or the floor." Brad's tone was light as he stepped into his pants but his eyes, when they met mine, were narrowed with anger. Not the hot fury that quivered through me but something cold and hard, like frost-covered granite. "He couldn't have seen anything unless he had X-ray vision."

"But when you stood up…"

"He would've gotten an eyeful of my manly posterior. Serves him right," he said, his voice muffled by his T-shirt as he yanked it over his head. "I'm going out there."

"I'm coming with you," I said. He glanced at me, frowning like he was unsure it was a good idea. "I won't wring his neck," I added grudgingly.

Brad looked like he wanted to say something else, but instead he shrugged and nodded, heading for the door. I followed him out onto the porch, shading my eyes as the sun hit them and peering across the street at the silhouetted figure inside the car. The concrete was cold under my bare feet as we walked along the driveway, and by the time we got to the road I was beginning to wish we'd taken the time to put shoes on.

Nelson slid out of the car as we strode towards him, me trying not to wince as the rough tarmac scraped the soles of my feet. If it bothered Brad he didn't let on, stopping in front of the car's bonnet with his arms folded and legs apart—a belligerent stance. "Nelson." Brad's voice was so gruff it was almost a snarl. *And he was worried about* me *being aggressive.* I really didn't want to have to intervene in a fight between my boyfriend and

a member of the Australian Federal Police.

"Peterson." Nelson nodded curtly. He wasn't wearing his uniform anymore; instead, he was dressed in black jeans and a plain but rumpled T-shirt. He must have gone home to change. Either that or he'd had the change of clothes in the car—though I couldn't imagine the long-legged man getting changed on his back seat. If he'd been coming off the night shift when he dropped past that morning, I didn't think he'd slept yet; his eyes were bloodshot and puffy with fatigue. A glance into the car revealed that each of the centre console's two cup holders held a takeaway coffee.

My attention snapped back to the conversation when Brad spoke. "Can we help you with anything, or do you just like harassing people in your spare time?"

The older man's steel-grey eyes narrowed. "You might want to watch your tone."

"Why? I'm pretty confident your boss would have something to say about you parking your butt outside Melaina's house when you're off-duty. You think *I'm* the one who's going to get in trouble here?"

"Ah, yes, your threat of a lawyer." Nelson looked around as if expecting a briefcase-wielding suit to leap out of a bush nearby and attack him with a sheaf of papers. "Where are they?"

"I was leaving it till tomorrow to call him," Brad said, his jaw jutting out dangerously. "It's Sunday, for Christ's sake."

Nelson opened his mouth to reply, and I stepped between the two men, my crossed arms in front of my chest tele-graphing my discomfort. "Stop it, both of you." Brad's mouth snapped shut, and I regarded the police officer, wary. "Nelson, why are you here? I already answered your questions this morning."

"Is that what you call your responses? Answers?" He rubbed his forehead, staring at me like he was trying to drill into my brain with his gaze.

"Yes. And you didn't answer *my* question. Why are you here?"

"I'm curious about your line of work. Heard you were working from home now."

I took a long, slow breath, letting the cool, late afternoon air fill my lungs before breathing it out through my nostrils. When I answered, my voice was steady. "Firstly, as Brad already pointed out, today is Sunday. I don't have any clients today. And secondly, if you are so curious about my dream therapy work, feel free to make an appointment. I charge fifty dollars an hour. Until then, please go away before I'm forced to call the police."

His right eye twitched at that, and I felt my own eyes widen in response. He didn't want me to call them. Was he even meant to be working this case anymore? The incident at Wattle Tree Park had been months ago, and as far as I was aware no one at the home had pressed charges after I'd put them to sleep. Sure, Ewan was complaining, but he'd also been committed and was being charged with arson. Hardly a reliable witness.

When *was* the last time Nelson had slept?

"Maybe you should make an appointment," I said softly. "How have you been sleeping?"

"Just fine," Nelson snapped, a muscle twitching beside his jaw. A memory hit me, sharp as a slap to the face: Ewan's face in the home, with a tic jumping beside his eye. I'd suspected Ewan might be blight possessed, but

174

couldn't get close enough to check, not without him drawing the nurses down on us. Nelson was close enough to be in range of my power. He didn't know to be wary. But did I really want to do this? Subdue a police officer on the street on a sunlit Sunday afternoon?

Can I afford not to?

"Have you been drinking that tea you bought from Serenity's?" I said, glancing at Brad. He frowned back at me.

"What? No." Nelson glowered at me. "I gave it to one of the ladies at the station. She's a new mum ... not that it's any of your business."

I rolled my neck from side to side as if stretching, taking the opportunity to look up and down the street. None of our neighbours were out on their lawns, although I couldn't guarantee no one was peering out their window. "It's just that you look rather similar to a client of mine, one who was suffering from terrible nightmares. Tired, peaky..." Beside me, Brad's eyes widened. *Good, he's got it.*

"I'm not having nightmares!" Nelson snapped.

"If you say so." I held my hands up with fingers spread, a soothing gesture. "You just call if you change your mind. Here, let me get you my card." I reached down, towards an imaginary pocket, and took a half-step towards the irate policeman.

"I already have your..." His eyelids slid shut as I exhaled a sigh onto his face.

Brad was ready, catching Nelson even as I stepped onto the verge. "Cross your fingers the neighbours are all watching footy," I said, opening the driver's side door. Nelson hadn't locked it.

"You're not going to take him inside?" Brad said with

a grunt, easing the tall man around the bonnet. I scooted back to him, lifting Nelson's feet so his heels didn't slam into the kerb and wake him up.

"Hell, no. I'm going to give him a confused dream about talking to us. Something surreal, to make him think he fell asleep at the wheel and this conversation was all in his head."

"I assume you're going to look for blights first?"

I nodded. "He's been out to Wattle Tree Park, and he's been around Ewan at the hospital. He could have been infected with a blight larva." The idea of a blight possessing someone with access to firearms made me shiver.

Brad's expression was grim as we manoeuvred the tall man into the driver's seat of his car. Brad closed the door softly while I crossed around to the passenger side, opening the door and sliding inside. The interior of Nelson's car wasn't as tidy as his personality had led me to expect. The floor was clear of the tiny pebbles and pieces of dry grass that clung to the carpet like burrs in most cars I'd been in, but the back seat was cluttered with empty takeaway food packets and receipts. It looked like someone had given a new car to an untidy person and the mess hadn't fully set in yet. Another sign of blight possession, maybe? Less attention to detail than usual? Certainly I'd never seen his clothes look anything other than neat before; now I had time to look, I saw his T-shirt was not only rumpled but had several small stains on it.

"Alright," I said to Brad through the open door. "I'm going in."

"Be careful."

"Always." I closed the door and got to work.

FALSE *Awakening*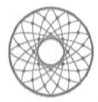

"He *wasn't* possessed." Brad stood by the lounge room window, peering through the blinds at Nelson's car. The sun was setting, bathing the street in an orange light before leeching the colours away, and all we could see of the constable was a vague silhouette.

"No." I threw myself down onto the couch. "There wasn't even any blight ichor. He's clean as a whistle. I feel like an idiot."

"Don't," Brad said. "I was starting to think he was possessed too. He's not acting rationally. But maybe we're starting to see blights in every dark corner."

"Yeah," I said, staring up at the ceiling. We hadn't turned the overhead light on, and it was growing gloomy. "Maybe he just really needed some sleep?" Nelson had been out cold for at least an hour now, and showed no signs of rousing. He'd wake up with a sore neck, but at least he was sleeping. And I'd given him a very nice dream—it had started with us chatting on the street before transforming into a three-person buddy cop movie, where we hooned around in a flying car and were all the best of friends.

I doubted the suggestion would work. He might not even remember the dream when he woke; the only reason Brad and Jen remembered the dream we'd shared was because we'd discussed it right after they'd awoken, before the memory could fade.

After a long, thoughtful pause, Brad turned to me. "I should go. I still want to talk to Belinda, see if the home called. And I need to iron some shirts for work tomorrow before I hit the sack."

"Okay." I grimaced. "I suppose I can't monopolise all your time."

"Not all of it, no," he said as he turned to get his shoes from beside the door. "Life does get in the way."

"Adulting is hard," I agreed.

"Speaking of adulting—" he glanced out the window again before sitting beside me to slide on his shoes, "—I'll call that lawyer tomorrow."

"Right. Okay." I wrinkled my nose.

After seeing Brad off, I put some shoes and a jumper on. There was no way was I going outside barefoot again, especially now the spring day was giving way to a chilly evening. I collected an empty clothes basket from the tiny laundry before heading into the yard to see whether the towels were dry.

Our yard was small, the tall photinia hedge that ran along the back fence warring with the clothes line for domination of the space. Smaller, scraggly bushes huddled along the sides of the yard: innocent bystanders. An odd assortment of bright, gemstone-hued bath towels and tea towels hung on the line, swaying in the evening breeze. I pulled them down quickly, making idle conversation with a sharp-billed magpie that strode to and fro in the shadow of the house. It ignored me, foraging in the long grass and loose clumps of dirt underneath a wall vent, occasionally lifting its head to warble.

A second magpie flew in low across the yard as I tossed the last towel into the basket. I ducked reflexively as it came in to land beside the first. Our local mob hadn't shown any signs of swooping yet, but, with spring in the air and babies in the nest, you could never be too careful.

FALSE *Awakening*

I'd known a kid at school who'd lost a chunk of his ear to a swooping magpie.

The second magpie jabbed its beak into the earth as well, and I frowned, leaving my basket on the path and easing closer, sneakers crunching on the grass. "What are you doing, Maggie?" I asked softly, not wanting to startle the birds.

One of the magpies lifted its head, swallowing something small and brown. A moth, already dead by the looks of things. It lowered its head to get another, and my stomach seemed to drop right out of my body as I realised what I was seeing. Those weren't loose clumps of dirt. That was a pile of moth carcasses. A big pile.

Mara.

Chapter Twenty

Mum stood beside me at the kitchen bench, staring at the bag, which bulged with dead moths. Their tiny carcasses were barely visible through the plastic; I'd double-bagged them, just in case. I would have triple-bagged them if we'd had enough spare plastic bags. Still, it was easy for me to imagine them, crammed in together, brittle carapaces crumbling under the weight of their fellows. "Are you sure you got them all?" she asked.

"I think so?" I wiped my hands down the front of my jumper. I'd been about to take the bag outside to the bin when Mum had come home, and I still really wanted to get rid of it. Even though I'd washed my hands, I could still recall those dry, dusty bodies beneath my fingers. "I mean, it was dark. Hopefully if there are any left, they won't make the magpies sick. The surface spray *said* it was animal friendly…"

"It was good thinking, spraying the vents too." Mum's eyes were narrowed but her head was cocked to the side,

a mixture of suspicion and interest.

"I think they came through a vent that time at Serenity's. At her old shop, I mean." I shuddered, hugging my arms.

"Are you sure the mara can't use the bugs now?"

"Relatively sure. At least, the ones that attacked us before stayed dead." Those bugs had been killed when I'd disrupted the hold the mara had over them, smashing each of the monsters in the head with a lamp. The memory of the two doughy-fleshed figures exploding into a mass of writhing, dying insects all over me and Brad made the skin on the back of my neck crawl with revulsion.

There'd been a lot more moths to clean up that time. This bag barely contained enough for one. But who knew how many the birds had eaten before I'd noticed?

"Good. Still, let's get rid of these, shall we?" Mum reached for the plastic handle on the exterior bag, and I flinched, stomach clenching. My cheeks burned as her gaze flicked back to my face, and she drew her fingers back. "What's the matter, sweetheart? The mara died. The surface spray worked."

I shook my head, biting my lip. "The insects died," I said finally. "The mara is still around somewhere. They're mostly incorporeal, like blights."

"Still, it can't get us here. And you sprayed the shop."

"I know."

"Then what's the matter?"

I didn't want to worry her, but ignorance wouldn't do her any favours, especially not now we were living together. It felt like I had a giant target painted on my back. I'd have preferred wings. "Last time this happened, Leander told me mara can't manifest like this unless an Oneiroi gives them the power to." My voice was barely above a whisper in the quiet room. Mum gasped, her hand flying to her mouth. I forced myself to continue. "They aren't as intelligent as blights, and usually they just wander from dream to dream, creating nightmares to feed off." I stared at the bag, feeling numb. "But if an Oneiroi gives them a boost, they can use insects to manifest a real body, using them as a sort of framework to build on. Then they can track down a specific person, someone the Oneiroi directs them to find, and create more serious nightmares. When they attacked Brad and me, they weren't just looking for a snack. They were trying to kill us. Stop our hearts."

"That wouldn't have worked." Was she trying to convince me, or herself?

"Mum..." I met her hazel eyes. They were tight with concern. Guilt was a heavy lump in my stomach and tried to freeze the words on my tongue, but the fear was worse. I swallowed. "I didn't tell you, after everything that happened. I didn't want to upset you."

Her knuckles curved around the edge of the bench, growing pale with the strength of her grip. She was holding on to steady herself. "Tell me what, Melaina?"

"That's how Uncle Ian died."

"*What?*"

"The coroner said it was a heart attack while he was sleeping. But Jat told me they found bugs in his bed. He didn't know what it meant, and I think Lacey has convinced herself that Uncle Ian brought a snack to bed and attracted them. But it has to have been a mara."

"Oh." Mum reached down and pulled a stool out, easing herself onto it. "Oh," she said again.

FALSE Awakening

"I'm sorry I didn't say anything sooner," I blurted, wringing my hands. "It happened while you were in that coma, and then Ollie got arrested and … well, it didn't seem to matter anymore how Uncle Ian had died." Mum had been upset enough at the news her beloved brother was dead and, even worse, that she'd missed the funeral. Why tell her he'd been murdered too? Even though she hadn't known it at the time, she and I had already avenged Uncle Ian when we'd dropped Ikelos in that lava.

Ikelos…

And there it was. The reason I kept staring at that bag of poor bugs like it was watching me with a thousand dead eyes. Because, if a mara had tried to enter our house, someone had sent it. And who else could it be but Ikelos?

At first, I'd assumed Ikelos was dead. I'd *wanted* to believe he was dead. But that bag of bugs meant an Oneiroi was hunting me, and I'd only ever met four, total. One of those was in jail. Another was heading back to Europe with an entire retinue for an alibi. One was Leander, who I'd once again grown to trust. And the fourth… Ikelos had to have sent the mara. He was the only one with a motive, and he'd done it before.

Mum was talking, I realised. I tore my gaze away from the bag. "…but I understand why you didn't. It just makes it worse, somehow."

"I'm sorry," I repeated. The words sounded almost as hollow as they felt.

"Have you warned Jen and Brad yet?"

"No." The thought hadn't even occurred to me, and that made me feel guilty all over again.

"Well, you do that while I get rid of this rubbish." She

stood, jaw tight and eyes narrowed as she took the bag by the handle and lifted it off the bench. The plastic bag bulged as the tiny corpses shifted, pattering against one another. "Ikelos infected both of them with blights—or, at least, Ewan did on his behalf. If Ikelos is still around, they need to know about it."

I nodded, reaching for the phone.

Jen was still at the library and would be there until late, but she promised to buy herself a small can of fly spray, joking that she'd keep it in her handbag instead of mace. Brad was horrified and volunteered to come back over, but I told him to stay at home with his sister. He promised to respray the exterior of his house straight away; it had been months since I'd done it for him.

When I hung up, feeling a little better after my best friend's good humour and my boyfriend's concern, I fixed dinner, a simple creamy carbonara that would leave us with enough leftovers for Jen to have some when she got home. But as I chopped and stirred, I considered Mum's comment about Ewan. No matter how I turned the ideas around in my head, I kept coming to the same infuriating conclusion.

Mum joined me in the lounge room for dinner, wearing a fluffy lilac dressing gown and matching slippers, her long hair caught up in a towel. The cream-and-garlic aroma riding the steam from my bowl made me realise how hungry I was.

I didn't want to consider that Mum and I were about to eat dinner on the same couch where Brad and I had—

Gah!

"Can I run something past you?" I said after shovelling the first couple of mouthfuls into my mouth. The pasta

was a little undercooked, but the sauce was delicious. "I'm hoping you can spot a flaw in my logic."

Mum nodded. "Go for it."

"Ikelos was using the nursing home to try to breed himself a horde of blights. A swarm?" I tipped my head to the side, wondering what the correct collective noun was, and then shrugged. "Ewan had access to Brad's grandfather and therefore to the breeder blight, which let him harvest the blight larvae."

"Have you ever wondered how Ewan did that?" Mum regarded the silent television as if it might switch on and reveal the answer. "Get the larvae from Mr Peterson, I mean?"

I stared at her with open-mouthed horror. "No. Gross, Mum!"

"What?" She took a sip of orange juice.

"It's just ... my boyfriend and Jen both ate one of those things, and I've been trying really hard not to think about the details. It's not sanitary."

Her gaze dropped to her food like that of a chastised child. "I hadn't thought of that."

"It's fine," I said, clearing my throat and trying to shove the mental image away. *Ew.* "Anyway, Ewan slipped the larvae to people who visited the home, like Larry. His aunt works there."

"Mim. I've met her. She's a Pets as Therapy volunteer."

I'd never been introduced to Larry's aunt, but I'd seen her before. She'd been unmistakable, with her brightly patterned cloak, wild hair and miniature poodle. "Right. And once I ran across Larry, I attracted Ikelos's attention, which led him to you." I still felt bad about that, even though, logically, I knew there was nothing I could've done to prevent it. "Leander said Ikelos might have left the city by now, given the Morpheus was here. Maybe he did. For all I know, Ikelos could've sent a mara after me from halfway across Australia. But what if he didn't leave?"

"We'll deal with it." Mum put a reassuring hand on the back of one of mine. They'd gone still against my bowl, my fork sitting idle amidst a twist of fettucine.

I wondered how Mum imagined we'd deal with it, but decided against asking. "It's not that," I said instead. "It's just … with Ewan in the mental health unit, unable to access Mr Peterson anymore, I'd assumed he was no longer of any use to Ikelos. But what if he's been hosting the exiled Oneiroi all this time?"

Thinking about the chain of events in this new light, I couldn't shake the conviction I was right. Ikelos had seen how effectively Ollie was able to hide from Leander in Mum's mind. After we'd thrown the exiled Oneiroi into the ephemeral lava, he'd been badly injured, and had retreated into a sleeping mind nearby. That night, after I'd put them under, we'd left both Ewan and Daniel in the recreation room at the nursing home; it made sense Ikelos would retreat to the mind he was most familiar with. What was it Brad had said to me afterwards? That when the police arrived Ewan had been raving about *nightmare monsters and his dark lord and how he'd get us all.*

Ikelos would have been mad with pain. Ewan had probably gone temporarily mad too. And once they'd both regained their sanity, they had already been in the mental health unit.

How long had it taken them to regain their senses? I recalled Ewan's nervous tic, the way it had abruptly

disappeared. He'd seemed steely, in control. Like a whole new person.

Did Ikelos somehow take over Ewan's body? The idea sent a shudder down my spine, a prickly feeling as if a swarm of ants was crawling and biting along my skin. I'd always assumed possession was a blight-only power and, as far as I knew, Ollie had never been able to possess my mother. But then, he wasn't a power-mad exile from a powerful familial line. Would it have even occurred to him to try?

Mum finally spoke, dragging me from my own dark thoughts. "I think you're right."

"Oh."

"You sound disappointed."

"I am. I was hoping you'd point out a flaw in my logic, tell me why it's silly. You were meant to assure me that Ikelos is dead, and maybe that Santa is real too."

Mum laughed. "I wish I could, sweetheart. Unfortunately, you know I'd be lying."

"Except about Santa, right?"

"Except for that." A smile twinkled in her eyes, but vanished with her next words. "We should visit Ewan tomorrow, see if we can figure out whether Ikelos is lurking in there. And you need to talk to Leander as soon as possible. Maybe he can get the Morpheus to come back."

"Nelson will freak if he hears that I've been out to the hospital again," I said. *Hang on ... Nelson!* My eyes widened. When I'd discovered the moths, I'd clean forgotten about the napping police officer in his car outside. Swearing, I put my bowl on the coffee table and knelt on the couch, peering through the blinds. Nelson's car was gone. "Huh." When he woke, I'd half-expected him to come up to the house, pound on the door and accuse me of goodness knows what. That he'd left instead was a relief.

"Huh?" Mum raised an eyebrow at me.

Leaving out the sex part, I told her about our second visit from the constable, and what I'd done. "I know it was risky, but I was sure he was possessed. He was acting so strangely. And he had this nervous tic, like..." My suddenly racing heart leapt into my throat and blocked my ability to speak.

Senior Constable Nelson's obsessive pursuit of me had begun after he'd been to see the former nurse in the mental health unit.

"Like what?"

"Like Ewan," I managed to choke out. "He was acting like Ewan."

Chapter Twenty-One

"*I*'m sorry." A tiny frown creased the skin between the nurse's manicured eyebrows. She wasn't the same one who'd been on duty during our previous visit. I'd have remembered the discreet tattoo on the side of her neck, half-hidden by a shock of ginger hair. "Mr Wright is no longer a patient at this facility."

I grabbed Mum's hand, feeling like the floor had dropped out from under me. "Wait, what?" I said. Or tried to say— the words came out in more of a squeak. Mum's lips pressed together until the pressure bleached them white.

The nurse pursed her own lips, looking from me to her computer screen and back again. "He was discharged yesterday."

"But…" I didn't know what to say. Constable Nelson had told me he'd been to see Ewan in hospital yesterday, but that had been mid-morning. Had Nelson known Ewan was about to be discharged?

"I'm sorry, we're just a little surprised," Mum said

smoothly, taking over when I continued to flounder. "We're family, and we didn't realise he'd been allowed to leave. He was rather, um, unstable when he was admitted." She dropped her voice to a whisper, as if she was sharing a scandalous family secret. "There was an incident with a fire, you know."

The nurse didn't seem impressed at Mum's attempt to draw her in. She turned back to the screen, clicking her mouse once and then returning her attention to us. Had she closed Ewan's record? It was a little pointless; we couldn't see the screen from the other side of the desk anyway. "His doctor wouldn't have authorised his discharge if she thought he was a danger to the community."

"And the police...?"

"Have been notified." The nurse smiled politely, although the expression didn't reach her eyes. "I'm sorry I can't tell you anything more. Have a good day."

Once Mum and I escaped the building, I swore vehemently, attracting a glare from an old man shuffling through the nearby carpark. I resisted the urge to flip him the bird; it wasn't his fault Ewan was on the loose with a probable Oneiroi hitchhiker.

"What now?" Mum said as we walked towards the street, where several cars crawled along, no doubt driven by people trapped in the maze of roads—and roadwork—around the hospital.

"An early lunch, maybe?" I kicked a pebble out of my way and it pinged off a nearby concrete barrier. We'd called Serenity first thing to swap shifts so we could bus it into the hospital. As a result, we had a couple of hours before we were due at the shop, which was a short bus ride from here. Monday mornings were quiet, so Serenity

hadn't minded. "We could catch the bus to Griffith, eat there before work."

"Good idea," Mum said, "but I meant about Ewan."

"I don't know. I don't have his address or anything." Daniel might have it, but I wasn't sure I could convince him to tell me what it was. Helping me navigate hospital bureaucracy was one thing; helping me track the man who'd burned down my place of work was another. I wouldn't risk it if I were him.

"We could try the White Pages."

"Yeah." I shoved my hands in my pockets.

"What about the Oneiroi? Can they help?"

"Leander's sent one of the other Oneiroi the Morpheus left behind to try to convince him to come back. The Morpheus, not Leander. He shouldn't be more than a couple of days away, though I don't really understand how travel in Erebus works."

"*Try* to convince him?"

I nodded, staring at my boots. Their purple laces were almost neon in the morning sunlight, and seeing them gave my spirits a tiny lift. "We don't exactly have proof. Just a hunch," I said, raising my chin and squaring my shoulders.

"Still, given how much effort the Morpheus put into pursuing Ollie for all those years, you'd think he'd be keen to catch the exile who's been organising to overthrow him."

It hadn't been that much effort, not really. Sure, he'd set Leander on Ollie's tail, but that had been all. Still, Mum had a point. Dad's crimes had been comparatively inoffensive. "So we just have to keep a slightly unhinged pyromaniac nurse and his uber-powerful dream spirit master away from us for two days. And maybe a slightly unhinged police officer too."

"More like five days. Maybe six," Mum corrected as we crossed the road, heading towards the bus stop.

"Huh?" I glanced at her.

"You didn't factor in the return trip, or the fact the Morpheus is still moving further away. Assuming the Morpheus is travelling slowly—which is probably the case since he's travelling with a retinue—and the other Oneiroi hoofs it, he'll be about three days' away by the time he gets the message. Then he needs to get back here again, which would take at least two days if he rushes. Maybe another three."

I rubbed my temples; listening to her sounded like one of those maths problems that involved two trains travelling at different speeds. But it also made sense. "Dammit."

"We'll be fine," Mum said. I wished she sounded like she meant it.

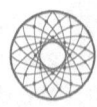

After Serenity swept out of the shop, leaving us in charge, I took advantage of a quiet moment to reply to a couple of client queries. Then I logged onto Facebook on the store computer, sending Daniel a chatty message that, among other things, asked if he'd heard that Ewan had been discharged. When he didn't reply immediately, I spent a few minutes figuring out how to search his list of friends. Sure enough, Ewan was there, but when I clicked on the smiling, two-tone-haired profile picture that pre-dated his arrest and hospital admission, all I could see were a few shares from different pages, and

one of Daniel's posts from several months before, which he'd tagged Ewan in. If Ewan had updated his page since he'd been discharged, I couldn't see it. There was also nothing to indicate where he lived.

A White Pages search also didn't turn up any hits for an "E. Wright", at least not alone. There were a few hits with an E and a second set of initials, but, as far as I was aware, Ewan wasn't married. *He'd better not be, given he asked Jen out.* I took a box of scented candles down from a shelf, grunting at the weight. Then I laughed at myself. Given he'd invited her out so he could drop a blight larva in her coffee, the fact he may have done so while married seemed like a lesser offence.

"What's so funny?" Mum asked when I came out to the shopfront, the box balanced on one hip.

"Nothing." I dropped it onto a stool and pulling a box cutter out of my back pocket to slit the tape. The mingled scents of vanilla bean and berries drifted up as I pulled open the flaps. "Has it been quiet out here?"

"As a graveyard." Mum wrinkled her nose. "I rearranged the incense alphabetically, African violet to ylang-ylang. Any luck on the computer?"

"No." I pulled out a couple of multi-coloured candles. "Normally I'm on board with people using social media privacy settings, but it's inconvenient when I'm trying to stalk someone."

"I can imagine," she said with a smile, coming over to help me write on the sticky labels we used for price tags.

I couldn't shake my sense of unease; every time the bell tinkled to announce a customer, I spun towards the door, half-expecting it to be Ewan, Nelson or both. After the vehemence of my reaction frightened a teenage boy into backpedalling out the door, Mum set me to working off nervous energy by restocking the shelves, cleaning every square inch of the store, and respraying the building's exterior vents and around the window sills and doorjambs with surface spray. I said a silent apology to any butterflies or bees in the area as I did that last task, trying not to breathe in the spray's sickly sweet aroma—but refreshing the spray did make me feel safer.

By the end of the day, the door glass was so clear it gleamed, and there wasn't a speck of dust even among the dream catchers: no small achievement given the dangling feathers seemed to attract the stuff. I was exhausted, but I'd worked off some of my demons. And at least I'd earned my salary.

I checked the computer one last time before shutting it down for the night. Daniel still hadn't replied. Maybe he was on shift.

"I'm thinking about getting a car," Mum told me as we locked up, packing the take into Serenity's safe and setting the alarm—another benefit of this new shop location. "I did get my licence before you were born, but I let it lapse after I went into the home. Do you think I'll need to re-sit the test?"

"I don't know," I muttered. "Probably?" I'd gotten my licence a couple of years ago but I rarely drove. A terrifying thought dawned on me, and I paused midway through dropping the shop's keys into my handbag. "You wouldn't need me to give you lessons, would you?"

"You don't have to look so horrified." Mum sounded vaguely offended. "I was a good driver."

Most people think they're good drivers. "I'm just not sure I'm ready for that responsibility," I said, avoiding

eye contact. I didn't want to teach anyone to drive—or remind them how to—for a long, long time. Not until I had kids and had no choice … and maybe not even then. I tried to force some enthusiasm into my voice. "Anyway, having a car would be awesome. You should go for it."

"I couldn't afford a new car, but I could get a decent—"

My phone buzzed in my pocket; I'd set the ringtone to silent. "Hold that thought," I said as I fished it out. *Justin Armstrong-Taylor.* "It's Jat." I hit the answer button. "Hello?"

"Have you seen Olivia?" My cousin's voice was low and fierce.

"Not since her party. Why, what's she done?" I'd seen posts from her in amongst my Facebook feed, but I'd been in a rush and hadn't paid much attention.

"She's missing."

Chapter Twenty-Two

We caught a taxi to Lacey's house. The driver muttered a startled oath as he pulled his car onto the very end of the long driveway. I had to admit the house did look magnificent; sunset's kinder light softened the harsh edges and lent the rendered concrete a gentle glow.

I wonder if Lacey's home? There was no way to tell; the house had a two-car garage so, if she was, her car was tucked out of sight. The idea of encountering her after she'd given us the cold shoulder at Olivia's party created a tangled ball of anxiety in my gut, but I straightened my spine and squared my shoulders. Hopefully she could put her attitude aside for Olivia's sake ... but, if she wanted a fight, I was ready for one.

Mum paid the driver while I slid out, stomping along the path that ran across the front of the building towards the imposing entryway. Justin must have been watching from the dining room window, because he opened the door as soon I began to climb the long stairs.

"Thank god you're here," he said, clattering down to meet me. "Mum's going wild!"

"What happened?" I gave him a quick hug. "Did they have a fight?"

"When don't they fight?" Justin said, rolling his eyes as my mother joined us. I offered her a twenty for the taxi, but she shook her head.

"Okay, anything more specific than usual?"

He shrugged, leading us up the stairs to the double doors. "Not really. Olivia's been quiet the last few days. Locked in her room even more than usual. We've barely seen her, but she's got finals in the next few weeks, and a big art history essay due, so..."

We paused in the foyer. The family room, visible through an open door, looked different. It took me a moment to realise what it was: the ever-present halogen lights weren't on, allowing a more natural pattern of light and shadow to fill the space. Lacey leaned against the back of one of the scarlet suede couches, which were less offensive than usual in the more subdued, fading sunlight spilling in through the floor-to-ceiling windows. Backlit by those same windows, she stood out like a crow on the beach in her dark jeans and a black knit turtleneck—the plainest clothes I'd ever seen her wear. Her face was drawn, looking older than usual, and she hugged herself, arms wrapped around her stomach as if she was in pain. But her dark brown eyes were dry when she looked at us.

I tensed, waiting for her to say something, make some biting comment, but she didn't. *Huh?*

"Come on," Justin said. I followed him into the family room, Mum at my side. "They're here," he mumbled needlessly, keeping his gaze fixed on his Nikes.

"Where is she?" Despite the abruptness of the words, Lacey's tone was measured. Either she wasn't mad we were here or she was trying to keep her temper under control until she had what she wanted from us. *Maybe both.* Had she asked Justin to call me? Was she really too proud to do it herself, even though she was clearly worried? I knew the answer to the second question, of course. I'd have to be the one to make the first move here.

"I don't know." Suppressing an irritated sigh, I walked around Lacey to sit on the roomy three-seater couch. Mum and Justin followed, sitting on either side of me, but Lacey just turned on the spot. At least her hands dropped from that stomach-clenching hug to press into the back of the other empty seat. "When was the last time you saw her?" I asked.

"I saw her yesterday morning," Justin said when his mother didn't reply immediately. "She came out to get a bowl of cereal just as I was leaving for soccer."

"I saw her a few hours later." Lacey's jaw tightened. "I think she snuck out last night, after we went to bed. I hoped she might've gotten in contact with you." There was doubt in her voice. She thought I was lying about not knowing where Olivia was; I was sure of it.

Irritation flared. "You know she's eighteen, right?" I narrowed my eyes at her. "She's an adult. If she wants to stay out—"

"She hasn't finished school," Lacey snapped. "We've … that is, I've spent far too much on her education for her to waste it now, right when she needs to focus, by gallivanting around with boys and staying out all night."

The words stung. I'd heard their ilk before; Lacey hadn't approved of my decision to drop out of university

after she and my uncle had paid for me to attend an expensive boarding school. Of course, by then I hadn't lived with them and they hadn't been supporting me financially, so they'd had no leverage over me.

I opened my mouth to snarl back at Lacey, but Mum spoke first, her voice calm. "Is that what you fought about?"

"No," Lacey said. Mum raised her eyebrows. Although she didn't speak, her scepticism was clear. After a moment, Lacey added, "Sort of." Her gaze slipped away from us to study the garden outside.

"Have you tried to contact her on Facebook or her phone?" I said.

"Obviously." Lacey flashed me a disdainful look.

"I have too," Justin added quietly. "She's not answering me either. I'm worried."

Mum crossed her legs and leaned back into the couch, knitting her fingers together and resting them on her thigh. Her casual pose surprised me. I felt about as relaxed as a cat staring down the jaws of a snarling, drooling Doberman. "What was the argument about?" she asked.

"I told you," Lacey said.

"No, you didn't. You said it was sort of about her gallivanting. I'm asking you for details."

"Why?" Lacey said. To my surprise, a faint blush coloured her cheeks, and I realised what Mum had seemingly already figured out. Lacey didn't want to talk about the fight.

"Because it's obviously relevant."

"I don't see how."

Mum sighed, a soft, resigned sound, and stood. "I

don't expect you to like us, Lacey, but we both care for your daughter. I know you do too, so I expect you to be able to find the decency to be polite. We just want to make sure she's safe. Why did you ask Justin to call if you don't want our help?"

Lacey glanced at me but didn't say anything.

"I expect calling me was Jat's idea." I looked up at Mum. "But she probably agreed to it because she thinks I'm a troublemaker, and all of us troublemakers run together."

"I thought she might reach out to you." Lacey looked as if she'd swallowed a slice of bitter lemon. "As family. That she might be looking for somewhere to stay."

"She hasn't," I said. Olivia and I got on well enough, but we weren't close. "Have you tried her school friends?" I recalled how happy Olivia had been at her party; she'd almost seemed to glow, and not just when we'd given her our gift. The expression of a girl in love? "Or does she maybe have a boyfriend?"

"She broke up with Sam almost a month ago." Justin picked at a loose thread on the hem of his jeans.

"A new boyfriend then?"

Justin shrugged, and Lacey shook her head, the motion stiff. "She didn't have a new boyfriend."

"Are you sure? She might not have—"

"I'm sure," Lacey said. If the words had been any harder they'd have serrated her lips on the way out.

Mum spoke, her voice gentle but her gaze intent on the older woman's face. "What was the fight about, Lacey?"

"She's pregnant, alright?" Lacey blurted. My mouth fell open, slack with shock. Beside me, Justin inhaled sharply. "The stupid girl got herself pregnant. That's

what we fought about. After I paid for her birth control and everything!"

Mum didn't look surprised; she simply nodded as if she'd suspected as much. "And you pressed her to have an abortion?"

"I..." Determination tightened Lacey's jaw and pride lifted her chin. But shame also coloured her cheeks. "She wants to keep the baby. I told her not to be foolish."

I stared at her. "No wonder she took off. It's her decision!"

"It's not just me saying it." Lacey balled her hands into fists on her hips as she glared at me with all the fire she could muster. "Sam wants her to get an abortion too."

"Jesus, Lacey." I leapt to my feet, glaring right back at her. "You're such a robot!"

"Better a robot than a deadbeat girl or her layabout mother. The last thing I want is for Olivia to turn out like Davina!"

The oxygen went out of the room ... or at least that was what it felt like as I gasped for breath. My hands clenched into fists, and I might have launched myself across the empty couch at my aunt, but Justin intervened, jumping up and looking between me and his mother.

"Stop it!" he yelled, his voice breaking. "Both of you, stop it! Olivia is missing, and I don't care if she's pregnant. She's my sister. I want her to come home!" He sobbed once, a strangled, choking sound, and then stumbled down the corridor towards his room.

Lacey looked like I had punched her after all. I knew how she felt, because I felt the same way, my chest aching and my stomach churning. "Jat..."

"Leave me alone!" His bedroom door slammed, and I

flinched. Lacey was as pale as parchment.

"Justin is right. Our priority right now has to be Olivia's wellbeing," Mum said. *How can she be so forgiving when Lacey just insulted us both?* But I could see the hurt, the anger, in the way her hazel eyes flashed and her nostrils flared with a slowly drawn breath. She just kept those emotions on a leash with a steely control I wished I shared.

Lacey seemed to deflate against the back of the couch, weary beyond her years. "You're right. I'm sorry. I'm just frustrated and worried, and it makes me want to scream."

"Well, now you've gotten it out of your system, why don't we go put the kettle on and talk about this like grown-ups?" Mum gave Lacey a small smile, and the other woman winced, but turned towards the kitchen.

"I'm going to go poke around Olivia's room," I told Mum as she started after Lacey. "See if I can figure out where she might have gone."

Mum nodded, understanding in her eyes. If I had to spend any more time with my cousins' mother right now, I really might hit her. One grudging apology didn't make up for her behaviour.

I hurried down the corridor, hesitating at Olivia's closed door before heading farther down to Justin's. I knocked tentatively. "Jat?" No answer. "Justin?"

"I said leave me alone." The words were muffled, barely audible through the bedroom door. I imagined him on his bed, his face stuffed into a pillow to muffle his sobs, and I ached to hug him the way I would have when he was younger and he'd scraped his knee. The feeling was made even worse by the fact that his tears were partly my fault. But I knew he wouldn't want me to see him crying. He had my uncle's stupid machismo bullshit to

thank for that.

"Okay." I hesitated, resting my head against the door and closing my eyes. "I'm sorry, Jat."

He didn't reply, so I trudged back to Olivia's room, feeling about an inch high.

I'd been familiar with Olivia's bedroom in my aunt and uncle's previous house, but by the time they'd bought this huge place Olivia had been in her teens and intent on maintaining her privacy when possible. So I wasn't sure what to expect when I cracked open the door.

The room was huge—not as big as the palatial master bedroom upstairs, but closer to a good-sized master bedroom in a regular house. A double bed sat against one wall, under a high window, a pastel pink and cream bedspread tucked in with military precision and mounded with pillows.

Beside the bed loomed a dresser backed by a mirror, bearing makeup, a small number of hair-styling products and a red leather jewellery box. The dresser too was pastel pink, but Olivia had seemingly tried to moderate the saccharine Disney-princess look by painting the front of each dresser drawer with blackboard paint and sketching pictures in chalk on them. On one, a Chinese dragon twisted in a sinuous knot, surrounded by cartoon flames. On another, a sun beamed down on a field of grass, dotted with smiling daisies and dancing butterflies. A heart in one corner had been smeared as if by an angry hand; maybe it used to contain someone's name. Her ex's?

The space on the opposite wall was dominated by an easel bearing a half-finished painting: the stylised silhouette of a tree wavered against a riotous background. The floor on that side of the room had been covered with a clear plastic protector. A second chest of drawers—this one less dainty and bearing pots of paint, brushes and an expensive stereo—sat near the easel. Beside it was a door; a quick peek confirmed that it led to a tiny ensuite that smelled of a citrusy shampoo.

The entire room was orderly; even the small bottles of nail polish and the tubes of paint were arranged in rows, coloured soldiers on parade. Olivia had never struck me as a neat freak—but then, Lacey had a cleaner come once a week. Maybe Monday was their day. If they'd tidied up in here, my odds of finding any handy scraps of paper bearing hastily scribbled names or addresses were greatly reduced. Even the waste paper basket was empty.

I looked in the closet. It was hard to judge, but it seemed as if Olivia had packed before leaving rather than just fleeing the house in tears: there were no jeans, and a conspicuous space gaped in the row of T-shirts on one shelf, as if she'd grabbed a stack to shove them in a suitcase. It was hard to tell from the shoes on the floor whether a significant number of pairs were missing; unlike me, Olivia owned more than one pair of boots and sneakers.

I closed the closet door and turned to the dresser. *Maybe she kept an old-school paper address book?* I doubted it, given she owned a smart phone, but you never knew. It was more likely that she'd have a diary or bullet journal, but if she did it would be well hidden.

The dresser was full of hats, accessories and under-garments. After confirming nothing was buried under-neath, I didn't look too closely at the profusion of satin and lace. The chest of drawers by the easel was more interesting: it contained sketch books and old canvasses.

FALSE Awakening

The top drawers were full of her older work. Based on the date painted or written underneath her name in the corner of each, it was from around when she'd started art classes in high school. I wasn't artistic, but it was interesting to see the difference between the stylised, almost cartoonish people in those early drawings and the more-realistic depictions in her later works.

When Mum came looking for me, a cup of coffee in hand, she found me sitting on the floor with my back to the wall, a large watercolour notebook from the bottom drawer splayed open on my lap. "What on earth are you doing?" She set the cup down on the carpet protector beside me.

"Looking for clues." I turned the page carefully. A big-eyed girl that was at least half kitten stood there, one hand on her hip. She looked as if she'd just stepped out of an anime. *Damn, Olivia's good.*

"Avoiding Lacey, you mean." Mum drifted over to the dresser, lifting the jewellery box's lid.

"That too," I admitted, glancing at the doorway to make sure my aunt wasn't lurking there. All clear. Still, I lowered my voice. "Sorry I abandoned you with her. She does bad things to my blood pressure."

"Mine too." Mum shrugged, poking through the jewellery, which clinked softly. "That ring we gave Olivia for her birthday isn't here. She must be wearing it."

"I'm glad she likes it." I put the sketch book to one side so I could safely take a sip of coffee. It was good: faintly nutty, strong and smooth. It was lucky I never had trouble getting to sleep, or having caffeine at this time of night would be a bad idea, and I never could resist the opportunity to try expensive coffee. "I hope she's okay."

"I'm sure she's with one of her friends. Lacey rang around those whose numbers she has and they all deny it, but I expect one of them is lying."

"I hope it's that simple." I nibbled my lip, setting the cup to one side and picking up the sketch book. "I wonder if she has one of those apps that let you find your phone? Maybe we could use that to track her down?"

Mum turned to me, eyes wide. "You can do that? I thought that only worked in cop shows."

"Not with my crappy old phone, you can't. But Uncle Ian got Olivia a new handset last Christmas. Jat was crazy jealous. I don't know exactly how they work, though."

"I'll check with Lacey. She might have already tried." Mum strode from the room, and I returned to looking at the pictures. I loved the soft colours in this notebook; some of the other sketchbooks had been done with bold inks, but these were gentler. A few seemed to be life sketches, while others were more imaginative. I didn't know whether she'd invented the characters herself or was painting from a reference, but the technique looked good to me.

Towards the back of the notebook, there was a two-month gap, and then the paintings took a darker turn. A face, tear-streaked, in profile. Wind-swept winter streetscapes. A darker version of the bright painting on the easel, one where the tree was gnarled and strange, the background muted. Looking at the dates, I felt a pang of sadness. They had been done in the four months after Uncle Ian passed away.

Guilt gnawed at me. I should have made a bigger effort to be there for Olivia and Justin after their father died. At first, I'd been so caught up in my own fear, knowing

he'd been murdered, believing an Oneiroi was hunting me, sending a warning. And after we'd saved Mum and neutralised Ikelos, I'd been busy helping her transition out of the nursing home and into a normal life, as well as dealing with the lack of an office in which to run my business. Still, those seemed like pathetic excuses now.

"I'll do better, Liv," I whispered to a painting of a strange dreamscape, twisted and gloomy. A single bright butterfly looked lost amidst the jagged rocks and clawing trees. "I promise..."

I turned to the next page and my blood froze, leaving me glued to the spot. The figure was a silhouette, the shape of the shoulders and hips distinctly male. Hair curled around his face, which was all in shadow except for a pair of amber-bright eyes. Wings fell down his back, orange smudged with black. Like those of a Monarch butterfly.

With my fingers numb with terror, I turned back to the previous picture: that lost, lonely butterfly. A memory surfaced: Olivia's sheer delight at the girly ring we'd given her, despite it being cheap compared to what she was used to. That had been a butterfly too.

Oh shit. I leapt to my feet, clutching the notebook to my chest, and bolted down the corridor, looking for Lacey.

I found her and Mum in the kitchen. Lacey looked a little less haggard than before as she wiped down the kitchen bench. She looked up as I thundered into the room, my boots raising a racket on the hardwood floors. "What is it?"

"Before, when you said you didn't want Olivia to grow up like Mum, what did you mean?"

Lacey hung the dishcloth over the faucet and straightened her spine as if facing a disciplinary committee.

Head high, soldier. "I'm sorry about that."

"Uh-huh." I waved the apology away. Mum crossed her arms, her expression disapproving. "What did you mean when you said it? Was it just the pregnant teenage single-mother thing, or was there more to it?"

Lacey blinked. "There needs to be more?"

"What's this about, Melaina?" Mum asked.

I slapped the notebook down on the granite benchtop. The book's leather exterior stuck to the slightly damp surface. Olivia would have yelled at me for that, but I didn't care. I flipped it open to the picture of the Oneiroi. Because that was what it was. I couldn't tell for sure whether it was the Morpheus or his brother, but the tremor in my hands told me which one my subconscious thought was more likely. The king of the Oneiroi had never shown an interest in my human family. Ikelos, though... "Look at this."

The two older women clustered around me, leaning in to examine the picture. Mum's eyes widened, and her hand flew to her mouth. Lacey frowned. "That's just one of Olivia's little paintings. She's going through a surrealist, fantastic art phase. She has such a vivid imagination. She always has, since she was a little girl. She wants to do art at university, you know." Her expression turned sour. "Or she did, until now. It's such an impractical choice, but I'd rather she did that than not study at all—"

"What about her dreams?" I demanded.

Lacey's eyes narrowed. "What about them?"

"She always has crazy dreams," Justin said from the door. His eyes were red and his fringe was mussed. "What's going on?"

"Does she always remember her dreams?" I looked

between him and his mother.

"She says she does," Lacey said, shrugging. "And she certainly seems to prefer sleeping to getting up and being a productive member of this household." She darted a glance at Mum. "But it's nonsense. No one always remembers their dreams."

"I do. So does Mum," I said. "It must be genetic."

"Oh no," Mum whispered, her gaze fixed on those burning Oneiroi eyes.

I nodded, agreeing with the despair in her tone as much as with the words. "Olivia is a lucid dreamer. She's pregnant. Ikelos is alive. And Ewan is missing."

Chapter Twenty-Three

"Who is Ewan?" Lacey demanded. Mum and I exchanged a look, and Lacey slammed the notebook shut. The sound made me jump. "Where is my daughter?"

"We don't know for certain," Mum said, at the same time as I said, "You wouldn't believe us if we told you."

"Try me." Lacey leaned against the counter, folding her arms and staring at us with fire in her eyes.

"We're talking seriously new-age stuff here. I know how much you hate that." I pulled my phone out of my back pocket. Maybe I could call Daniel, see if he was off shift. I needed Ewan's address straight away.

"Does this relate to your dream therapy business?" Justin came into the room, passing the three of us to enter the kitchen proper.

"Yeah." I didn't look up, thumbing through my contacts.

"Tell me," Lacey demanded, covering the phone screen

with her hand so I had to meet her gaze.

"Fine." I put it on the bench, gathering my thoughts. The process made me feel like a sheep dog must, trying to gather an unruly flock. How on earth was I going to explain this to Lacey? She was practically a card-carrying member of the Australian Sceptics, and she'd always hated my line of work.

"Melaina…" Mum's tone was heavy with warning.

I shook my head. "She wants to know. And, if we're right, Olivia may be in danger. And her baby, too. Besides, Leander's not going to rat on me for telling."

"What?" Justin squeaked, dropping a plastic bottle of juice onto the floor. The orange liquid splashed wildly around the interior but, fortunately, the lid held. "Danger?"

"I said 'may be'." I tried to smile bravely, but it felt more like a grimace so I stopped. "She'll be fine, because I'm going to find her. I'm a regular old superhero."

"You're not *that* old," he said, picking up the juice. Behind him, the unattended fridge door swung closed with a soft thud.

"Just a little bit old, right, Jat?" I heard Lacey draw breath and hurried on. "Like I said, this isn't stuff you're going to believe, Lacey. But just … for the purposes of my explanation, even if you don't, please realise there are other people who do. It's important."

She nodded, pressing her lips together.

I took a breath. *Might as well dive straight in.* "There are creatures called Oneiroi. They are spirits who live in people's dreams and can manipulate those, um, dreams. Mostly, the Oneiroi stay in their own world and are pretty harmless to the human dreamer." *Except they have the ability to set blights and mara on you, and can create nightmares in their own right.* But that was a dark, scary rabbit hole that I so wasn't going to go down just now. "The thing is, though, if a person is a lucid dreamer and a female, an Oneiroi who spends a lot of time in her dreams while she's pregnant can sort of ... shape the foetus so it's born with Oneiroi powers. Not all their powers, but some."

"Right," Lacey said flatly.

"Remember, other people believe it," I reminded her. "Ewan certainly does. He used to be a nurse at Wattle Tree Park."

"He's the one the police were investigating for burning down Serenity's New Age Gifts," Justin added, sloshing juice into a glass. I glanced at him, surprised. "What? I pay attention to stuff."

I gave him a half-smile before turning back to Lacey. "Jat's right. Ewan was also taking advantage of the patients at the home—"

"Taking advantage of them how, exactly?" Lacey turned to Mum, horror blooming in her suddenly wide eyes.

"Not sexually," Mum said. "He was using the home as a place to build a powerbase for his Oneiroi master."

Lacey rubbed one of her temples with a hand; the other was wrapped around her middle as if keeping her reactions to herself was a physical struggle. I was impressed she hadn't started yelling yet.

"Ewan knows Mum and I are lucid dreamers," I said. "The fact Olivia is too, and is already pregnant, makes her vulnerable. Ewan will want her for Ikelos. His master."

"And you ..." Lacey gestured from Mum to me "... you believe all of this? Possession? Mutated babies with dream

powers?"

"I learned first-hand that it's true," Mum murmured, her glance sliding across to me.

The room fell silent as both Lacey and Justin stared. It was Justin who spoke first. "You have dream powers?"

"I told you I was a superhero." The room seemed too bright. How was I having this conversation with these people? I'd worked so hard to avoid it, not because of Justin but because of his mother. I'd been sure she'd have me committed. Looking at Lacey's calculating gaze now, I wasn't so sure I'd been wrong.

"That's why I slept for so long." A flush bloomed on Mum's cheeks as her gaze dropped to her hands. They twisted together on the benchtop. "There was an Oneiroi in my dreams."

Lacey snorted.

"Anyway," I said with a scowl, "all of this means we need to find Olivia. I don't think she's in physical danger—"

Justin frowned. "But you said…"

"It's her mind I'm worried about. And the baby's. Even then, we've got a bit of time, I think…" My stomach tightened at the idea of my bubbly cousin, unaware of what she was getting herself into, putting herself in the hands of Ewan and, worse, Ikelos. Did she think he was some supernatural Prince Charming, come to sweep her off her feet? He was certainly handsome enough, if your tastes ran to tattooed and sinister.

"Can your dream powers help you find Olivia?" Justin asked.

"Sadly, no. As far as superhero powers go … well, on a scale from one to Superman, I'm somewhere around a zero point five."

"What *can* you do?"

I opened my mouth to answer—but, before I could, Lacey's self-control snapped. "This is ridiculous." She threw her hands in the air. "Stop filling my son's head with nonsense. I need actual genuine help to find my daughter, not pseudo-spiritual fairytales. If you're not really going to help, get the hell out of my house."

"Show her." Mum brushed my shoulder with her fingertips; when I looked at her, she shook her head. My aunt and I had a similar temperament despite not being biologically related. Maybe there was something to that nature versus nurture thing I'd ignored in science class after all. "She's not going to believe you unless she sees proof," Mum told me, "and her scepticism is wasting time."

She's right. I rolled my shoulders back, trying to ease the tension there. "Are you volunteering?"

"It can't be me," Mum said. "She'll assume I'm faking. Again."

I winced, but had to agree. I looked from Lacey to Justin. "I basically have two powers. One is the ability to shape a person's dreams—"

"We don't have time to take a nap," Lacey said.

"—and the other is to put them to sleep by breathing on them," I continued. "Something about them inhaling my breath puts them to sleep." Justin opened his mouth, a glint in his eye, and I grinned at him. "Yes, I brush my teeth. It's not garlic breath."

"Garlic would only work for vampires anyway." Justin put the juice back in the fridge.

"Anyway, the point is that I can prove it to you. That I'm part Oneiroi."

"By putting one of us to sleep?" Justin asked.

"Yes."

His hand shot into the air. "I volunteer as tribute."

"I'm not sure..." Lacey said as Justin circled around the bench and came to stand before me. "That is. Um. What are you going to do to him?"

"Put him to sleep. Don't worry; it's safe. So long as he's sitting or lying down." I looked at my cousin. "Otherwise you'll fall."

"Oh. Makes sense," he said. We trailed behind as he tromped out to the family room, throwing himself onto the scarlet couch. "Can I have a dream about bikini babes?"

"Jat," I said with a sigh, perching on the edge of the seat beside him. "I can't give you that kind of dream."

"Why not?"

"Because ick?"

Lacey stood near us, shifting from foot to foot.

"What are you worried about?" Mum asked, sitting on the other couch. "After all, if we're lying to you, nothing will happen. Right?"

Lacey studied me. I'd seen that look before, on some of my more sceptical clients. Wondering what the trick would be. "There's more than one way to knock a person out," Lacey said finally. Mum hissed an irritated breath.

"I'm not going to drug him or smack him on the head." I held my hands up, fingers spread so she could see they were empty. "This is all natural." *Supernatural. Whatever.*

Still keeping my hands in the air, I leaned over Justin, putting my face within a foot of his. Those tear-reddened eyes widened, clearly unnerved. "Relax, cuz," I said. "I'm not going to kiss you." And then I breathed on him.

I was familiar with the effect my power had on people;

I'd been using it since my teens, when I'd discovered it was a great way to sneak out of my boarding house after curfew. Still, conscious of my aunt's nervous, suspicious gaze, I watched with a critical eye as Justin's eyelids slid shut and the tension eased out of his face, his muscles growing slack. A deep, sighing breath slipped between his lips as they softened, parting to reveal a hint of teeth. Slowly, his head listed to the side.

"Very funny, Justin." Lacey stepped forward until her shadow fell over her sleeping son. "Justin?" He didn't react, and her gaze shifted to me, realisation dawning in her eyes. "He's really asleep."

"Yes," I said, speaking quietly. "They go straight into a deep sleep when I do that, so they tend to be oblivious to what's going on around them. Still, he'll wake up if you shake him or speak loudly enough. You know, if you're worried about him."

Lacey caught her bottom lip between her teeth, staring at her son's relaxed face for several long moments. "No. Let him sleep for now. It's been a stressful day, and we need to talk."

I stood, and we filed back into the kitchen.

"Now," Lacey said, turning to me and Mum. The scepticism and irritation were gone, replaced with a sharp-eyed determination. "How are we going to find Olivia?"

Chapter Twenty-Four

I wish Daniel had just checked his damned Facebook
messages. Butterflies spiralled in my stomach as
I drove home along mercifully quiet streets in my uncle's
car. My uncle's very expensive, limited-edition muscle
car, which was the burnt orange of a smoky sunset and
cost more than my annual salary. Several years' worth
of my annual salary. That was why I clung to the steering
wheel with a white-knuckled grip and had turned the
radio off. I didn't want any distractions. I'd barely driven
a car in years, and never one that smelled of leather and
was probably smarter than I was. And surely an auto-
matically dimming rear-vision mirror and heated seats
were overkill?

The fact Lacey hadn't sold the car in the months since
my uncle's death was telling, and made me even more
afraid of scratching it.

*If Daniel had just answered me, I wouldn't be driving
this ridiculous vehicle.* I'd checked my Facebook page on

Lacey's computer to confirm Daniel hadn't replied, and had then called Wattle Tree Park. Daniel wasn't at work, but was expected in later. I'd left a message for him to phone, but really? Couldn't he just live on social media like everyone else seemed to?

The plan Lacey, Mum and I had come up with had involved Mum staying with Lacey and Justin—it turned out Olivia hadn't logged off her social media accounts on her PC, which had given them a handful of fresh leads to pursue. Since Jen wouldn't be home for hours, I'd suggested I go to our place, in case Olivia reached out to us there.

What I hadn't told any of them was my half-formed plan to go out to Wattle Tree Park later in the evening, once Daniel was at work. I was pretty sure I could bluff my way in to see him. And, if he wouldn't help me, I would be able to put him to sleep so I could go through the home's records. Ewan's address would be on file there.

Mum and Lacey were better off out of it. I didn't want to get Mum in trouble, and Lacey ... well, for the first time in years, I thought she might actually bail me out. If Constable Nelson found out I'd gone back into Wattle Tree Park again, after hours and in a visit that resulted in mysteriously sleeping nurses, I'd definitely need a lawyer. And, unlike the one Brad had spoken to today, Lacey might even represent me for free. *Maybe*.

I breathed a shaky sigh of relief when I took the key out of the ignition, feeling more than hearing the engine shut off. Giving the steering wheel an uneasy pat, I shouldered my bag and slid out of the driver's seat, peering down at the keys to mash the button that activated the central locking.

I jumped almost out of my skin when someone strode across the lawn towards me.

Olivia? But that first, hopeful thought fled when I realised the approaching figure was male. I backpedalled, bumping into the side of Uncle Ian's car. The car alarm began to wail, the lights flashing. In their strobing illumination, I took in the shabby, dishevelled appearance of David Nelson. He wore tracksuit pants and a creased T-shirt. Stubble shadowed his chin, and his eyes ... his eyes stared out of his head like a man possessed. And I knew what that looked like.

"Get away from me," I yelped, darting to the side, away from the hands I expected to grab me, choke me.

Instead, he paused on the edge of the driveway. Those hands covered his ears, and his face scrunched up as though the sound pained him. "Please shut that off," he shouted over the screeching alarm.

Blight-possessed people can't talk... Still, I made sure the car's bonnet was between me and Nelson before thumbing the alarm off with a shaking hand. "What do you want?"

"I need to know. Is it true?" His face was suddenly in shadow, but his rasping voice carried despite the protesting, rapid-fire bark of a dog several houses up.

"Is ... is what true?"

"I spent the day talking to some of your clients." He shifted his weight from one foot to the other. "Several of them claim you put them to sleep during your therapy sessions. Herbal teas, they said. I thought it was hypnosis. But one, a Mrs Blackwood, saw you put her granddaughter under by just breathing on her. Is it true?"

I tried to think of a clever answer: some way to diffuse

the situation, a plausible excuse. But he'd seen the footage of me doing exactly that at Wattle Tree Park. What was the point? "Yes," I said with a sigh. "It's true."

"I knew it." He ran a hand through his hair. It stuck up in clumps, like it hadn't been washed for days. "He told me ... you'd been messing with my dreams. He said the footage was proof." He stepped forward, and I took an equal step backwards, my boot sinking into the garden on the far side of the driveway. A few stray autumn leaves we'd never swept up crunched beneath my heel as he pleaded, "Make it stop."

"I didn't ... wait, what? *Who* said?"

"The man with the burning eyes."

I stared at him. My first incredulous thought—that Nelson's dreams had been clean when I checked—was swept away in the sickening realisation that only blights left residue, not Oneiroi. Had Ikelos been hiding in Nelson's mind while I poked around in there, watching me? My stomach churned.

"He comes to me when I sleep, fills my head with nightmares of you," Nelson continued. "Says you're a devil, a witch. Says I should arrest you, or... But he's a symptom, a figment. Not my friend. And you can make him go away."

Or? I swallowed, my glance flicking down to his hip before returning to his tortured expression. He wasn't wearing his gun belt, and the bulge on one side of his pants seemed more key-sized than gun-sized. Still, I took a slow breath, kept my voice even. "How long have you been dreaming of him?"

"About a week." One of Nelson's hands scratched at his stubble; the other hung loose at his side, though the

fingers flexed, a restless, anxious gesture.

"Since you went to visit Ewan?"

He nodded. *Scratch, scratch.* "You believe me?"

"Of course I do," I said. "Do you believe me when I say I'm not a witch? I haven't been giving you nightmares." *Technically true.* I'd given him a pretty good dream, actually. Or it had started out that way, at least—I wasn't so sure how it had ended up.

He nodded again. "There's no such thing as witches."

I laughed, a nervous sound borne of the adrenaline still coursing through my system—and then jumped when a screen door banged a few doors up. A man yelled and the barking dog fell silent, the night still.

We can't do this out here. I squared my shoulders. "You'd better come inside before my neighbours complain. I'll try to explain what's going on."

The hair on the back of my neck prickled with unease as Nelson followed me up the short footpath connecting the driveway to the front door. "That's a nice car," Nelson commented. "It's not registered to you."

"Well, no." I unlocked the front door, gesturing for him to precede me into our darkened house. Of course he'd known the car wasn't mine. He'd done a lot of digging into my life. "It was my uncle's. His wife loaned it to me."

"Nice loan. Still, it has to be rough getting it under the circumstances. Sorry. About your uncle's passing." He stopped in the entryway, and I shut the door behind me. To our right, the lounge room was filled with orange shadows from the streetlight outside. I remembered my panic that Nelson had seen Brad and me in there. A blush scalded my cheeks, and I had to clear my throat before I could speak.

"The kitchen is straight ahead," I said, flicking the entry light on so he could see where he was going. "I'll fix you a coffee while we talk."

"Not a relaxing herbal tea?" Nelson's tone contained a trace of self-depreciating humour as he ran a hand along the doorjamb until he found the light switch and turned it on. Although he was clearly fatigued, his gaze still took in the contents of the benches: a microwave and our coffee machine took up one corner each, while the remaining space was filled with other small appliances, a grocery list, an empty coffee mug … the usual clutter of life.

"No, no tea." The knot of tension between my shoulders eased when I entered the kitchen proper and he remained on the other side of the bench, sliding onto a stool with a soft groan. I snatched up the mug, placing it in the sink to deal with later. "Honestly, I've rarely seen someone in more need of a good night's sleep than you," I said. "And I wish I could help you out with that. But I'm more worried about you falling asleep than staying awake at this point."

"Why?" He blinked those bloodshot eyes, his fingers drumming on the benchtop as I retrieved a clean mug and turned the coffee machine on.

"Because the man with the burning eyes is an actual thing, not just a symptom of your sleep-deprived mind. He's a spirit named Ikelos."

"A spirit."

"A dream spirit, yes." I kept my tone matter-of-fact. I didn't want to antagonise the constable. Even if he didn't have his gun on him, I was sure he could physically subdue me in half a dozen different ways. *I so need to*

learn self-defence. "And if he's been in your dreams enough times, he might be able to possess you. If you fall asleep, it will be easier for him." I was pretty sure of that last part. It was definitely true for blights … although I had seen Ikelos slide into an awake Ewan as easily as I'd slide my hand into an oven mitt. *That's because Ewan is his minion. The ease of familiarity.* At least, I hoped so. Otherwise, inviting Nelson inside might have been a very bad mistake. "How do you have your coffee?"

"White and none."

"Right." The coffee machine thrummed as I pulled the milk out of the fridge, turning over in my mind how much to tell the constable. I really didn't want to go into my parentage if I could avoid it. "Ikelos doesn't like me much. He sees me as a threat due to my work. If he possessed you…" I grimaced. "Well, let's just say I've had my fill of being choked."

Nelson's fingers stilled, and he sat up a little straighter. "Brad Peterson. Your boyfriend. Is *that* why he attacked you last winter?"

"Yeah." It was a blight, but Ikelos had been directing it, so it totally counted. "Though he wasn't my boyfriend at the time. I wasn't lying to you when I said I'd never met him before that night. We hooked up later, after I helped him."

Understanding widened Nelson's eyes, and he seemed to be regarding me in a new light. Less *abused girlfriend and co-conspirator* and more … something else. Fingers crossed it turned out to be something good; *helpful and trustworthy dream therapist* would be a lot better than *unstable lady in need of medication.* "That's why you didn't press charges," he said.

"Yup. Because it wasn't Brad's fault. Same as it wouldn't be your fault if you got possessed and tried to kill me. Still, even knowing that, I'd rather avoid it if it's all the same to you." I gave Nelson a small smile, standing sideways as I frothed the milk so I could keep an eye on him.

Nelson rubbed his eyes. "Is this for real?"

"Unfortunately, yes." I finished making Nelson's coffee, giving him time to think. He was willing to hear me out, even if he wasn't quite convinced yet. I wasn't sure I'd have even gotten that much from him if Ikelos hadn't targeted his dreams, seeded them with nightmares. He had too much of a logical, ordered mind, despite Serenity's glimpse of his astrological tendencies the month before.

In a way, Ikelos had done me a favour.

"I expect it'd be a lot easier to believe I was scamming you somehow," I said, sliding the coffee across the bench to Nelson. I withdrew my hand quickly, before he could reach across and grab it. "Hypnosis and hallucinogenic drugs; that sort of thing."

"I had considered it. But I never drank that tea you sold me, and you haven't had access to my house."

I blinked. I had no doubt he'd double-checked. "You didn't really give the tea to someone at work, did you?"

"No." He regarded the coffee for a long moment before taking a cautious sip. His willingness to drink it felt like a victory. A small one, sure, but a victory nonetheless. "I wanted to have it sent for testing," he added, "but I couldn't think of a way to justify it. So I binned it."

The reminder that Nelson had access to resources I didn't struck me like a slap to the cheek, widening my eyes and filling me with sudden energy. *He could help*

find Olivia! "Ikelos, your burning-eyed man, is working with Ewan Wright. More accurately, Ewan works for him. He's Ikelos's hands in our world. And I think he might have abducted my cousin."

Nelson's gaze sharpened to steel. "What?"

"Her name is Olivia Armstrong-Taylor. She's eighteen, and she's been missing for about twenty-four hours."

"Has this been reported to the police?"

I nodded. Lacey had been on the phone to them when I left. "But the connection between her and Ewan ... well, it's nothing the police can pursue as a lead. I don't think they'll find her."

"The connection. It's this Ikelos?"

"Yes. I found evidence that he's been in her dreams too. Drawings of him."

"What does he look like?"

Nelson's tone was casual, but I knew a test when I saw one. Fortunately, I knew the answer. "Eyes like embers. Wings like a Monarch butterfly. Tribal tattoos." His eyes widened, and I suppressed a surge of grim satisfaction. "I think ... well, Olivia's of particular interest to him."

"Why?"

"She's pregnant. And she's related to me."

"You said he has a grudge against you." I nodded, biting my lip, and he frowned. "How is the pregnancy relevant?"

I hesitated. "Ewan and Ikelos ... well, they believe they can subvert the baby. Bring it under their control."

"Are they right?"

"Yes," I whispered, hugging myself as a shudder ran down my spine. If Ikelos could possess Ewan after a few months of residence in his dreams, how much control would he gain over Olivia's child after nine months? Would the baby have any autonomy once it was born? Or would its personality be put to sleep, subsumed by Ikelos? Ollie hadn't done that to me—but then, Ollie wasn't an evil bastard. "Do you have Ewan's address?"

"I do." Nelson ran a finger along the rim of his mug, though he studied me through lowered brows. "You want to go out there?"

"Yes. Tonight. I can't be sure he'll have taken her there, but it's the only lead I have. And he has no reason to assume the police will piece it together. Or that I will. Olivia and I ... we aren't that close. And she's been keeping a lot of secrets lately."

"Why not let the police handle it? I can call it in right now; they'll send a car around to see if she's there."

"Because Ikelos is a dream spirit. Even if they do find Ewan and Olivia, how are they going to tell if she's possessed? This isn't a supernatural cop show. You can't call me in as a consultant or whatever."

He hesitated. "I could get fired for this..."

"I know." I waited, my arms folded, for him to make his decision. I didn't beg, even though I wanted to. Nelson didn't strike me as the sort of man who'd give in to what he'd regard as emotional blackmail.

"Okay," he said. "But I want in."

Chapter Twenty-Five

"Leander, I don't know if you can hear me. But, if you can, get your skinny butt to this mirror right now." My reflection stared back at me, looking irritated and a little alarmed. Behind it, my back-to-front bedroom was both familiar and distressingly empty of Oneiroi. With the curtains drawn, the mirror was the only reflective surface in my new bedroom. It hung on the inside of my wardrobe door, where I could be sure it wouldn't capture a reflection of myself without me being aware of it. I'd grown to trust Leander during the past few months, but I still couldn't be sure he wouldn't sneak a peek at me getting changed if given the chance.

I closed my eyes and rested my forehead on the glass, breathing out a sigh. "Seriously, Leander, I need you."

No answer. I opened my eyes, using a thumb to wipe away the condensation my breath had left, and pulled the wardrobe door wide open, swinging it so the mirror faced the side of my chest of drawers. There, I'd taped a piece of paper from the kitchen notepad with a scribbled note explaining what we believed: that Ikelos had been hiding inside Ewan's mind and was now squatting in Olivia's. I hoped Leander would see the note and bring the cavalry to help. Despite my brave words to Nelson, I wasn't confident I could prise Ikelos out of Olivia's dreams on my own.

First step: get her away from Ewan and back home. I'd worry about the second stage later.

I pulled on a comfortable knitted jumper over my band T-shirt and turned to my bedroom door, heading up the corridor to find Nelson still sitting on the stool at the kitchen bench. "I don't know why you needed to get changed," he said, taking in my more casual clothes.

"I'd been in that outfit all day." I wrinkled my nose. "It was gross." *And you seeing me talk to a mirror might make you change your mind about the whole giving-me-Ewan's-address thing.*

"You say this to the guy dressed like a hobo." He smoothed down the creased front of his T-shirt with a restless hand.

I shrugged, grinning as I hooked my handbag over my shoulder. "But you're a comfortable hobo, am I right?" He frowned, and I hastened to add, "Comfortable is good. I'd live in yoga pants or trackies if I could get away with it."

"It's fine. Believe it or not, I would too," he said. "Still, I didn't even think you owned a pair of sneakers till now."

"Well, what else would I sneak in?"

"Those are meant to be sneaky?" he said with a laugh, gesturing to my feet.

I looked down at them, clad in gleaming white and hot pink below the hem of my dark jeans. "They're auditorily

sneaky."

"True, that." He stood, pulling his keys out of his pocket.

I raised an eyebrow at them, jingling my own—well, Lacey's—keys in my hand. "No offence, officer, but you're not driving. You know what the ads say about driving while fatigued. It's as bad as driving drunk. Let me handle it."

His lips pressed together, and for a second I thought he was going to object. Certainly he was the more experienced driver by a long shot. But when he did speak, his answer wasn't the one I expected. "I'm not going with you."

"But you said—"

"If Ewan has taken Olivia against her will and I come with you, it could be spun as an illegal search. Hell, it would be. The chances of us landing a conviction go way down."

"I don't care about a conviction. I just want to get Olivia home!"

"I know." He handed me a piece of paper. On it, he'd written an address and, below that, a mobile phone number. "Ewan's address and my number. If you're asked, you got the address from somewhere else. I know I gave you my card a few months ago, so you have reason to have my number. I assume you didn't keep it?" I shook my head, pressing my lips together. I'd tossed the card in the recycling the next day. "Didn't think so. Copy the address onto another piece of paper."

He was being paranoid, but I obediently transcribed Ewan's address onto the back of a loyalty card in my purse before programing Nelson's number into my phone. "And where are you going?" I asked, handing him his original sheet. He scrunched it up and stuffed it in his pocket.

"Home. If you get to Ewan's place and find your cousin

is there, text me with all the details, like it's the first time we've discussed it. I'll call a unit to respond." He smiled, an expression that was at least half grimace, as we turned towards the front door. "I'll do my best not to fall asleep in the meantime."

"Oh, hey, about that. I had a thought. You probably *are* safe to sleep now, if Ikelos has set up permanent residency in Olivia's head like I think he has." Ollie had been in Mum's mind constantly while she was pregnant with me. A quick departure to mess with Nelson's dreams might invalidate the entire nine months' work. I didn't think Ikelos would risk it.

Nelson sighed, a wistful sound, as we stepped out into the night. "I hope you're right, though I won't test the theory till I hear from you. These nightmares ... I've never experienced anything like them."

"Well, after this, if you're still having issues, let me know. I really can take nightmares away." I pulled the front door closed.

Nelson cocked his head, his expression hard to read in the gloom. Finally, he shrugged. "Sure, why not?"

It wasn't exactly a ringing endorsement, but we'd come a long way in the last hour or so. And I didn't need him to believe I could fix his dreams in order to do so. I just needed him to not arrest me for trying. "Drive safe, okay?"

"I only live a few minutes from here. I'll be fine."

He squared his shoulders and I wondered whether he was trying to convince me or himself. Still, he was doing his best to make it look like we hadn't conspired tonight; I could hardly order him a cab or drop him off, leaving his car on my street. I saw now, as he strode towards it, that he'd parked it several blocks up, in front of an empty

playground. No wonder I hadn't spotted it when I'd gotten home—especially given how focused I'd been on not scratching Uncle Ian's car on our concrete letterbox. *Sneaky bugger.* The thought was as admiring as it was grumpy.

Once Nelson slid into the driver's seat I turned to my own car, regarding it with faint trepidation. I climbed inside and turned the engine—and heater—on, letting it idle as I pulled my phone out of my bag.

No way was I going to Ewan's house on my own.

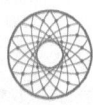

"I still can't believe you told him," Brad said, his gaze fixed on the display of the GPS we'd found in the glove box. When I glanced at him, the device's green and white glow lit up his face in the dark car interior. "How'd he take it?"

"Remarkably well, all things considered," I said, "though I didn't tell him everything. Still, if Nelson turns out to be on our side, you'll be able to call off your lawyer before you rack up too big a bill." I flicked on the indicator even though the road was almost empty, easing the car around a roundabout and into the suburbs.

"Let's see how tonight goes first. I might need him to get us off a trespassing charge if Ewan catches us peeking in his windows."

"Yeah..." We drove in thoughtful silence for a minute, the GPS's clipped British instructions the only sound in the car. When Brad laughed softly, I tipped my head to the side, risking another glance at him. "What?"

"Remember how, when we first started dating, I told

you Belinda said I always go for the bad girl?"

I grinned. "And Jen said the same thing about you. That I go for bad guys, I mean. Not that you're a girl. Obviously."

"Well, I was just thinking tonight proves who the real bad influence is. I never needed a lawyer until I met you."

"It's hardly my fault," I huffed, tapping my fingers on the steering wheel. "Besides, I never needed one till I met you either."

"I'm not complaining." There was a teasing note in Brad's voice. "I like it when you're the bad girl."

"Oh, do you?" I replied with a laugh.

"*In one hundred metres, turn right. Then you have reached your destination.*"

I didn't feel like laughing anymore.

Taking a leaf out of Constable Sneaky's book, I drove further up the street, parking the car in front of a mostly empty block. The skeletal frame of a house loomed behind wire fencing and canvas. "He's home," Brad said as I turned off the engine. "His car's in the carport, and the light in the front room is on."

"Bugger. It would've been easier to check the house if he was out."

Brad opened the glove box to slide the GPS in. I jammed my handbag in on top. "We'll have to come in from the back yard," he said. "Unless you want to just knock and push past?"

I shook my head. "He won't let us search the house. No way." My mobile phone buzzed in my hand as I switched it to silent.

"Maybe you could, you know..." Brad blew out his cheeks, puffing loudly.

I raised an eyebrow at him. *I don't look like that … do I?* I shook off the thought. "If I could get the jump on him, sure. But if he sees it's me, he won't unlock the screen door. He knows what I can do. I'm hoping we can glimpse her through a window or something; then we can text Nelson."

"Let's hope he doesn't have a dog," Brad said as we climbed out of the car. I locked it and slid my phone and keys into a pocket of my jeans. If we were going to engage in criminal trespass, I wanted my hands free.

The night seemed icy after the car's toasty warmth—I'd by now grown fond of the heated seats. Beside me, Brad was dressed in black jeans and a navy blue hoodie with the hood up. He grinned like a schoolboy about to engage in a prank; the expression brought a smile to my own face, and I slid my hand into his. I loved that he hadn't questioned my conviction that Ewan had Olivia, even though it was almost entirely based on speculation and gut feeling, a justification thinner than the paper on which Olivia had painted Ikelos.

I was going to feel like an idiot if she'd taken off to Sydney with a mate or something.

Trying to look like a couple out for an evening walk, the two of us strolled back along the street on the other side of the road from Ewan's place. He lived two blocks from the corner, his house one among many small, brick veneer places: the sort a real estate agent would describe as "cute" or "cottage-like". The blocks were small enough that the left-hand wall of each building formed part of the adjacent property's fence line. Carports rather than garages were the norm, and each front yard was tiny. Blue light from the television flickered through the cracks in the venetian blinds, but there was nothing to indicate Ewan was actually in the front room, let alone whether Olivia was with him.

"There's not much scope for sneaking," I muttered as we reached the corner and turned right, out of sight of the house. "No big trees to skulk behind, and just that side gate behind the carport."

"There's a sensor light over the front door too," Brad said. "If we try to get past the car to get to the gate, it'll probably come on."

"Crap."

"Yeah. Still, I got a good look at the layout on the GPS screen. Cross your fingers that the neighbour behind him isn't home." Brad led me down the street and we turned right again, back onto Ewan's street, but this time at the other end: the street was a circuit, shaped like a bent bobby pin with both tips touching the feeder road. We slowed as we approached the third house along: the place that shared a back fence with Ewan's. This house had an empty double carport and the lights were off. *Bingo.*

"You ready?" Brad whispered.

Was I? This could land us in a lot of trouble. We'd already gotten an unofficial warning against trespassing once, for the incident at Wattle Tree Park. If someone called the police other than us, I doubted we'd get off so lightly a second time. But I couldn't shake the mental image of my bright, bubbly cousin in a sleep coma of the sort Ikelos had trapped Mum in, her muscles wasting away as her belly swelled and the Oneiroi forced his way into the baby's psyche, gnawing into it like a grub into an apple. I pulled out my phone. "Give me a sec."

"What are you doing?"

"Drafting that text to Nelson." My fingers flew across the keypad. "I want to have it ready if she's in there, just in case." I didn't say just in case what. Careful not to hit send, I turned the phone off and slid it back into my pocket. "Alright, now I'm ready." I put on an American accent and swaggered forward. "Let's be bad guys."

Chapter Twenty-Six

Sneaking into the yard of Ewan's neighbour proved easier than I'd expected: their gate was unlocked and we weren't greeted by a snarling, slavering hellbeast on the other side. In fact, the only sign of animal life was a sleepy hen clucking itself to sleep in a chook pen over the fence. Surely not in Ewan's yard? A breeze rustled the top of a tree in the back corner of the garden. I gestured towards it and we crept into its shadow, my eyes straining, and failing, to pierce the blackness. As if to underline the point, a leafy twig scraped my forehead. I hissed between my teeth at the sharp sting, batting the offending bough away.

"You right?" Brad breathed, standing so close beside me that I could feel his body heat.

"Yeah," I said quietly, touching my face gingerly. It was sore but not damp with blood. "Just a graze." Who knew they'd have a guard tree? I felt around in the gloom, finding a sturdy lower branch. The bark was smooth

under my fingers. "I'm going over. Watch my back."

"Always."

The twigs above me rustled more vigorously as I tested my weight on the branch. It held. "My back, not my butt," I muttered, glancing at Brad.

"I can't do both?"

I flashed him a nervous grin that he probably couldn't see, but didn't answer. Instead, I placed my hand on the top of the cool metal fence and my sneaker on the branch, using the former to steady myself as I climbed onto the latter and peered through the dangling foliage into Ewan's yard.

At first it was hard to see much of anything; the street-lights didn't penetrate this far. But the moon was a gibbous almost-disc overhead, and soon my eyes adjusted, able to pick out details in the dim, bluish-silver light.

Ewan's lawn was in dire need of a mow, its spring growth an unrestrained tangle of grass and spiky weeds. A native bush that might be a bottlebrush sprawled like a drunk on a bender against one fence, and the obligatory clothesline filled the centre of the yard, at one end of a cracked footpath. The other end of the footpath connected to a laundry door; to the right of it stood a long window, dark, its curtain drawn. Probably a bedroom.

The toe of my sneaker squeaked against the metal as I climbed from the branch, heaving myself over the fence and dropping into a weedy garden bed on the other side. Brad soon landed beside me with grunt of pain, going to a knee in the dirt. I offered him a hand and he took it to stand, wincing as he shifted his weight. I tilted my head at him in a silent question. "I'm fine," he whispered. "I just haven't climbed a fence in ten years. I'm out of practice." He peered around the yard. "No dog, at least."

"Yeah." I realised I was hunching over, as if expecting a blow, and forced my shoulders back. "Let's go."

Careful to lift my feet so my sneakers didn't whisk through the tangled, knee-high plants, I eased my way over to the footpath, breathing a little easier when the soles of my shoes touched concrete. As uneven as it was, the path seemed safer than the long grass. At least I could see where I was putting my feet.

With Brad in my shadow, I hurried to the bedroom window, trying in vain to peek through the gap in the undulating curtains. No joy; they had been closed tightly. Gesturing for Brad to stay where he was, I crept around the side of the house, closer to the gate and carport. More windows: another bedroom and what was probably a kitchen window beside a glass sliding door. All of them were covered. *Ewan couldn't have left one curtain open?* Exasperated, I returned to Brad, shaking my head in response to his raised eyebrows. He stood by the back door, leaning against the brick wall with all his weight on one leg, the other knee bent in a pose that I suspected was meant to look casual—though I was sure he was favouring it. *He's sprained it. Shit.* Going back over the rear fence would be a nightmare. Hopefully we could sneak out the front gate after all.

"Maybe we will have to go around the front and knock," I whispered, my gaze slipping past my boyfriend to the laundry door. What were the chances...? I stepped past Brad. My nerves thrummed with energy as I reached for the doorknob. It was cool in my palm as I held my breath and turned...

The knob rotated easily, and I gasped as the door swung inwards, bumping almost immediately against

some obstruction. Crouching so I could feel around inside, I found a mound of clothes inside the door, covering the laundry floor in front of the washing machine. *Gross.* I wiped my hand on my jeans and then leaned my shoulder against the door. Slowly, slowly, I pushed, hearing fabric slide across the floor as the pile shifted. From the other end of the house the television chattered, canned laughter covering the small sounds as I made a space wide enough that we could slip through.

At least, I hoped it covered the sounds. It was hard to tell over the thundering of my pulse in my ears.

Brad's eyes were wide as I glanced back at him. He indicated the door with a tip of his head. "What about your ankle?" I breathed.

"I'm not leaving you."

I wanted to kiss him, but settled for a grateful smile as I turned back to the door and the black room beyond.

I'd thought crossing the moonlit, tangled grass had been tricky, but it had nothing on scrambling over an uneven pile of washing that stank of sweat and stale deodorant. At least I was able to steady myself by resting my hand on the top of the washing machine.

The hallway was mercifully clear of obstructions, its carpet cushioning my footfalls as I moved out of Brad's way.

An open door stood to our left, to the bedroom whose window I'd seen down the side of the house. Holding my breath, I poked my head in the door, glancing around. It was the master bedroom; an unmade bed dominated the space. A single bedside table was wedged into a corner, so cluttered that I feared there'd be a landslide of tissues, socks and electronics if I went near it.

I shook my head at Brad, too nervous to risk speaking, and he turned to the door on the opposite side of the hall. This one was closed. *The other bedroom?* It had to be. He reached for the handle and eased the door open. It scraped across the carpet, the sound so faint I could barely hear it.

Brad's sharply drawn breath as he looked into the room was louder. For a moment, he froze in the doorway, and I had to stand on my toes to see over his broad shoulder.

This bedroom was smaller, lit by a softly glowing lamp on a green-topped folding table in one corner. The table was much neater than the one in Ewan's bedroom, bottles of pills arranged in an orderly fashion, a roll of tubing coiled in the corner. Next to the bed a metal stand loomed. A drip stand, currently empty.

In that bed lay Olivia.

Before I knew I was moving, I'd shoved past Brad, hurrying to my cousin's side. She lay on her back, her chest rising and falling in the slow, even motion of sleep. Her chestnut hair spread around her head and shoulders, pretty as a picture—and a clear indication that she hadn't been tossing and turning. Her skin was pale, the yellow lamplight unable to lend it more than a cursory warmth. Her hands were folded across her stomach, on top of a white hospital blanket. Her left hand bore a ring: the butterfly ring we'd given her sparkled on her ring finger as if it were a wedding band, a placement I was sure wasn't accidental. When I brushed her bare arm with my fingertips, her skin was cool but not cold.

"Holy hell," Brad whispered. "He actually did it."

"Yeah, he did." I whipped my phone out of my pocket,

pressing a button to activate the keypad. The message to Nelson was still open on my screen.

"Melaina." My cousin's voice was raspy. I turned back to her, jabbing the send button with my thumb as I did so. "You came," she said, blinking sleepily.

"Of course I came," I murmured, shoving my phone in my back pocket and stepping close, grabbing the corner of the blanket to pull it back. From the fabric visible at her shoulders, I could see she was clothed. *Small mercies.* "Let's get you out of here."

Olivia cleared her throat and then smiled at me, lovely as a china doll. The lamplight reflected in her pupils, giving them an orange glow that sent an uneasy chill prickling down my arms. "But I don't want to go," she said, her voice clearer, louder. I shushed her but she shook her head. "Don't you see? I'm going to have a baby, and it's going to be special. Chosen by my new lover for great things." Her hands slid across the blanket where it covered her belly—a belly as flat as it had ever been. If I hadn't known she was pregnant I'd never have guessed.

"Ikelos isn't your lover, Olivia. He's … he's a parasite. He wants to steal your baby, make it his vehicle in this world. Like it's a car, not a person. Your child deserves better than that."

Olivia stiffened. At first, I thought I'd offended her and she was pulling away, but the reaction was a whole-of-body one, like she was in the grip of a seizure. Her fingers curled in the folds of the blanket and her limbs tensed. Her gaze slid away from my face and the muscles of her face tightened.

"Oh," said a disembodied voice. A familiar voice. "I'm not *that* bad, surely."

I whipped my head around to search for the source of the sound. And, in the reflective surface of the drip stand pole, I saw him—or, rather, a slice of him, a line that ran down the centre of his body, like I was peeking through a door left ajar. *Ikelos.* His only garment was a loose, knee-length skirt fashioned from strips of leather, like something I'd expect to see on a Roman centurion in a movie. Black tribal tattoos covered what I could see of his bare chest.

Despite all that bare skin, there was no sign of the injury Mum and I had inflicted on him. No sign of burns.

My heart leapt into my throat, thundering there like a panicked bird. When my gaze locked with his burning orange one, his eyes narrowed. "You can see me? Curious."

Brad took a step forward, following the line of my gaze to the drip stand. "Is it him?" he whispered. "Ikelos?"

"Who else would it be?" Ikelos replied.

I swallowed my panic. Ikelos was in Erebus. I was awake. *We're safe.* "He can't hear you," I told the Oneiroi, my voice little more than a squeak. It had clearly missed the memo about us being safe. "Seeing an Oneiroi in a reflection is a half-breed trick. It doesn't work for humans."

"Interesting."

Did the fact I could see Ikelos in a reflection mean he'd abandoned Olivia's dreams? Or was this a projection? There was so much I still didn't know about how Oneiroi powers worked.

Ikelos rubbed his chin with the ball of a thumb. "Fortunately, I have other ways to communicate with my pet human." Satisfaction was heavy in his tone, and I spun, a warning on my lips.

FALSE *Awakening*

A dark-haired figure loomed behind my boyfriend, grinning cheerily as he lifted a glittering object. I stepped forward, hand outstretched. Brad started to turn as the glittering object descended, piercing his clothing, driving into the meat of his shoulder. A syringe, quickly depressed.

Brad staggered, and Ewan laughed. "Nighty night," he crooned as Brad reeled, slamming into the wall. A picture fell to the floor with a crash.

With a wordless cry I stepped forward, my hands curling into fists.

Or I tried to. But Olivia's cool hand snatched one of my wrists, pulled me back towards the bed. Her face was still a stiff mask, her gaze fixed on the room's far wall. She was even more like a doll than before.

"Let go!" I tugged, but she clung to me, her hand a shackle. "Brad!"

"Melaina," Ikelos said, the tone conveying his disapproval. His voice seemed louder, richer, some of that resonance I remembered from our previous meeting creeping back into it.

Ewan watched with an appraising eye as Brad slid down the wall, his limbs gone boneless, his eyelids fluttering as he fought to keep them open. Panic warred with fatigue on his face. Fatigue won, and his eyelids slid shut.

"What did you do to him?" I cried, gripping Olivia's fingers with my free hand, trying to prise them backwards, digging my nails into the flesh of her thumb and the back of her hand. She didn't flinch.

"He's just taking a nap." Ewan plucked the now-empty syringe from Brad's shoulder. The tip was a dark red in the poor light. "I'm not a murderer."

"No," Ikelos said with a laugh as warm as a blanket

straight from the dryer. I cringed away from the sound. "He leaves that to me."

Olivia's other hand snaked out, grabbing my other wrist and holding it tight. "Let me go!" I braced my feet and tugged backwards. "Olivia, are you even in there? Can't you see how stupid this is? You're being used!"

In reply, my cousin yanked me back towards her with a fierceness I hadn't known she was capable of. I stumbled, sprawling across the bed. Her knees dug into my ribs, knocking the breath from my lungs.

"Olivia isn't home," Ewan said. Gasping, I twisted my head to the side, trying to keep him in view. "She isn't feeling a thing right now, but she'll be sore later. You might want to ease up on her." He paused, his head tipped to the side. Listening to silent instructions from Ikelos? "Right." His hand slid into my back pocket to draw my phone out, lingering for a moment on my arse. I kicked backwards, growling, my sneaker scraping against his shin. I wished I was wearing my hard-soled boots so I could really do some damage. "Bitch," he spat, dancing out of reach and examining the screen of my phone. "She texted the cop."

"Well, that's inconvenient," Ikelos said. His voice tickled my ears, the way a too-loud bass track does: like your insides are vibrating apart.

Shuddering, I tried to yank my hands free. My fingers were growing numb with the strength of Olivia's grip. How was Ikelos doing it? He had to be possessing her. But he couldn't speak through her lips? That suggested his control wasn't perfect. The thought gave me new strength, and I redoubled my efforts to free myself. "Olivia!" I yelled, almost in my cousin's ear. She didn't even blink.

"Can you bring them both?" Ewan asked. From the corner of my eye, I saw him turn my phone over and remove the battery. He dropped both halves into a rubbish bin underneath the table. I kicked backwards, but he stayed out of range.

"No," Ikelos said from the drip stand, for the first time letting me overhear his instructions to the nurse. "We'll have to leave the girl. But this will be better."

That tickling feeling doubled in strength. Now it felt like a small insect had crawled inside my skull. I wanted to claw at the insides of my ears, but my hands were immobilised. Panic flared, hot as a supernova, and I screamed, thrashing like a wild thing. I grabbed the end of Olivia's hair and yanked, tried to claw at her eyes, not caring that I was hurting my cousin. That she was an unwitting vessel for something else. But the feeling I struggled against wasn't on the outside. It was inside me. *He's inside my head.*

"A lucid dreaming Oneiroi half-breed, already prepared," Ikelos said with a smile, his reflection leaning forward, his gaze catching mine, tangling it up so I couldn't look away. The force of his will shook me until I felt like I would fly apart.

As if I were nothing more than a brittle leaf caught in a whirlpool, I was drawn down into unconsciousness.

Chapter Twenty-Seven

I slumped on a park bench, legs outstretched before me, and stared through heavy eyelids at a nameless lake. Overhead and behind me arched a timber trellis smothered with trailing vines. Bees droned, though I couldn't see any inside my shallow cave of leaves and wide-petalled flowers. The sun beamed down outside my shelter, warm enough that I could feel the radiant heat beyond the scraggly edge of my patch of shade, but a water-cooled breeze reached me, ruffling my fringe and brushing my cheeks.

I yawned, rubbing my eyes, and stretched until my fingertips skimmed across the glossy leaves on either side of me. The air was rich with the aroma of honey-suckle. I was content. I could stay here forever.

Overhead, a currawong rustled in the branches, its crooning song melancholy, and I realised—

I'm not content. Something is wrong.

I rubbed my temples, frowning at the lake's glistening,

light-dappled surface. *Where am I? How did I get here?* I struggled for a moment to recall, but my thoughts were muddled and slow. I was waiting for someone, wasn't I? Had I organised a lunch date with Jen? My mum? No, that wasn't right. Was Brad meant to be meeting me? Why couldn't I remember?

A memory of Brad, sliding bonelessly down a wall, flashed across my mind's eye, driving me to my feet. Grass rustled beneath my boots and the leaves around me sighed in the playful breeze: *hush, hush.* Pressing my lips together, I shook my head violently. I would not hush. I stepped forward, into the sunlight.

The breeze faded, the hot air blanketing me, dragging my limbs downward with warmth and the suddenly overwhelming, saccharine sweetness of honeysuckle. I blinked, and forcing my eyes open again took conscious effort. But something had happened to Brad, and *why couldn't I remember?*

I looked around. Now that my field of view wasn't restricted by the trellis-cave, I could see that the lake had no end, stretching away until it faded from view, the way computer game scenery does at the edge of its render distance. The water's surface was empty, as was the grassy park—the flower-covered trellis was the only feature. A sun-filled park on a beautiful afternoon should be full of people. Where were all the people?

"I'm dreaming, aren't I?" I said, looking up at a brilliant white sky. Despite the glow all around me, warming the top of my head and bathing my arms in golden light, there was no sun overhead. "Yup, dreaming."

A flutter of movement drew my gaze back to the trellis. A butterfly danced from one rosy-pink flower to the next, touching down briefly before moving on. Its wings were black with white splotches, and I blinked with surprise. I'd expected it to be black and orange, and why would that be, and, oh god, *Ikelos had taken over my mind*.

Rage, iron-tangy and hot, flooded my mouth and set my pulse to racing. The artificial daylight seemed brighter as I spun, searching for some sign of the Oneiroi, some way out of the dream he'd trapped me in. When he'd invaded Mum's mind, he'd locked her inside a fragment of dream within a dream. From the outside, it had looked like a dying wattle tree, a timber cocoon. What had it been like from the inside? Sleepy afternoon sunlight and the dull drone of bees?

"Like hell," I growled, throwing a hand out to point an accusing finger at the trellis, the butterfly. I imagined it gone, destroyed in an eruption of flame as hot as my fury at Ikelos and his presumption. And fire *did* bloom, uncurling like a hand at the base of the trellis, its orange fingers grasping at the vines. But it wasn't the inferno I'd imagined. Smoke, heavy and acrid, wafted out of the cave as the flame bit into green wood. Energy slipped from me, leaving me a little bit sleepier, my limbs a little bit heavier.

"This is my dream," I whispered. That vine should have exploded in a shower of sparks and burning splinters. It shouldn't have cost me anything. Something—or someone—was interfering with my ability to fully influence the dreamscape, dulling the usually keen edge of my wrath. I was so used to having total control over my own dreams, control without cost, that the concept left me a little breathless.

Or maybe that was the smoke.

FALSE *Awakening*

I needed to get away from the heat and honeysuckle. Even now I could feel them insinuating themselves into my thoughts, attempting to lull me back to sleep. I clenched my hands, nails biting into my palms, each tiny crescent of pain helping to keep me alert.

I willed my real body to wake, my real eyes to open and—

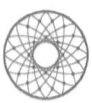

Lying, curled on my side: a stiff foetal position.
A fabric-lined box.
Windows.
Lights sweeping across the roof.
Trying to move.
Barely the twitch of a finger.
"She's awake." My own voice. My own voice? But deeper, somehow. Richer. "But not for long."
My eyes slid closed again.

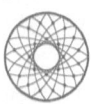

—the currawong took flight from the top of the trellis, launching itself with a beat of its black and white wings. Its call—a single, descending note, repeated over and over—tugged my gaze skyward as it flew up, circling twice beneath the ceiling of the formless white sky ... and disappeared, its song cutting off mid-note.

It couldn't have left. It was an ephemera, not a real bird. But perhaps my subconscious was trying to show me something. *You can fly in your dreams,* I'd told Felice. *You just have to will it.* And yes, I'd taught myself to fly in dreams, but in my dreams I could also explode trellises into kindling and leaf fragments with a thought. Flying wouldn't come free. What if my energy gave out when I was mid-air? The grass was soft underfoot, but it covered a layer of hard earth that would make short work of me if I hit it from a height.

"What the hell," I said. "I've never had a proper falling dream before anyway."

Imagining myself to be as light as the smoke particles floating upwards on the column of heated air above my fire, I threw myself skyward. I cheered when my boots didn't immediately thump back to Earth, turning my gaze towards that whiteness, the perimeter of the dream I was trapped in. But it didn't grow any closer. I didn't soar so much as bob a couple of metres off the ground like a deflating helium balloon.

Muttering curses against Ikelos and promises of what I was going to do to him when I found him, I floundered upwards, kicking my feet and flapping my arms: the world's most graceless bird. I must have looked ridiculous, and for a moment I was glad Leander wasn't there to make fun of me. Of course, if he'd been there, I wouldn't have been doing this in the first place. He had wings.

Beside me, the column of smoke dispersed as it rose. The stink of it tickled my nose, but it drove out the lulling honeysuckle aroma. I considered glancing down to see how far I'd come but dismissed the idea with a shudder. My previously blasé approach to flying, and to heights in my dreams more generally, had been based on my confidence that I wouldn't ... no, *couldn't* fall. I felt no such confidence now. Instead, I kept my gaze fixed on the smoke.

By the time I reached the dream's white ceiling, my

arms and shoulders ached with effort. Sweat prickled my brow, and my lungs burned. It wasn't cooler up here, not like it should be at higher altitudes. The heat closed in around me, squeezing the breath from my chest.

Gritting my teeth, I flung myself into, and through, the white ceiling, passing into it as though into a bank of fog. The heat dropped away like a discarded blanket. My weariness remained. I floated for a moment, staring around me. I'd seen this sort of thing before: unformed dreams, stripped of even their proto-dream. I'd met my father for the first time in such an environment. That meant this was a place Ikelos hadn't shaped. Not yet, at least.

Feeling a surge of triumph, I again willed myself to wake up.

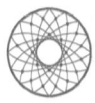

My eyes flew open, a surge of panic stiffening my limbs. The sheets rustled beneath me, and I realised where I was. In my house. In my own bed. The familiar scents of home reached me, replacing the stink of smoke and the cloying scent of honeysuckle: the fresh, white floral aroma of our laundry powder arising from my pillow; the more distant smell of coffee and ... was that *bacon* coming from the kitchen? My mouth watered. *Time to get up, before Jen and Mum eat it all.*

I groaned and stretched like a cat, trying to shake off the befuddled haze of the dream. My limbs felt heavy and tingly, like they were in a post-anaesthetic daze. I stiffened as I remembered the needle in Ewan's hand, Brad slumping against the wall. Had Ewan drugged me? How had I gotten home?

As if summoned by my thought, Brad appeared in the doorway, holding a steaming cup of coffee. Better him than Ewan. "Good morning, sleepyhead," my boyfriend said with a gentle smile, coming into the room and placing the coffee cup on the bedside table. He looked good, and smelled even better when he leaned over to give me a kiss.

"Brad. You're okay!"

"Of course."

"How did I get home?" I asked, struggling to a sitting position and reaching for the cup.

The bed dipped as he sat beside my bent knees. "Constable Nelson got your message. He came for us."

"And Olivia?"

"She's fine."

"Oh. Good." I sipped the coffee. It tasted different than usual: weaker, almost watery. Had he short-changed me on the beans? But I appreciated the gesture. I could get used to coffee in bed. "What happened to Ewan?"

Brad shrugged, running a hand down my calf. Even through the blanket the sensation was delicious. Outside, the wind sighed through the treetops. It sounded almost like the ocean, but the nearest beach was a two-hour drive away. The sound relaxed me, helping the tension seep out of my bones. I was safe. "Nelson's handling it," he said. "How are you feeling?"

"A bit sluggish." I put the coffee back on the side table. I could make a stronger one later. "Did Ewan drug me?"

Brad shook his head, his hand running up my leg towards the knee, leaving me tingling. His dark eyes were smoky as he regarded me. "Jen isn't home," he said with a serious look.

"And Mum?"

"She's asleep," he said.

I glanced at my window; the curtains were drawn but a bright light seeped in around the edges. Daytime. She'd no doubt been up half the night, helping Lacey look for Olivia, worrying about me. Still, disappointment turned my mouth down at the corners.

"She's a very deep sleeper," Brad assured me, his voice husky as he leaned over to kiss me again. Even as his tongue parted my lips, his hand slipped between my knees, pressing against the blanket, against my core. I gasped, a warmth blossoming inside me. "And we can be quiet," Brad added, his lips moving against mine.

"Quiet as church mice," I whispered, lifting one of my sluggish arms to curl my fingers into his hair. Brad would be just the medicine for this lassitude gripping me. He really knew how to wake a girl up.

"Quieter." Brad's hand was still massaging. "Though I love to hear you squeak."

"Squeak?" I protested, sliding back down under the blanket, drawing him after me. "I do not squeak."

"Oh, really?" Brad slid his free hand under my shirt, the fingers brushing up my side to cup the swell of my breast, to lightly pinch my nipple. The other hand stayed where it was, circling slowly. "I bet I can make you squeak. Though I prefer it when you're louder." His eyes twinkled. "When you scream."

I reached for him with a growl, tugging at his shirt, the button of his jeans. I craved his touch, the silken heat of his body against mine as we moved together. *I wish clothes came off as easily as they do in the movies. All these pointless zippers and buckles!*

253

Our clothes were on the floor, and I felt a moment of dizziness as hands that had been struggling with tight denim were suddenly grasping Brad's erect hardness. "Oh, Melaina," Brad groaned as my fingers clenched reflexively in surprise. "I want you so badly."

"I..." I was naked too, and the hand that had massaged against the blanket was now working at the slick core of me. The sensation sent pleasure shooting through me like bursts of light, but something was wrong. Had I ... had I blacked out for a moment?

Brad rolled, pulling me on top of him. I faced the window, and my eyes locked on the narrow strip of light between the curtains. It wasn't just bright; it was white. Fog pressed up against the window pane? But that gusting wind would blow away any fog, wouldn't it?

Oh no. No, no, no.

I was still dreaming.

Propped up on my elbows, I looked down at Brad. He stared up at me, his lips parted and his lids heavy with desire. "I love you."

For a moment, I considered letting the dream run its course. Desire flamed through me. I wanted my boyfriend so badly that I ached to think of it. The sensation of him pressing up against me, waiting for me to ease down onto him, made me almost crazy with lust.

A tiny frown tightened the skin between Brad's brows. "Is everything okay?"

I wanted to kiss that frown away. I wanted to lose myself in him. But this wasn't Brad. And me losing myself ... that was exactly what Ikelos wanted. Me, distracted. Not fighting him for control.

Reaching up, I yanked the curtains open,

half-expecting to see the flame-eyed Oneiroi lurking outside, pressed up against the window like the world's nastiest creeper. But all I saw was the press of white fog marking the edge of the dream.

"Melaina, what's wrong?" The desire on Brad's face faded, replaced by a concern that seemed so real. So very real. My chest clenched with pain. But I couldn't do this with him here.

With my eyes burning, I bent down, kissing him on the lips. I blinked and a tear fell, making a wet circle on the pillow beside his ear. "I'll find you, Brad, I promise."

Brad's chocolate eyes widened. "But I'm right—"

I willed the ephemera that looked like my boyfriend to disappear.

I collapsed onto the sheets on my hands and knees, my heart aching even more than my nether region did at Brad's sudden absence. My throat tightened, but I swallowed the sobs. For a few moments, I'd felt safe and loved. But it hadn't been real.

Wiping savagely at my cheeks with the back of my hand, I re-examined my room with narrowed eyes. Now that I was … undistracted, there were signs that it was a dream, signs other than the watery coffee and the fogbank at my window. The numbers on the clock radio were a nonsense jumble, and the small pile of unpaired socks that usually nested by my dresser was missing. Was there no washing machine sock monster in dreamland, or did Ikelos lack the power or insight to create a truly authentic representation of my house in my dream? It wasn't like he'd seen the original, after all. At least, as far as I knew.

Not wanting to waste yet more of my energy reserves on creating clothes, I slid out of bed and marched to the wardrobe, yanking it open. A glance at the mirror inside the door showed only my reflection. Disappointment surged; even though I was buck naked, I would have been glad to see Leander just then, if he'd get me out of there.

My mouth gaped as I examined the wardrobe's contents. A rack of identical clothes greeted me: knee-length A-line dresses made of a white fabric with butterflies cavorting around the hem: caramel brown, jade green, blue and yellow, and one familiar black and orange one. I barely owned a dress, let alone one covered with butterflies. Curling my lip at the Monarch butterfly, I snatched one of the dresses out and scrambled into it. At least it fit.

My socks and underwear drawers were empty, but the underwear I'd been wearing before was in a neat pile in the corner, where I'd apparently wished it away to during my make-out session with the fake Brad. I couldn't see any socks or my boots, so I spent a thin thread of energy to will them onto my feet. When the room swam for a moment, swaying as if I stood on the deck of a ship, not bland beige carpet, I wondered whether I should have gone barefoot, even if my boots did make me feel more confident.

Too late now.

Clenching my jaw, I stomped out into the corridor, glancing left and right in case the Oneiroi had left nastier delaying tactics than my sexy-arse boyfriend and a lack of shoes. The corridor was empty. To my left, Mum's bedroom door lay open. I glanced inside … and froze.

I expected to see her bedroom: spacious, decorated in cream and soft peppermint tones, about as messy as my own. Instead, the door opened onto another familiar space, albeit one I hadn't seen for a few months—Mum's old room at Wattle Tree Park. The empty king-single bed

was near the door, while her little table crouched underneath the window, its sole chair a lonely sidekick. I drifted towards the window, my gaze caught by something outside. Not a wall of white mist but a dreary, winter-cold garden full of wattle trees and other native shrubs. One of the trees was dying. A chill crept over me.

"Mum?" I murmured, my fingers brushing the glass. The smooth surface was so cold it stung my fingertips, as if I'd trailed them in icy water, and the smell of my mother's perfume tickled my nose. I wanted to smash through the glass, barrel across the frost-covered lawn, and tear her free of that tree prison.

I turned my back on the lie. She wasn't out there.

The lights flickered, plunging the room into blackness. Even the natural light from the window disappeared, though the distant sound of surf pounding on rocks remained. I gasped, taking a step back. The table struck the back of my thighs and—

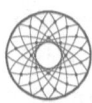

"Melaina?"

"I don't think she can hear you."

"Well, have you got any other bright ideas, moth boy?"

"Not really, no. Melaina?"

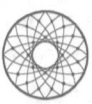

—with a fluorescent hum, the lights flickered to life. The bed was no longer empty. Mum lay on her back, arranged in a pose that reminded me of Olivia's when I'd found her in Ewan's spare room: Snow White in her glass coffin.

With her black hair flowing around her pale face, Mum fit the role even better than Olivia had.

The urge to protect my mother, to cross to her side and brush a loose strand of hair from her cheek, was so strong that I took half a step towards her before I realised I was moving. This was another ephemera, a dreaming figment created to delay and upset me. *Just walk away,* I told myself. *She's not real. Even if her chest is rising and falling with sleep, and she's ... snoring?* What if it really was her?

There was one way to be sure.

Gritting my teeth, I willed my mother out of existence.

The blanket fell onto the sheets with a soft thump and a gentle puff of perfume-scented air. I staggered, catching myself on the bed's chilly metal frame, my grasping fingers knocking a clipboard to the floor with a clatter. Instead of medical records, the clipboard's top sheet was covered with a child's scribbled drawings.

I couldn't keep doing this. If I ran out of energy, I wouldn't be able to fight Ikelos even if I could track him down.

I breathed slowly through my nose, my eyes closed, until the world righted itself and my pulse slowed. I was stronger than this. I had to be. I opened my eyes and marched from the nursing room ward and back into the hallway of my house.

The hallway opened into our tiny kitchen, which was empty of people. I raised my eyebrows, surprised. I'd half expected to find an ephemeral Jen next. The room was rich with the smell of food. Beside the empty stool was a plate heaped with breakfast, ready to eat. Bacon and eggs glistened on perfectly cooked toast, while tomato and avocado were neatly sliced and piled on the side. A

glass of juice, its sides slick with condensation, towered beside the plate.

Hunger stabbed at my belly as though I hadn't eaten for days. But the food's unnatural freshness made me even warier than before. Even if fake Brad had fixed it, it shouldn't have that straight-off-the-hotplate look.

Still, it wouldn't hurt to just grab a quick mouthful, would it? A slice of tomato to go?

I shook my head, narrowing my eyes at the plate of food like it was a slavering blight. This was another trap. Ikelos was getting desperate.

I turned towards the front door, throwing it open. Seeing the fog there, I sighed with relief. It wasn't some other pocket of dream.

Real fog might have drifted in through the open portal. This white mist stayed in a white wall just beyond the threshold.

I stepped into it.

Chapter Twenty-Eight

When I opened my eyes and found I was back in my bed, I swore in a way that would have earned a disapproving tut from my mother and a boxing across the ears from Uncle Ian. *Maybe I'm really awake this time...?*

I studied the room, my scowl growing as that tiny flicker of hope died. The coffee cup was missing. But so too was the clock radio ... and, when I checked beneath the blanket, I discovered I was still wearing the white dress, the hem crumpled from sleep. Several of the butterflies bore creases across their brightly coloured wings.

Growling, I snatched up one of my pillows and hurled it against the wall. Then I buried my face in my hands, struggling to contain the tears searing the back of my eyeballs, the frustration closing my throat. Ikelos had trapped me in a maze. A maze not made up of cultivated hedges or upright logs bound together—I could smash my way out of one of those, even in the real world, or

scale the side. No, this maze was built from pieces of my own subconscious mind. I was sure that, if I could find the middle, I'd find him, squatting like a fat spider at the centre of its web. Only, instead of trying to catch flies, he was trying to steal everything that was me. The webs weren't sticky snares; they were lines of control, slowly spreading, taking over my body, one function at a time. Locking me down while he stole my voice, my ability to walk, to *think*.

I scrambled up and turned to the window, the mattress shifting beneath my toes. My goddamn boots were gone again. Tearing the curtains aside, I saw that same, white-backed glass, blank as a sheet of paper. Hands balled into fists, I smashed it, my arms as powerful as pistons because I willed them to be. Shards of glass flew all around me, scratching my cheek, slicing my toes, and I plunged out the window—

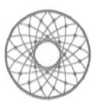

Two voices. "Melaina?"

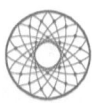

—and woke up in my bed. The window was intact, my face unbloodied. I tried to open my eyes but the lids felt impossibly heavy. I couldn't even twitch a finger, roll my head to the side. *Am I paralysed?* I recalled the syringe in Ewan's hand. It seemed so long ago. *Drugged?* Or was I still sleeping?

Panic fluttered in my chest, my belly. Adrenalin-fuelled energy fizzed along my veins. I directed all of it to opening my eyes. The clock radio was back, but this time the display wasn't jumbled letters but a word, written in blocky lines.

SLEEP

"No." The word came out muffled, as if my mouth was full of cotton wool. My tongue felt huge and dry.

SUBMIT

"What, like an essay or something?" I ground out the words. "I already quit uni." I reached out, shoving the radio to the floor with a crash. "Let. Me. Out!"

Head spinning, belly churning, I staggered upwards again, bracing myself as well as I could on the uneven surface of the bed. I hooked my hands into claws and grabbed the edge of the window frame. Teeth bared, I peeled the window back as if it was a giant sticker pasted over a hole rather than cracking glass and splintering timber. The edges of my vision faded to grey as the last of my energy flowed from me, and I heard Ikelos laughing, felt his webs coiling tighter as I toppled out the window, dizzy, falling—

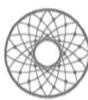

"Melaina!"

—and someone caught me, their warm arms holding me. I was limp, as cold as a corpse. Too cold even to shiver. Was I dead? Could I rest now?

FALSE *Awakening*

Slowly, heat seeped back into me. Awareness returned. I was lying on a bed, my bed, on top of the covers. Brad cradled me from behind, spooning me. I recognised the smell of him. I recognised the freckle on his hand, which rested on my upper arm. I recognised the contours of his body where it pressed against my back, my legs.

"Not again," I moaned, trying to toss his hand away. It might as well have been made of steel for all the effect I had on it.

"Melaina! It's us." Brad stroked my hair back from my face. The tender gesture brought tears to my eyes. I didn't know if I had the energy to banish another ephemera. I was sure I didn't have the willpower. "You're safe now," he murmured.

"Don't lie to her," Leander said. The bed shifted as he sat down on the other side, gazing at me with worried green eyes. His wings hung down behind him, a living cape. His clothes were matt black, a subdued hue that was very unlike him. At least the tight pants and vest were his traditional style. "She's not safe. None of us are."

His words were so frank—so close to my own, despair-tinged thoughts—that they cut through my grief. I stared at him through spikey lashes. "Are you real?" I whispered.

"As real as I always am." A smile quirked the corner of his lips.

"How can I believe you?" I said with an unladylike sniff. "That's what an ephemera would say."

"Will me away."

"I don't have the energy." A sigh slipped out of me. I knew I sounded pathetic, and I hated it. But I was so, so tired.

Leander leaned down, reaching past Brad's hand to lay his fingertips on my cheek. The touch was as gentle as the brush of a moth's wing, as warm as a candle flame just out of reach ... and with it came a thin thread of energy, trickling into me like molten silver. It didn't fill the void completely, but it helped. The despair receded. My eyes widened, and Leander nodded, seeing my realisation.

But I had to be sure. I closed my eyes and willed both Leander and Brad to vanish.

They didn't.

"You're really here!" I turned, kissing Brad fiercely, before leaping up and throwing myself into Leander's arms. His returning hug was gentle, unsure. "How did you find me?"

"I'm an Oneiroi," Leander said as I sat back, gripping Brad's hand. My boyfriend propped his head up on his other hand so he could see both me and Leander as the Oneiroi spoke. "I don't need to be near a person in the real world to find their dreams."

"So you haven't found my body?" My stomach sank.

Leander shook his head, his lips pressing together in a thin line.

"Then how are *you* here?" I asked Brad. He was, I saw with relief, wearing full-length striped pyjamas. I wasn't sure I could handle the awkwardness of seeing him naked with Leander sitting right there beside us. I might self-combust on the spot.

"Leander brought me into your dream." Brad regarded my clothes with a bemused expression of his own. I was still wearing the damned white butterfly dress.

"But why? Please don't take this the wrong way, Brad, but I know bringing you in isn't exactly energy efficient."

I raised my eyebrows at Leander. "Aren't you burning energy we could've used to fight Ikelos?"

"I needed his help," Leander said with a theatrical sigh.

"He found your dream," Brad added, his expression a trifle smug, "but Ikelos had shielded it, and Leander needed help getting through. Apparently, your subconscious trusts me more than him."

"Oh." I looked from one man to the other, feeling like I should be embarrassed or worried. But the tension I'd felt between them the first time they'd met seemed to be gone. Maybe breaking into my mind had helped them to bond. I wasn't sure whether to be pleased or horrified.

"The upshot is that Ikelos and Ewan still have you, and we don't know where," Brad continued, his expression grim. "Nelson is doing his best to find you, but I think he's floundering. Do you have any sense of where you might be?"

"None." I scrunched the portion of hem over my knee up in my hand, hiding the Monarch butterfly from view. I would have willed it away but didn't want to squander the energy Leander had spared for me. "The one time I came close to consciousness, I was lying on the back seat of a car, but I couldn't move. I didn't get a look out the window. The only other thing I've noticed ... well, it might not be relevant, but that ocean noise? It doesn't seem to fit with the rest of my dream."

"Ocean noise?" Leander tipped his head to the side.

"Yeah, you know? Surf pounding on rocks, waves on sand?" The sound had been present since the first time I'd dreamed of waking in my house; it was so constant I'd almost grown used to it.

"I know what it sounds like," the Oneiroi said, exasperated. "You can hear the ocean now?"

I nodded. "You can't?"

"No," Leander said.

Brad shook his head. "Me neither. Is it possible it's something you're hearing in the real world?"

"Maybe. You think Ewan's taken me to the coast for a holiday?" I tried to force a laugh, but it fell flat.

Leander looked at Brad, who shook his head, sitting up straight and wrapping his arms around my shoulders. "No. Nuh-uh. We just found her. I'm not leaving."

"You're the only one who can tell Nelson." Leander leaned forward. "Perhaps Ewan has a property at the beach."

"On a nurse's salary?" Brad said with a snort.

"Or maybe he has a relative who owns a holiday home," Leander pressed. "Brad, you *have* to go. If I've taken your dreaming mind so far from your body ... well, it might not be safe."

A chill crept over me. I eased myself out of Brad's arms, turning so I could see his expression. "Brad, where are you?"

"Asleep in your bed, actually." Brad looked around the dream equivalent with a critical eye. Was he noticing the subtle differences too? "But don't worry about it. Jen's looking after me. And I'm not leaving."

"Actually, you are," Leander said.

Brad's eyes narrowed, his jaw tightening as he stared at the Oneiroi. "You're going to kick me out?"

"If I have to." Leander crossed his arms and squared his shoulders, his wings rustling together behind him. Then he glanced at me and his expression softened. "But

I'd rather have your agreement. If you won't do it for your own sake, do it for Melaina's. The longer Ikelos possesses her ... well. Let's just say that this tiny corner of dream we're in is small and getting smaller."

My skin prickled and the room seemed to grow darker. I was unsure whether it really was, or if it was just my panic. Of course, here, the latter could cause the former as easily as the other way around. "What happens when it vanishes?" I said, my voice shaking a little.

Beside me, Brad's mutinous look faded. He prised my fingers from around the hem of my skirt, taking my hand in his again.

"I don't know for sure." Leander's gaze slid away from mine to regard the blank cupboard door behind me.

"But you have a theory," I said. "Tell me. Please?"

"Best-case scenario? You will remain, but he'll have complete control over your body and mind whenever he wants it. He'll be able to slip in and take over at any time."

"Oh."

"There's more." Leander wouldn't meet my eye. "He might still want to breed himself a half-Oneiroi, lucid-dreaming offspring. He's never been one to be satisfied with the power he has. An army of Oneiroi-controllable humans who he can send anywhere? Who he can offer to other Oneiroi to possess in exchange for their fealty? That's something he'd definitely be interested in." He swallowed, his Adam's apple bobbing. "So once he has established control of you, he may go after Olivia again. Or..."

Brad swore.

"Not or. *And.* He'll do both," I whispered, afraid that if I spoke any louder I'd throw up all over myself. "Go after Olivia and ... and give me to Ewan."

"We won't let that happen," Leander promised, shuffling across the bed so that he was right in front of me, his wings spread wide. With Brad to my side, I felt a little bit safer—but the icy feeling in the pit of my stomach remained. I remembered Ewan taking the opportunity to grope me while he was retrieving my phone. I had no doubt he'd do as Ikelos demanded, and gleefully.

"I've been trying to break free." I clutched at Leander's arm with my free hand. "He's too strong for me."

"But not for us," Leander promised.

"That's why I need to stay," Brad said, a desperate note to his voice. "I can help you."

"No, you can't, and you know it," Leander said. "You being here is costing me energy I could be using to help Melaina. You got me in and I'm grateful for that, but you need to go. Get Nelson to investigate where Ewan might be holding her. Think of it as a two-pronged attack: us in Erebus and you in your world."

Brad stared at me, his heart in his eyes. "Melaina, I..."

"I know." I slid both arms around his waist and leaned my head on his shoulder. I didn't want him to go either. What if I never saw him again? But if I—my body—really was at the coast, that meant Leander had dragged Brad's mind at least one-hundred-and-fifty kilometres from Canberra. That couldn't be good for him. I swallowed and said, "But what Leander's saying makes sense. Just ... make sure Nelson finds me."

"I love you," Brad whispered into my hair, clutching me against him. "Come back to me."

"I will." I laughed, hating how mirthless it sounded. "Make sure I have somewhere to come back to."

I didn't want to let go of Brad. From the ferocity with which he clung to me, I knew he didn't want me to either. Finally, Leander cleared his throat and I withdrew, wiping my eyes with the back of my hand. "Before I go," Brad said, looking past me to meet the Oneiroi's gaze, "is there anything I can do to give Melaina some of my energy, like you did? To help her against Ikelos?"

I opened my eyes wide, shaking my head at Leander. *Say no*, my expression said. Brad would need everything he had to make sure he got back to his own body in one piece.

"Yes," Leander said. I glared at him, and he grimaced. "But not too much. We need you to wake up too, remember?"

"Fine. How do I do it?"

"Give me your hand." Leander held his own hand out, palm up. Brad gripped it, and Leander held out his other hand to me. When I hesitated, both men scowled at me, their faces wearing an identical look of impatience: brown eyes and green narrowed, brows furrowed, lips pressed together.

I realised in that moment that I loved them both. Not in the same way, no; my feelings for Brad blazed as hot as an autumn bonfire, while those for Leander were closer to the comfortable heat given off by a smouldering log in a bed of embers. But I *did* love them. With my heart flipping in my chest, I reached for Leander's hand with one of mine, taking Brad's free one in the other so that we formed a triangle.

"What's that smile for?" Brad asked me.

"Nothing," I said. I hadn't even realised I was smiling. "Just remember, don't give me too much."

"I won't," the two of them said together, before sharing a self-conscious laugh.

"Ready?" Leander added.

Brad and I nodded.

For a moment, nothing happened. Then Brad's lips parted in a gasp, showing me a glimpse of his teeth. His pupils dilated, and his fingers clenched in mine. I glanced at Leander, worried something was wrong, but the Oneiroi was serene beside me, his legs crossed and his eyes closed, long lashes brushing his cheeks.

The power flowed into me, and I forgot to worry.

Leander's energy was usually starlight silver. It tasted like cold spring water, tangy with minerals. It smelled like snow under wan sunlight. But now it was tinged with green: the same snow, only in the dappled shade of a pine forest. Airy and cool, woody and brisk. Was that what Brad's energy, his spirit, felt like? Surprise thrilled through me. I'd assumed he'd be the sweet, smoky brown of expensive chocolate or the invigorating aroma of coffee.

I'd gotten the invigorating part right, at least. As the power flowed into me, my skin tingled and my senses expanded until I felt like I could float away. Slowly, Brad's lids drooped, his lips going slack and full. I'd seen that sleepy, satisfied look on his face before ... but never in the company of others. A blush burned my cheeks.

"That's enough." I squeezed Leander's hand to bring his attention to me.

Leander's eyes flew open, and he regarded me with surprise. The tips of his ears flushed red and the flow of energy stopped. Beside us, Brad's head lolled to the side. "Leander," I said, exasperated, gesturing to Brad with the hand whose fingers intertwined with his—though I

didn't let go. "You can't send him back to his body like this. He'll sleep for a week!"

"I…" Leander blinked at Brad. "You're right." He frowned, and slowly Brad roused, as if from sleep. Leander was giving some of his own energy back to Brad; I was sure of it. It was a curious sensation, like feeling the flow of a river through the soles of your shoes when you were standing beside it. The power didn't pass through me, but it shivered my bones regardless.

"Is it done?" Brad blinked sleepily, looking between me and Leander. A frown pinched his brow. "What?"

"Nothing." Leander released both Brad's and my hands, shuffling back so far that I worried he'd fall off the edge of the bed. "It's done," he added, rubbing his hands on his pants.

I rolled my eyes and turned to Brad, placing my palms on his cheeks and kissing him full on the lips. "Thank you. Now, make sure you go straight home, young man," I teased. "No going past the mall to hang out with your friends."

"Yes, ma'am," he said with a grin that quickly faded. "Though I'm not sure how to get there."

"Can you take him back to his own dreams, Leander?" I asked.

The Oneiroi shook his head. "If I leave you, I might not be able to find my way back in again. But I can help… Here." He stretched out awkwardly from his position on the edge of the bed, gripping Brad's shoulder. "Close your eyes. Can you see the thread?"

"Yes." Brad's hand waved in the air beside him, fingers outstretched and running from his chest in a straight line out the bedroom door. "It's pretty. Reminds me of a field of grass blowing in the wind. Shimmery."

"I can see that," Leander said, nodding. "Now, follow the cord. It will lead you back to yourself. And remember, tell Nelson about the beach."

"Okay..." And, without opening his eyes or saying goodbye, Brad faded from view. The only sign he'd been there was a depression in the blanket where he'd been sitting.

Taking a deep, trembling breath, I exhaled through my teeth. Would I ever see him again? I jumped, startled, when Leander's hand slipped into my own. "You'll be back with him in no time." His gaze was intent on my face.

"You..." My throat felt tight, like someone was squeezing my windpipe closed. I swallowed and tried again. "You can't promise that."

"I just did."

"Hey, what was that all about before, with the energy transfer? You looked like—"

Leander swivelled on the bed, standing and rolling his shoulders back. "Never mind that now. Let's go serve Ikelos his eviction notice."

"If you say so." I grinned.

Chapter Twenty-Nine

I wriggled my bare toes on the carpet and smoothed the rumpled hem of my dress. Now I was full of swirly silver and green energy, Leander-filtered Brad-y goodness, I considered willing the dress to change into something more suited to my style. But I'd need every scrap of energy I could muster. The fact my boots were gone again, lost in the transition between dreams, irritated me. I'd paid good power for those.

Leander regarded me strangely, looking me up and down.

"What?" I said. "I know, dresses aren't my thing, and my legs are milk-bottle white, but…"

"It's not that," Leander said. "It's the butterfly pattern."

I wrinkled my nose. "It's so cutesy I might die," I admitted. "I figure either my subconscious had butterflies on the brain or Ikelos is trolling me. Or both. It could be both."

"And not a single moth among them." He pressed his hand to his chest. "I'm hurt."

"Speaking of moths, where are the other Oneiroi? You mentioned the Morpheus left others as reinforcements."

"He did." Leander edged around me, the tips of his wings tickling the tops of my feet, and strode to the door. He leaned out, peering into the corridor. "But I ... well, I couldn't get Brad's help if they were with me. Not without them reporting me to the Morpheus." His voice grew sombre. "I would have been happy to be reported if they'd have helped you first, like I did with Ollie and your mother. But I know these people. They're sticklers for the rules."

"It's okay," I said, my voice soft. "You wouldn't be much good to me in jail. But ... could we get them in now he's gone? Send up a Bat-Signal?"

"A what?" Leander glanced at me over his shoulder.

"A Bat-Signal. You know. A request for help that can be traced back to the source, like a beam of light at night. Think of a lighthouse, only ... bat-shaped."

"Oh. Right." Leander scratched behind his ear. "Unfortunately, the void of Erebus isn't good at carrying a signal. It must be the lack of bats." He said this last part with a dead serious expression that made me think he was teasing me.

I wrinkled my nose at him, deciding not to take the bait. "So can we do it? I mean, I can see the light of dreaming minds from a distance through Erebus. Clearly, something can get through, even if it's just light waves."

He turned towards me. "What you're seeing is your own mind's interpretation of—"

"Uh huh," I interrupted. "Can you do it?"

"Yes. I think so." He hesitated. "Maybe."

"Maybe" wasn't very reassuring, but I didn't think we had a choice. I'd seen Leander go up against Ikelos before,

and that had been when my friend had been at full strength, with my father at his side. They'd been creamed, trussed up and tortured before I could do anything to stop it. Now, when we were both sub-par? I'd take a maybe chance of reinforcements. "What do you need?"

"We have to find the perimeter of your dreams." He paused, lifting his nose like a dog scenting the air. "This way."

To my surprise, he didn't lead me towards the front door of the house, or even the laundry; instead, we hurried into Mum's room. Dreams often reset themselves, especially traumatic ones, and I braced myself for the sight of her in the nursing home bed, but it remained empty.

How could you so casually destroy me?

The thought, spoken in Mum's voice, was so filled with pain that I took an involuntary step towards the bed. "I didn't," I said. "You weren't real."

I felt real. That's how I know how much your betrayal hurts.

"Melaina?" Leander stood by the window. Behind him, the pane of glass had vanished; he must have willed it away rather than smashing it. Cold air from the winter garden flowed in like a tide, an invisible wall of ice that set goosebumps to prickle at my flesh. "Are you alright?"

"I'm fine." I rubbed my temples with my fingertips. "Just a guilty conscience."

You could bring me back again, Mum's voice suggested. *Will me back from the void. Please. It's so dark here.*

Gritting my teeth, I hurried to Leander's side. "Or maybe not," I said. "I think Ikelos is messing with me."

"How?"

"I'm hearing things." I leaned against the table, taking

a deep breath. "Thoughts designed to delay us."

"Good." Leander brushed the outside of my arm, his palm as warm as an electric blanket on a cold night. "That means we're on the right track. Ikelos is afraid."

He's not afraid of anything, Mum spat in my head.

"I think you're right." I smirked.

"Still," Leander said, "let me know if it gets too bad."

I lifted my chin. "I've got this."

"Give me a bit of space," he said. Even though I knew it was silly, I scooted back onto the desk rather than crossing back to the bed, as if that would keep Ikelos out of my thoughts. Leander folded his wings back so they stuck out, horizontal to the ground, before climbing through the window frame and into the nursing home garden. Shivering, I hurried after him.

From inside the room, the garden had looked cold, but at least the sun had been up to give the day a veneer of warmth. Now, as my feet hit the ground, crunching on frost-covered grass that was slick and sharp against my soles, night fell. The transition was as fast as a Hollywood scene change, the sun sliding from the sky and stars winking to life around us. I half expected to see the moon float into the air like an escaped balloon, but the heavens remained moonless.

Leander turned at my sudden hiss of breath, taking in my summery clothing with a frown. "Don't waste energy on it," I said before he could do anything extravagant, hugging my arms across the front of my chest. "That's what he wants you to do."

"You're no good to me if you're frozen to death."

"I'm not. I'm at the beach, remember?" My teeth didn't seem convinced; the words came out chopped into little

pieces by chattering.

Making a curious sound that was half laugh and half snort, Leander returned to my side. Before I could object, he picked me up, one arm beneath my knees and the other behind my back. My breath huffed out and I hesitated, debating whether to struggle. But my feet no longer felt like I was walking on knives, and Leander's arms were warm through the thin fabric of my stupid dress. Did he carry a bubble of heat around with him, or was he spending a tiny bit of energy to project a sphere of warmth for my benefit? As my shivering subsided, I decided not to ask.

Instead, all I did was raise my eyebrows at him. "You're loving this whole damsel-in-distress thing, aren't you?"

"I'd prefer you in your kick-butt boots and warm clothes to a dress," Leander said, the muscles in the arm I could see flexing as he held me tight against his chest. He seemed distracted, his face turned upwards. Thankfully, he didn't notice me ogling him. "Brace yourself," he added.

That, and the flaring of his wings, was all the warning I got before he launched both of us into the midnight sky.

The gardens were a frost-covered fairytale beneath us as we broke through the trees, paths lit by in-ground lamps whose candlelight-yellow glow flickered and danced. The trees swayed and sighed in a breeze I couldn't feel. Seasonally inappropriate wattle blooms like tiny yellow pompoms sent forth a scent that was what would happen if a rose and a lavender gave birth to a perfumed baby: sweet, relaxing, rich, fresh.

The scene was so picturesque and enticing that I wanted to ask Leander to land. We could conjure up warm clothes and hot cocoa and then wander the winding paths. I even opened my mouth to suggest it ... and then closed it with a snap of teeth, tearing my gaze away. Wattle never smelled that good in real life. And those path lights were meant to be electric. "Sod off, Ikelos," I muttered, looking up at the star-strewn sky instead. That seemed to be where Leander was headed, not across the wall but straight up. His gaze was fixed on those distant stars, his face showing no hint of strain though my long-limbed frame wasn't exactly feather-light.

As if triggered by my thought, Leander grunted with surprise and we dipped in the air. I clutched at his vest for a moment before releasing it, embarrassed. "What's going on?" I asked as sudden perspiration beaded his forehead.

"Don't know. You just got..." He paused, apparently thinking better of what he'd been about to say. "Don't know."

I just got heavier. I felt lopsided in his arms, like something was pulling me—us—downward.

Something *was* pulling me downward. I peered towards the ground, ignoring the spin of vertigo, and saw that a part of my dress hem was hanging straight down, as if someone had sewn lead into the fabric. At the heaviest point, dragging us lower, was the Monarch butterfly. I swore.

"What is it?" Leander said between puffing breaths. His shoulder muscles, already well-defined, now bulged with the strain of keeping us steady in the air. We'd stopped climbing higher.

"Ikelos is playing silly buggers," I said. "Do you have a knife?"

"What? No. Want me to make one?"

FALSE Awakening

I shook my head. "All good." Leaning to the side, I grabbed the hem just above the butterfly, gripping the fabric in my fist.

Melaina, look out! Mum's voice cried. My gaze snapped to the ground and I saw—really saw—how high Leander had carried us. The home's gardens were still picturesque, but now they were also distressingly far away, like a postcard photograph taken from a helicopter. My own helplessness crawled into my throat, sharp and bitter with fear.

Get him to land before you fall, Mum begged.

"We're on the right track." I swallowed the panic, closing my eyes. "Ikelos is getting shrill."

Shrill?!

I could have created a knife—in the same way I could have flown if Leander had dropped me, which was how I knew the panic was irrational. It would be expensive, but I could do it. Still, there were cheaper ways to rid myself of the leaden butterfly, and hopefully of my faux mother.

I reminded the fabric of how thin it really was, especially in a contoured line around the Monarch. The reminder was backed by a needle-thin sliver of energy.

It was enough. The dress fabric parted with a tearing sound. I opened my eyes in time to see the fabric butterfly plummet towards the earth like a dropped rock—exactly the way a piece of fabric shouldn't. Leander and I shot upwards as his powerfully beating wings no longer had to strain so hard to bear us higher.

A glance at what remained of my dress told me it was only missing a piece about as large as my hand with my fingers spread. Relief flooded through me. I'd worried I'd be naked from the waist down.

"We're here," Leander said, glancing at me before hastily returning his gaze to the starlit heavens. They seemed to flicker, like real stars … but it wasn't the planet's atmosphere generating that effect. It was the edge of my own dreaming mind, an invisible curtain, creating the illusion. I couldn't detect the boundary in any other way and wondered how Leander had done so.

"How close are we?" I asked, regarding the dreaming minds warily. I'd been out there before, with Leander and my father. It had been beautiful. But another hadn't been vying for control of my mind at the time. Now, embracing that sparkly vista seemed like … surrender.

"Close enough." Leander's voice rumbled in my ear. His wings had fallen still and we hovered, a kite cradled on an updraft. The ocean sounded closer now; I almost imagined I could smell the tang of salt water. "If you reach out your hand, you can touch the edge."

I shuddered. "So … about that Bat-Signal?"

"Right. What we're going to do is make your mind glow brighter than it does now, so it washes out the light of all these other dreams."

"You told me once that I glow pretty bright already." What he'd actually said was that I was a bonfire surrounded by fireflies. The memory sent a curl of warmth through my chest, and my thoughts flashed back to sitting on my bed, holding hands with Brad and Leander.

"It does, but we need it to be brighter. Think of the sun during the day. It's a star, but its light hides all the other stars from view. You will be a beacon to the other Oneiroi, a sign that Ikelos is hiding here. They won't be able to ignore it."

I hesitated. "Won't that also attract blights?"

"Blights require a physical infection, and there's no way Ikelos would let that happen. He's not looking to share you with another possessing creature. He doesn't play well with others."

"Mara then?" I persisted. The idea of posting an "open home" sign for all to see suddenly didn't seem like such a great idea. Was this Ikelos's hesitation, I wondered, or my own? Could he be that subtle?

Leander shrugged, the gesture lifting me against him. "I'd rather deal with Ikelos and the mara with reinforcements than just Ikelos without reinforcements. Mara aren't so bad if they haven't been given a boost by an Oneiroi and, again, Ikelos has no reason to do that. He's trying to take over your mind, not kill you."

"That's reassuring ... I think." I shoved my hesitation aside. I'd known this was the plan. I'd suggested it. There was no sense in backing out now. Besides, what alternative did we have? "Let's do it."

"Stretch out your hand until you feel resistance."

I extended the arm that wasn't pressed against Leander's chest, willing it not to tremble as I reached past his face and brushed the sky. The resistance presented by the barrier was so faint I barely noticed it, similar to the feeling of tension on the surface of a crystal-clear pond. The only sign the tips of my fingers had broken through was the way that the stars in the distance wavered and danced, distorted as if they were pebbles on the bottom of that pond. Beyond the barrier, my fingers felt a little warmer than the rest of my hand. "Now what?"

He hesitated. "I've never tried this before," he admitted. "But try imagining the edge of your dream glowing as brightly as the sun."

I closed my eyes, imagining myself turning up a dimmer switch in a darkened room. *Come find me, Oneiroi! Come fetch your exile out of my head. I don't want him.* Energy flowed up my arm, sparking and dancing like static electricity, draining out of the reservoir Brad and Leander had given me. I grew weaker by the second.

I'd hoarded the power for this reason, to use it against Ikelos ... but the idea of letting that final piece of Brad and Leander go made me ache with despair. And so, greedily, I kept a small piece for myself. Not enough to make a difference—a single glowing coal after the heat of a fire. It warmed my heart.

When I opened my eyes, I expected to see the heavens ablaze with light. But the sky was unchanged. "Did it work?"

Leander frowned. His hair brushed against the inside of my arm as he shook his head. "No." He looked around, desperation filling his voice. "It should have. I was so sure. Maybe ... maybe Ikelos is blocking it? Absorbing it?"

I followed his gaze. The creeping sense of surface tension, the edge of my dream, had eased down my fingers, from their tips to the middle of my palm. "The bubble's getting smaller, isn't it?" I'd known it was—Leander had told me so—but *feeling* it shrink around me, a tightening noose, filled me with dread.

"You have to try again," Leander begged, his eyes mirroring my fear back at me.

"I have barely anything left," I whispered. He seemed to blur, and I didn't know whether it was because of the sudden rush of fatigue or because my eyes had flooded with tears. "Leander, I'm sorry. I can't do it."

"Of course you can," Leander said, and I felt energy flow into me from all the places where he touched me:

down my arm, across my back, along the back of my knees. Compared to what I'd spent, the quantity of power was a thimbleful. He was running low too. If his wings hadn't been a part of him, we'd have tumbled to Earth. Sudden fatigue scribbled shadows beneath his eyes.

"Stop it," I demanded. "You have to go, fetch the Oneiroi back here. I'll ... I'll hold him off till you return."

"We don't have time," Leander said. "You know we don't. Please, Melaina, try it again."

"I..." I didn't know what else to try. Usually, picturing what I wanted and spending some power on it was enough to get it done. I'd turned that stupid dimmer switch up to eleven. It hadn't worked. What else could I try?

Nothing. This is the end.

My gaze dropped from Leander's eyes to his lips. If I was going to die here, or be forever imprisoned in my mind while Ikelos strutted around in my body, I would at least have this memory to sustain me.

Before I could think it through, I pulled my arm backwards, from where it was pressed between Leander and myself, and slid it around his back, between the strong line of his wings. My traitorous fingers curled in that hair, so soft and silky, and I drew his head down to mine. Slowly, so he could pull back if he wanted to.

He didn't want to. Our lips met not in a crash but in a tender kiss, as gentle as anything I'd ever felt. He exhaled a soft *oh* against me, and kissed me deeper, his tongue flickering against mine as we tentatively opened our mouths to one another. A fire roared to life within me, ignited by that single ember of Brad-and-Leander coal and fuelled by my desire for the Oneiroi. A desire I'd carried for years but only today acknowledged. His fingers tightened around me, pressing into my ribs and thigh, and I kissed him harder, stoking those flames higher.

My other hand trailed above us, drifting on the surface of a pond. As Leander clutched me and we kissed, I sent that roaring flame out into my dreams. I wasn't clinically adjusting a switch. I was burning with desire, with love, and even, yes, with the heat of shame at what Brad might say when I told him, because of course I would tell him … if I lived long enough.

My eyelids had drifted shut as we kissed, and I only realised something had changed when a brightness pressed against them, green and silver and blue, shifting like the aurora australis.

My eyes flew open. Leander's face filled my vision, the flecks of gold in his green eyes clear and sparkling as he stared at me, his expression full of a hundred storming emotions. Light haloed his head. The sky above us burned, shifting between emerald, sapphire and diamond hues, the stars no longer visible.

"Told you that you could do it," he said, his lips moving against mine.

"No!" a voice howled. It came from everywhere and nowhere. It was inside me and all around me, crawling into every corner of my being. I clutched my ears to block out the atonal reverberation, though the gesture didn't help. Leander's cry was barely audible, despite coming from right beside me.

A wall of wind knocked us towards the ground, a slap from a spiteful child.

Chapter Thirty

The world spun around us—light above, darkness below, and then the reverse. Leander spread his wings with a snap and then screamed as they were torn back. The sound seared my soul.

We crashed into a stand of wattle trees rather than the hard earth or the frozen concrete of the path. Twigs tore at my skin, my hair. Small, spikey leaves pricked me like needles. The air whooshed from my lungs as a branch caught me across the stomach, my body folding around it.

"Leander," I gasped as soon as I was able, staring around me. The world seemed to tip and slide. I blinked, trying to clear my vision. Above me, the branches clattered in the wind, but I thought I heard my name, a thread of pain running through it. "Leander?"

There, on the other side of the rough-barked trunk. Was that him? A flash of pale grey, a shadow blacker than the dappled light weaving beneath the trees. I slid from my branch, reaching for the earth with my bare toes, and wobbled around the trunk. Moving hurt: I was all bruise, the deep pain accented by the stinging of a dozen cuts.

But when I saw Leander, I forgot about my injuries. He'd hit the same tree, but hadn't been as fortunate as me. A long branch, stripped of leaves, protruded wetly from his shoulder. One wing was pinned at an awkward angle behind him, calling to mind uncomfortable memories of dead moths on display in glass frames. His other hand clutched at the protruding branch, his fingers stained dark. The tang of blood and the spicy-sweet, true scent of the wattle blooms filled my senses. Bile flooded my throat.

"Ouch." Leander forced a smile.

"Oh god." I reached out a trembling hand, brushing his hair back from his clammy face. "We have to get you down from there so I can heal you."

"No." Leander shook his head before biting his lip, probably to contain a gasp of pain. "Ikelos is coming. You have to hide until the others get here."

"I'm not leaving you."

"But—"

"No!" I reached for the trunk, splaying my fingers against the rough surface. Leander was too heavy for me to lift, but there was another way to get him down. "Help me," I begged the tree, feeding it a thread of my hoarded energy. The tree quivered in response, and I ignored my dizziness and reached for Leander, steadying him as the branch dipped, lowering him slowly. When his feet touched the ground beside mine, the branch snapped cleanly from the trunk, adding the sticky scent of sap to the iron tang of blood.

FALSE Awakening

Leander sagged against me, and I staggered into the trunk under his weight, adding yet another scrape to my collection. "Steady." I helped him sit with his uninjured shoulder against the tree. "We need to get that branch out of you."

Before I could command the dream to help, Leander's jaw tensed, and then he reached behind his back and yanked. The branch seemed to come away cleanly and with a wet sound, though I couldn't help but wonder where all those leaves had gone. Were they still inside him? Nausea churned in my belly.

With his face grey, Leander closed his eyes. "Ouch," he said again; this time the word was barely a whisper. Behind him, the branch thumped to the ground.

I wasn't sure what would happen if I spent my last store of power healing Leander. Normally, if I ran out of power in someone else's dream, I was shoved back into my own head until I recuperated. I'd never run out of power in my own dream before. Until today, until Ikelos had moved in and rearranged the furniture, I'd never had to pay to make changes to my dreams. Would I be kicked out of my own mind? Would it give Ikelos free rein to take over everything that I was?

At that moment, seeing Leander bloody and helpless, I didn't care.

I knelt beside him, placing my hand over the wound. *Heal*, I told it, pouring what power I had left into his body. As I did so, Leander reached for me, brushing a finger along a stinging cut at my temple.

And a curious thing happened. I felt the energy flow out of me, sensed its absence even as the wound began to close. But, at the same time, Leander's silvery power flowed back into me. My skin tingled as my cuts healed; the deep bruise at my stomach twinged and then fell silent. I frowned at him and he stared back at me, a tiny smile curving his lips. His fingertips glistened with blood from my cut even as my hand was covered in his blood.

I opened my mouth to swear at him, call him an idiot ... but then the energy changed colour, took on a green tint that was Brad's and a blue tint that was mine. It was the power I'd just poured into him to heal his wounds. It should have been spent, gone forever. But it wasn't. His eyes widened with realisation as I gave him back that blended mix. We'd created a perfect loop between us, where we could repair our bodies and no energy was spent.

It wasn't as much power as I was used to, and I doubted I could change the rest of the dream and have the same effect as I was having on him. But it was better than nothing. I took Leander's bloodstained hand with my own, afraid to let the link be severed in case we couldn't recreate it. "Come on," I said, urging him to his feet. "We need to bunker down before—"

The top of the tree we were sheltering beneath exploded, showering us with shards. A huge face peered down: a face with burning eyes and surrounded by wild black hair that danced like Medusa's snakes. Huge wings flared, almost blocking out the sky—but the light Leander and I had ignited still burned, opalescent, at the edges.

"Oh, shit," I whispered. Ikelos had clearly been watching monster movies; he was the size of a giant, and just as bad tempered. "Run!"

We set off through the home's grounds, darting this way and that as Ikelos took swipes with a giant fist, obliterating trees and pounding bath-sized craters into

the earth. I hoped he got a splinter. I hoped the seeming randomness of his attacks meant he didn't know where we were, rather than that we were being herded.

With the circuit of energy flowing like a river between Leander and me, I didn't grow tired. My breath didn't ache in my lungs and, when a flying branch scored my arm, the cut healed instantly. But we couldn't hide forever. We skidded to a stop when we reached the edge of the trees, a wide stretch of grass and path between us and the wall of the nursing home. If we went out there, Ikelos would spot us in an instant.

"We have to fly. We'll be harder to hit," Leander urged me, flaring his wings and preparing to scoop me up.

I shook my head, taking a half-step backwards. "No. If we go up there it's a matter of time till he gets lucky. We don't have the energy to fight him. We have to hide."

"Where?"

I looked around. The stand of trees behind us was being rapidly reduced to kindling. We couldn't get to the nursing home and back into my house without being spotted. Up was out; we'd be swatted like bugs. *Again.* That left ... "How about down the rabbit hole?" I gestured between the snarled roots of a tree, begging my dream to provide us a means of escape.

I staggered against Leander, who also wavered as our mutual reserves were sapped. But, sure enough, light began to glow from between the roots: the steady, dusty yellow light of an old electric bulb. Peering down, I spied a space both familiar and strange—my old dorm room from boarding school, minus the door and window and with a scattering of dirt on the desk beneath us. A neat little burrow with a single bed and a closet full of school uniforms that wouldn't fit me anymore.

Beyond the trees, the crashing sounds of Ikelos's tantrum increased in tempo, growing abruptly closer.

"He felt the change to the dream." Leander's voice was tight with urgency. "Get down there, quick!"

I turned, sliding along the grassy lip, dislodging another shower of dirt as I slid onto the desk. Tiny stones plinked against the wood varnish and the tops of my feet. Leander leaned down and planted a quick kiss on my upturned face.

"Be safe, love," he said. And he let go of my hand.

"Leander, no!" I lunged for him, trying to grab his leg, his ankle. To pull him down to hide with me. But he hopped out of reach, past the tree line and into the air. Looking through the grass that was now level with my eyes, I saw him fly up, weaving erratically to dodge a sudden blow from a huge fist. And he wasn't alone: he held me in his arms, cradling me much as he'd done before. I rubbed my eyes and looked again. Yes, that was my bare foot, my tattered white dress.

He'd projected an illusion of me and was leading Ikelos away. I knew how little energy he had left. He was practically defenceless; the only thing that remained to him was his agility as he darted to and fro, distance rendering him small. His wings were no longer grey but instead reflected the light of the sky above. He looked like a butterfly, like a member of one of the most powerful Oneiroi bloodlines. Like a prince.

"You're too late," Ikelos bellowed, his voice so loud that another shower of dirt fell, dusting my feet and calves and staining the hem of my dress. "Another few minutes and these dreams will be mine."

With my heart in my mouth and my ears ringing from the Oneiroi's roar, I stared up at the shimmering arch of sky that was the boundary of my mind. It looked as far away as ever … but the top of it was brushing Ikelos's madly twisting hair. Had it been doing that before?

It hadn't. I knew it. I had to do something. I wouldn't die, hiding in a room that had been my sanctuary as a teen but was now a dead end. An oversized coffin. Panic clawed at my throat as I scrabbled at the crumbling lip of grass and dirt, planting my forearms in the soil and heaving myself upwards. My toes clawed at the dorm room's wall, tearing a shred of paper from a forgotten band poster. My upper body strength *sucked.*

I was half out of the hole when Ikelos roared, a sound filled with triumph. My heart froze in my chest as I looked up. He'd caught Leander, caging my friend between the fingers of his hands as if Leander really was a butterfly, one he'd snatched out of the air. Slowly, Ikelos brought his palms together, peering between his fingers, presumably to watch as Leander struggled against being crushed.

The howl of fury that followed told me the exact moment that Ikelos realised he didn't have me trapped too. He smashed his hands together so hard the sound cracked like thunder, echoing off the nursing home wall behind me. The world seemed to tilt sideways and the colours to fade as something limp and grey tumbled from Ikelos's hands, shaken away with the same indifference as I'd flick drops of water from my fingers after washing up.

"Leander!" I scrambled the rest of the way from my hole, reeling and weeping as I ran across the grass towards the place where Leander had landed, smashing a park bench into shards. I expected a huge foot to stomp down on me at any moment. The ground continued to shake and Ikelos continued to roar, but I made it to Leander's side unharmed.

The sight of him with a branch spearing through his chest had left me trembling. This was so much worse. His legs, tangled amidst broken planks of wood, were broken, bent at unnatural angles beneath him. His wings were shredded. I fell to my knees, ignoring a stab of pain as a splinter gouged my calf, and grabbed his hands. He lifted one of them to his lips and kissed my palm, leaving a red smear behind.

"Leander," I sobbed. "You stupid idiot."

"Th-there's my girl," he said, blood bubbling at his lips when he smiled at me.

Smiled... *What?*

"Look. At Ikel—" He coughed, a wet, painful sound. "Ikelos."

Wrenching my eyes from Leander's face, I turned to see what he was talking about.

Behind me, a normal-sized Ikelos spun and cursed in a glowing web of light that was closing in on him. At different points around the web, all around as well as above and below, a dozen moth-winged Oneiroi hovered, slowly rotating and glowing like avenging angels. The reinforcements had come. My heart soared. I might actually make it through this alive and in possession of my own body.

Inside the web, Ikelos shimmered, as if a heat haze had sprung up between us. The Oneiroi rotated faster, something almost frantic in their dance.

Ikelos vanished with a faint *pop* of displaced air. The Oneiroi let out a collective groan and disappeared too.

Dammit. I turned back to Leander. "He escaped,

didn't he?"

He nodded, wincing.

"They'll catch him." I placed my hand on Leander's ashen cheek, reaching for the reserve of power; with Ikelos gone, my access to it was fully restored. I poured energy into Leander as fast as I could channel it. His eyes opened wide and he shoved my hand away, breaking the contact. "What are you doing?" I snapped. "Heal yourself."

"You have to wake up," Leander demanded. "Don't worry about me; I can take care of myself. You have to wake up *now*."

"Why? He's gone. I—"

"*Now!*"

He took the reserve of energy I'd given him and used it to kick me out of my own dream.

Chapter Thirty-One

The first thing I became aware of was the howl of fury. Was I still asleep, fleeing Ikelos as he fought to take me over? No, the sound lacked the resonant, penetrating quality of Ikelos's voice in my dream. It was human.

And it was getting closer.

My eyes snapped open to regard an unfamiliar ceiling. I tried to sit, but a wave of dizziness swamped me, shoving me back to the bare mattress on which I lay. Taking a slow, shuddering breath, I gingerly turned my head. White, seashell-patterned curtains were drawn across a window, bright sunlight spilling around their edges. They billowed slightly, stirred by a breeze that carried the briny tang of the distant, sighing ocean. The seashells blurred and shimmied as my vision wavered.

Daytime. It's daytime. Ikelos had possessed me at night. How long had it been?

A snarl and the sound of shattering glass from down

the hall were all the incentive I needed to try moving again. More slowly this time, I eased myself up onto my elbows. I felt lightheaded, my muscles were stiff with disuse and my mouth tasted dreadful, but I was able to slide to the edge of the bed and place my feet on the carpet. My bare feet. Again.

Ugh. Maybe this is *still a dream?* I tried willing my boots onto my feet. A twinge of discomfort between my eyes and a lack of boots told me I was either awake or out of juice. At least I wasn't wearing that stupid dress anymore; in fact, I was in the same clothes I'd been wearing when I broke into Ewan's house with Brad: dark jeans and a band T-shirt, all rumpled from sleep. Another mark in the "I'm really awake" column, then. There was no sign of my knitted jumper or pink and white sneakers.

Wavering on my feet, I crept to the door and peeked out. A scuffed timber-floored corridor stretched in either direction. The crashing, which sounded a lot like a toddler having a tantrum, came from the right. *Nope.* Turning left, I kept one hand on the wall to steady myself and placed each foot as carefully as if I were treading through a Lego minefield. Beach-themed pictures in cheap frames hung on one side of me; on the other side, another bedroom door stood open. The room was empty, but showed signs of habitation; the bottom bunk held an open suitcase, its contents spilling across the mattress. A sleeping bag lay open on the top bunk, a chrysalis after disgorging its butterfly.

The thought of butterflies made me shudder. But my fear turned to relief when I glimpsed the top of a bannister at the end of the corridor. A set of stairs, going down. I was going to make it. I was—

"Melaina." The snarled word froze my blood in my veins. I spun, and the world tilted. My hands thumped against the wall as I braced myself.

Ewan stood at the other end of the corridor. He wore beach shorts, a T-shirt and a murderous look. His hands clenched into fists and his eyes narrowed as he regarded me with pure hate.

"Hi, Ewan," I croaked, easing backwards towards the stairs. My voice was rusty with disuse. "No need to show me out."

"Ewan isn't here," he said, taking a step that matched my own. "I shoved him in a cellar, way down deep." He reached a hand up and tapped his temple. "I can barely hear him screaming."

"Ikelos?" I whispered, reaching blindly behind me for the handrail. I wasn't sure I could manage the stairs without it—but my fingers grasped at air. Not close enough.

"Who else? You drove me out with your swarm of gnats. I moved to this body and now they *won't leave me alone!*" He swatted at the air as if shooing away a cloud of biting, whining things. One of his hands smashed into the plasterboard, leaving a crescent-shaped dent. When he withdrew his hand, blood smeared his knuckles. He didn't seem to notice.

Taking advantage of his distraction, I scooted backwards, grabbing the cool railing with a trembling grip. *Get it together, Melaina.*

Ikelos turned his hate-filled glare back on me. I froze. "I tried to move again," he said. "There's a baby napping not too far from here. Milk dreams and hazy colours to hide in. But they've hemmed me in. Trapped me. How

dare they? Who do they think they are?"

My mind flashed back to the memory of the twelve Oneiroi forming a pattern around Ikelos, spinning a net closed. Had they managed to complete their snare once he'd jumped into Ewan?

"Well, you were pretty keen to have a human body," I said, not taking my eyes off Ewan ... well, Ewan's body. I eased my way down onto the top stair by feel. "Maybe you'll like it."

"Not this body. Not a weak human body, cut off from Erebus." Ikelos's gaze skittered along the walls as he took in the photos of beach chairs and surfers. His top lip curled with contempt.

"Go," a voice urged, as faint as a whisper.

My heart leapt. *Leander?* I wanted to look around for him, hunt for his face in a reflection, but I didn't want to give Ikelos the opportunity to jump me. How I'd ever confused Ikelos for Ewan in the nursing home was beyond me now. Even as distracted and confused as Ikelos was at that moment, his presence was clear in the raised chin, the rolled back shoulders. Ewan had been a skink. Ikelos was a crocodile.

"Go now."

Ikelos didn't react to the other voice. After several tense heartbeats, I turned, starting down the stairs as fast as my dizziness would allow.

"Stop!" The roar echoed off the glass window at the middle landing, making me flinch. Heavy footsteps followed, thundering like my pulse in my ears.

A cheap ceramic vase filled with dry grasses sat on the window sill. I grabbed it in both hands, turning and thrusting it out just as Ikelos reached me. White shards and brittle seed heads flew around us as the thin ceramic shattered against his chest. My fingers stung with cuts as he staggered backwards, the breath *oofing* out of him. I fled, my lungs heaving for air.

The patch of sunlight falling from the stairwell illuminated a section of corridor tiled in white. The rest of the house's ground floor was only dimly visible, the curtains drawn. I blinked as I entered the gloom, my vision adjusting to the dimness. My head swam as I whipped it from side to side, trying to guess which way the exit lay. If I could get out, I could attract attention. Get help. A floor-to-ceiling curtain caught my eye and I lunged for it, tearing it back. A window. A grassed back yard. *Shit!*

The sound of Ikelos clambering to his feet sent me scrambling down another corridor. I darted through an open doorway into a cool room; a combined bath and shower took up one corner, while a washing machine and dryer towered to my right.

"Come back here, bitch!" Ikelos appeared in the doorway. I slammed the door in his face, locking it with a savage twist of my wrist.

The doorknob rattled. Then the door trembled as he pounded on it. I eyed the lock, which was smeared red by my bleeding hand. It seemed sturdy, but even as I—*thump!*—stared, the doorframe showed signs of weakening, the timber giving a little with each—*thump!*—blow.

The window over the sink was too small for me to squeeze my shoulders through, but I darted to it anyway, tearing it open and pressing my face up against the dusty screen. "Help me!" The words tore at my throat. "Somebody, help!" The sole response was the furious bark of a

nearby dog. Was everyone at work? What day was it?

Where was Leander? The mirror only showed me my own reflection.

Thump!

I fumbled for my pocket before remembering Ewan had taken my phone.

Thump!

The doorframe splintered. I heaved an empty laundry hamper into the bathtub and then drew the curtain around it. Desperately trying to slow the frantic gasps of my breathing, I squeezed myself in between the dryer and a tall, freestanding broom cupboard.

The door gave with a crash, flying open and hitting the other side of the dryer. With a roar, Ikelos launched himself at the shadowy, hunched shape behind the curtain. I darted out of my hiding spot, planting a bare-footed kick on his backside. I'd never kicked anyone in my life and there was no strength in it, but his balance was off. He toppled forward with a yelp. I ran out the door.

"This way!" that voice cried from my right. It was female, I realised. *Not Leander.* Disappointment stung as I dashed towards the sound. The corridor dead-ended in another curtain-covered wall. *Please be a door. Please be a door.* If it wasn't, I was screwed.

I yanked the curtain back so hard that one end popped off its hook, the curtain slumping like a drunkard. Behind it was a glass sliding door. I'd hoped to see a concerned neighbour, preferably one holding a cricket bat, but the paved area outside was empty. Overlayed on it, instead of my own, frightened reflection, was an unfamiliar female Oneiroi.

I unlocked the door and yanked, but it didn't give.

Her movements frantic, the Oneiroi gestured up and to my right. I looked at where she was pointing, seeing a bolt set at the top of the door. My fingers slipped on it at first, but I gripped it tight and yanked downwards. It slid open with a click.

Something heavy slammed into my back. My head cracked against the glass, pain blossoming behind my eyes. The world went grey at the edges, swimming with tears of pain. I turned just in time for Ikelos's second punch to hit me in the stomach. I doubled over, gasping. His next blow would be downwards, to the back of my head, I was sure of it. I couldn't lift my arms to protect myself. This wasn't about incapacitating me so he could try to possess me. He couldn't do that anymore, trapped as he was.

He's going to kill me...

"Hey, Ikelos," the Oneiroi shouted, her voice right behind me.

Ikelos snarled, shoving me back into the hall, and launched himself at the glass. I expected him to burst through it like a villain in a movie, but it was safety glass and he bounced off it. The other Oneiroi flinched, grey wings twitching, and then laughed.

Ewan's face twisted into a visage of such fury that he barely looked human. His eyes narrowed to slits and he bared his teeth in a snarl, spit flying as Ikelos growled something incomprehensible. Balling his fists, he attacked the window.

Swallowing to stop myself from vomiting, I crawled away from the door. The Oneiroi in the reflection kept up a stream of taunts, presumably knowing Ikelos couldn't get to her, trying to keep his focus on her and away from me. Had

Leander sent her? Was he okay, still tucked away in a corner of my subconscious, or was he bleeding to death?

My stomach felt like one huge bruise. So did my forehead. What did internal bleeding feel like? Leander wasn't the only one who had to worry about bleeding to death.

I had to deal with Ikelos fast.

The bathroom tiles were cold against my hands and hard against my knees. Gasping for breath and with my ears ringing, I scrambled to my feet and staggered to the broom cupboard. It swung open easily and I searched the contents for weapons. The broom and mop wouldn't do me much good. The laundry detergent might, if I could get it in his eyes. The—

Ah ha.

My trembling fingers wrapped around the white plastic handle of a steam iron. It felt twice as heavy as it should have, and my hands shook as I lifted it from the shelf. Its cable unravelled, tapping against my shin as I shuffled back out into the corridor.

Ikelos saw my reflection in the glass as I came up behind him. He turned.

Screaming, I swung.

The iron caught him in the temple with a dull, wet sound. He teetered, blinking at me, confusion puckering his brow.

Then he fell.

Chapter Thirty-Two

I perched on the edge of my hospital bed, my feet dangling, clad in my trusty boots. Jen had packed them for Brad—along with my toiletries and a change of clothes—before he'd driven from Canberra to the district hospital where I was being treated. I'd never been so glad to see a pair of shoes. I'd nearly cried.

Although that may have been the pain medication.

My head ached from where I'd smacked into the glass door, my stomach was mottled with bruises, and my fingers were covered in sticking plasters. At least none of the cuts had needed stitches, but my right hand had been more badly cut up than my left. Typical.

Brad limped into the room, closing the door behind him. "We have to wait for the doctor to do his rounds. They won't discharge you until then." I nodded glumly, and he frowned. "I'm not going to argue with them, Melaina. It's a long drive home. Concussion is serious."

"Two hours. And a suspected minor concussion. But

I don't think it is—my memory is fine." I shuddered. "I wish it wasn't."

"I don't want you hurling in the car," Brad teased, brushing my cheek with a feather-light touch. I studied his face, still glad to be seeing it in the flesh, not as an ephemera or a projection of his dreaming mind. As I did so, I ran the uninjured side of one hand across the textured surface of the woven blanket on which I sat.

This is real. And I'm safe.

I'd escaped. Selena, the Oneiroi who'd helped me, had assured me Ikelos was trapped, tucked away in Ewan's head: a tick burrowed into a tender patch of skin, but with walls all around. Ewan himself was in a coma in another hospital ward, under police guard. The doctors thought I'd caused his condition, belting him with the iron, but I knew differently. So did Senior Constable Nelson. I'd told him the truth when he took my statement on the kidnapping.

He hadn't written that part down, though, and somehow I doubted he'd shared it with the local police.

The thought of Ewan, trapped in a possessed nightmare with his master, struck me as a suitable repayment for what he'd done to my family and friends. Not to mention me, although I hadn't suffered as badly as most of them. Ewan hadn't even had me for a full day in the end, and I wasn't badly harmed. In fact, Ikelos had protected me … up until he'd tried to bash my skull in.

Thinking of my friends made me bite my lip. I hadn't seen Leander in my dreams last night—though my dreams had been foggy, probably clouded by the pain medication. At least I didn't have a snoring neighbour sharing my room to keep me awake; although I didn't have private health insurance, Nelson had secured me a single-bed room. I'd threatened to kiss him by way of thanks, which had *definitely* been due to the pain medication.

I started when Brad took my hand, holding it tenderly. He sat on the bed beside me. "He'll show up," he said, guessing the train of my thoughts. "You'll see." His tone was low and reassuring. I wanted to believe him.

"He saved my life. I wouldn't have escaped without him."

Brad's fingers squeezed mine and, although the gesture was gentle, I winced. He immediately released my hand with a grimace of his own. "Sorry."

I shrugged it off. "They're fine. Stupid cuts. Next time I have to delay a pursuer, I'll use something sturdier than a cheap vase."

"Make sure you do," he said, a twinkle in his eyes. Then his smile faded. "I wish I could've done more to help. I couldn't even give the police a useful lead in finding you."

"It's not your fault. I *was* at the beach." Ewan had broken into an empty vacation home; there hadn't been a connection, financial or familial, for Nelson to find. The police had only found me after I'd staggered into the street, dizzy and confused, and a fisherman heading out to the nearby boat ramp had spotted me and dialled triple zero.

"Still, if I'd been there, maybe Leander wouldn't have been hurt."

I looked up to meet Brad's despondent gaze, biting my lip. I didn't want to tell him. I didn't want to risk him leaving me here, with an ache in my heart to go with my other pains. But if I didn't tell him straight away, the secret would gnaw at me. The longer I left it, the bigger a deal it would become. "Brad." I drew a wavering breath.

"There's something I have to tell you."

He blinked, his gaze sharpening on me. "Uh oh."

"I, uh." I swallowed. "You know how I told you I was able to light up my dream so the other Oneiroi could find us? Well, I tried it using the power you and Leander gave me, but it wasn't enough. So I generated more by ... by kissing Leander."

Brad's Adam's apple bobbed as he swallowed. "Like, a peck on the cheek, or...?"

"Or." I gripped his hand, afraid he'd pull away and disappear like that banished ephemera.

"So you did it to save yourself?"

I shook my head. "I didn't know the kiss would generate the power," I said, my voice barely a whisper. "I thought I was going to die. I was scared, and he's one of my best friends."

"Would you have kissed Jen if she were there?" Brad's tone was light, but there was a twist to his lip that told me he wasn't thrilled at my revelation.

"Maybe..." I said. *Though probably not with tongue.*

Brad looked away, and my heart shrivelled inside. I'd ruined everything.

"Tell him that, if it makes him feel any better, he can kiss me too."

The voice came from the window behind me. I spun, gasping with pain as my abused midsection reminded me not to get overexcited. The greeting I'd been about to speak turned into a grunt of pain.

"Articulate as always, Melaina," Leander said with a laugh.

"Leander. You're alive!"

"Apparently." Unlike me, the Oneiroi didn't have any

obvious signs of an injury, though his honey-brown skin was paler than normal and his eyes bore shadows that matched those under my own. "Go ahead, tell him."

"Seriously?"

"Yes."

Brad was watching me with a guarded expression that froze as, cheeks hot, I relayed Leander's message. To my surprise, my boyfriend's ears flamed red and his eyes widened.

Despite everything, the guffaw that burst from Leander's lips was music to my ears. He was alive.

"He's laughing at me, isn't he?" Brad muttered.

"No," I lied. "Whatever gave you that idea?"

"I've met him. Twice." Brad's gaze went to the window, where I knew he was seeing the hospital carpark rather than the grinning Oneiroi. "I'll think about it and get back to you," he said, eyebrows raised.

Leander stopped laughing, and I stared at Brad in shock.

The Oneiroi coughed. "As delightful as this is, I was hoping to talk to you about something else."

"What? Is it Ikelos?" My stomach tightened, threatening to propel the dry toast I'd choked down all over the bedspread. Visions of the rogue Oneiroi coming for me in my dreams made my hands clammy. Or was he rampaging through the hospital in Ewan's body?

Brad stood, glancing at the door.

"It's not Ikelos," Leander said. "At least, not directly."

"What do you mean, not directly?" I asked, my voice sharp.

"There's a reward for his capture, actually," Leander said. "The Morpheus is due back here tomorrow, but he's

already sent a messenger to say we can ask a single boon of him for Ikelos's arrest."

I waved Brad back to the bed and he sat, his gaze flicking between me, the window and the door. "Not one each?" I asked.

Leander shook his head.

"Tight arse," I muttered. Still, a boon from the Morpheus... It wouldn't be particularly useful for me. None of his gifts would affect the real world—so what could he offer me that I couldn't conjure for myself? But, for Leander, it was a huge deal. "You should take it. Get yourself a promotion so you don't have to spend your days hunting fugitive Oneiroi in the far corners of the world."

Leander shook his head, folding his arms. "I have a better idea."

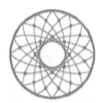

Jen and Mum collected the dinner plates, despite my protests. "Rest," Mum told me, pointing at the couch with one hand as she balanced a stack of plates on the other.

"But you cooked," I protested.

"Doctor's orders," Mum said with a shrug and a smile. "You can make it up to me next time I have a cold or something."

"You better believe it." I slumped onto the couch with a grimace. I'd been home for three days and felt a lot better. I could use my fingers so long as I was careful, and laughing no longer felt like I was being punched all over again. But I chafed at the inactivity. I hadn't gone back to work yet; my bruises had turned a lovely greenish yellow that made me look like an extra from a zombie movie, and I didn't want to frighten either my clients or Serenity's. I could at least clean up after dinner, but Mum insisted on mothering me. She'd told me she was making up for lost opportunities. It was kind of sweet. Annoying, but sweet.

"Davina's making tea," Jen said, darting back into the room and flopping down beside me. She lowered her voice, leaning in. "Is it tonight?"

"I think so," I whispered, grabbing the remote and turning the television on to cover the sound of our exchange. "Leander wasn't sure of the specifics."

"It's so romantic." Jen grinned from ear to ear. "And you are officially the best daughter ever."

"Maybe," I said.

"You're not feeling bad about accepting Leander's offer, are you?"

"A tiny bit. He could have secured himself the best posting in Erebus. Like, wall-to-wall dreams of ski bunnies. Whatever took his fancy."

Jen regarded me for a moment, her blue eyes soft. "He doesn't want that. Because then he'd have to leave you."

My heart gave a kick in my chest. Was she right? Brad still hadn't accepted Leander's offer to make out, though he hadn't refused it either. I wondered if he'd let me watch...

Still, all I did was raise an eyebrow in reply. "And you know this because...?"

"I know stuff." Jen took the remote from me and flicked channels. "I think it's crap that the Morpheus can't release your dad," she muttered. "What good is a boon that comes with restrictions?"

"There are rules, apparently," I said dryly. "They can't

waive Dad's punishment for breaking the law. But they *can* relocate his prison." Leander had assured me that Dad's imprisonment in Mum's dream wouldn't send her into a coma the way Ikelos's had Ewan. It had something to do with her being a lucid dreamer and Dad being less heavy-handed than Ikelos. That second part was definitely true. Dad had lurked in Mum's dreams for more than twenty years, and she'd been fine. Overly sleepy, but fine.

I hoped Mum didn't choose to go down the hypersomniac route again. I didn't think she would. Yes, she missed Dad, but she had built a life that was about more than him. She loved working at the shop, and had made several friends her own age. She and Serenity had even started a book club together.

"What's the point of being king if you can't ignore the rules?" Jen complained, jolting me out of my thoughts. "The Morpheus needs to watch himself some *Aladdin*. Jasmine's dad figured it out in the end."

"I don't think they have Disney in Erebus."

Jen glanced at me. "Are you kidding? I bet it's all ice palaces and Polynesian princesses. Little girls dream too."

I laughed.

Later, after we'd watched a movie together and eaten copious amounts of jelly and ice cream that Jen insisted was medicinal because they served it in hospitals, Mum stood. "I'm off to bed," she said, stretching. "I've got a double shift tomorrow."

"Okay," Jen said. Thankfully, Mum didn't notice her knowing look.

I managed to keep my own sentimental smile off my face too. Go, me. "Goodnight, Mum."

"And to you, sweetheart." Mum covered a yawn with

the back of her hand, turning to go.

"Mum?" I called after her.

"Yes?" She paused in the doorway, her black and silver hair framing her face: still Snow White, but middle-aged and comfortably dressed.

I let myself grin. "Pleasant dreams."

The end

Acknowledgements

*L*ike *Lucid Dreaming, False Awakening* has been a long time coming. I'm delighted to be able to share with you the second (and probably final) instalment in Melaina's story—although I'm going to miss the sound of her not-so-delicate footfalls as she stomps her way through my imagination. She's left some big boots to fill.

Firstly, let me fire the party cannon for my excellent support team (Pinkie Pie won't mind). Stacey Nash, Kim Last and Craig Lawrie, who read the drafts in various states and gave me valuable advice and encouragement— thank you. I adore you all. Group hugs!

Also, thank you to my wonderful editor, Lauren Clarke, who has an eye for plot holes, asks all the hardest questions and spots even the tiniest errors. Seriously, you guys—she noticed that an apostrophe was the wrong font. An *apostrophe*. She is truly my people.

The cover is brought to you by the aforementioned Kim. She has done all my book covers to date; her eye for design and her talent for turning my bumbling suggestions into something beautiful leave me constantly in awe. If you're in need of a cover designer, look up 'KILA Designs' on Facebook.

Thank you to my friends and family for putting up with my inattention and vacant looks, for letting me rant over Messenger, and for waving pompoms most enthusiastically: Mum, Dad, Kristy, Ali, Craig, Karen, Cassandra, the BC09 girls (especially Nicole, Isla's biggest fan!) and the AOR girls.

And finally, as always, thank you to my son, Nathaniel. There is more laughter in my life when you are with me.

About the author

Cassandra Page is a mother, author, editor and geek. She lives in Canberra, Australia's bush capital, with her son and two Cairn Terriers. She has a serious coffee addiction and a tattoo of a cat—despite being allergic to cats. She has loved to read since primary school, when the library was her refuge, and adores many genres—although urban fantasy is her favourite. When she's not reading or writing, she engages in geekery, from Doctor Who to AD&D. Because who said you need to grow up?

www.cassandrapage.com

Review for
Isla's Inheritance

"Witty, fun, and faerily spooky, this first instalment is perfect for fans of the fae and those who like their urban fantasy a bit light-hearted. I was literally laughing out loud at several points in the book. However, things are not all fun and games and witty banter. There were some serious creep-out moments, and wonderful twists and turns in this beautifully Australian urban fantasy."

– 5 star review, Carissa at Amazon